Not A
Stranger

Not A Stranger

A Novel by
John R. Feegel

NAL BOOKS
NEW AMERICAN LIBRARY
TIMES MIRROR
NEW YORK AND SCARBOROUGH, ONTARIO

Published simultaneously in Canada by The New American
Library of Canada Limited

The first chapter of this book appeared in the Signet paperback
edition of *Malpractice*, the author's previous novel.

 NAL BOOKS TRADEMARK REG. U.S. PAT. OFF. AND FOREIGN COUNTRIES
REGISTERED TRADEMARK—MARCA REGISTRADA
HECHO EN HARRISONBURG, VA., U.S.A.

SIGNET, SIGNET CLASSICS, MENTOR, PLUME,
MERIDIAN and NAL BOOKS are published *in the United States*
by The New American Library, Inc., 1633 Broadway, New York,
New York 10019, *in Canada* by The New American Library of
Canada Limited, 81 Mack Avenue, Scarborough, Ontario M1L 1M8

Library of Congress Cataloging in Publication Data
Feegel, John R.
  Not a stranger.

  I. Title.
PS3556.E32N6   1983   813'.54   82–24666
ISBN 0–453–00435–0

Designed by Sherry Brown

First Printing, June, 1983

1 2 3 4 5 6 7 8 9

PUBLISHER'S NOTE

For homicide detectives and medical examiners, who often see more of each other than of their own families.

Not A
Stranger

1

It was late on a gray Saturday afternoon, and for Birmington in November it was cold. Tyrone Lewis was tired and his feet hurt from standing on chilled concrete with only thin sneakers and worn tube socks to cover them. His feet wouldn't have complained if he had played pickup basketball behind the school with the rest of his friends. But here at the Crossdale Shopping Center the impending sunset was almost cruel. The sun was not big and yellow and warm, but hesitated reluctantly at the edge of the earth and brightened only the center of the gray shroud that covered the rest of the sky.

"Mind, you don't eat none of them chocolate bars," his mother had told him that morning as he left the house. "Thems fo' the church. And you has to get a dollar for every one of them. Yo' hear?"

"Yas, Mama." There was no hope of escaping his assigned duty with more protests. He had voiced them all when she had announced that she had volunteered his services to the Lord. The Clara Diggs Memorial Society of the African Methodist Episcopal church, a scant three blocks away from Tyrone's house, had decreed that several hundred dollars would be raised before Easter to repair the organ. To accomplish this economic miracle, the ladies had purchased an appropriate quantity of chocolate bars from a wholesale house that specialized in charitable causes. Their product was distinctively shaped, packed ten to the box, and bore the name of the church, school, or cause it allegedly supported. In fact,

it was three or four times more profitable for the candy re-
packager than it was for the anonymous chocolate maker or
for the laborers in the Lord's vineyard. But the salesman had
not explained that to the ladies at the AME. In fact, he sold
them not only several cases of chocolate but also a lifetime
supply of embossed car deodorizers that could be dangled
from rearview mirrors.

Tyrone was twelve and was the fifth child of nine born to
Bessie and Tom Lewis. He was a soft-spoken boy because
Tom would not abide children's noises around the house. Each
of them had learned to do as he was told, ask for nothing,
eat what was put in front of him, and to move out the minute
he was old enough. As a result, Tyrone was the next-to-oldest
still at home. His seventeen-year-old sister, Chanelle, was
restless and ready to leave, but determined to be the first in
the family to finish high school.

Tyrone's stomach growled and he looked longingly at the
remaining chocolate bars in his box. He had sold five, and the
money was burning a hole in his pocket. Bessie had given him
a quarter for lunch and other necessities, but it was gone by
ten in the morning. At two he had carefully swiped two
apples from the vegetable display of a large grocery chain
store. But all of that was long gone as well.

He knew no one had seen him lift the apples, but the
unmarked patrol car across the parking lot bothered him just
the same. There was a man in it and it had been there on and
off since noon. Tyrone and all the other little black boys
could spot an unmarked car from two blocks away. The city
was too cheap to buy convincing decoys and too regimented
to let these stripped-down Fords become dirty or dented.
They might as well have painted them blue and white like
the rest of the cruisers.

Tyrone walked to the end of the sidewalk outside Eckerd's
Drugstore and stooped down to read the clock inside. Sale
or no sale, he had agreed with his mama, a deal is a deal. At
a quarter to six he could close up and head home, confident
that he had made God happy and that he would not be asked
to sacrifice another Saturday for at least two months. (He

didn't know about the car deodorizers scheduled to go on sale immediately after the new year.) The time on the clock made him smile. It was close enough. He was sure God did not measure eternal rewards in ten-minute intervals. He squatted down on the sidewalk in front of the drugstore and carefully refolded the flaps of the box. It would be passed on to his brother James, who at age ten had been assigned to three hours' sale duty in front of a white Baptist church on the other side of town. James had bargained for the Sunday duty because it was short and got him the use of the bike. He also knew that white Baptists bought candy from little black boys if you caught them in front of their church, in full view of their well-dressed friends. In fact, Tyrone and James had sold some items over there when Bessie and her AME friends had no drive at all going on. (Calendars stolen from funeral homes were always good for a quarter.)

Tyrone did not see the unmarked car slide up behind him, amber parking lights only, as he reached the far side of the shopping complex. The macadam beneath his feet was a little warmer than the concrete had been, and he was headed home. Why should he care about the soft hum of a Ford on his heels? The parking lot was half-filled with cars anyway. If the cop wanted to talk about apples, Tyrone knew he could duck between the cars and escape. The trick, his older brother had told him, was not to run too soon. You had to wait until the cop had stopped and was busy with his paperwork.

The unmarked car rolled up next to Tyrone, keeping pace with him as the driver lowered the window.

"Where you goin', boy?" the stranger behind the wheel said.

"Home," Tyrone replied. He kept walking.

"Hold up a second. I needs to talk with you." The man's inflection was a fair imitation of a Negro dialect.

The boy clutched his box of chocolate bars a little tighter to his chest as he stopped. " 'Bout what?" Nobody seen me take them apples, he thought to himself.

" 'Bout some of them missing children," the man said. "You know about that?"

3

"Uh-huh."

"There's been eleven boys 'bout your age that ain't never showed up again. You know that?"

Tyrone nodded. He'd heard. Everyone had heard. From the church to the newspapers to special lectures in class to the nightly news on TV, everyone had heard: young black boys missing—some found dead; no clues, no leads.

"Don't it scare you none to be out here all alone, knowin' about them boys? We got cars staked out all *over* the place, and look at you. Walkin' along like it was a Sunday promenade." The man leaned out of the car slightly and gave Tyrone a closer inspection. "What you got in that box?"

"Candy. For my mama's church." He clutched the box a little tighter. He had placed the five-dollar bill inside.

"Your mama's church?" the man said incredulously. "What kind of a church prays with candy?"

"They *sells* it," Tyrone said firmly. "To fix the organ by Easter."

The man nodded slowly. "What's your mama's name, boy?"

"Bessie. Bessie Lewis."

"*I* knows Bessie Lewis. I knows 'bout everybody in this part of town."

"You does?"

"Sure do. The police chief made that part of my job. He says, 'Sam, if you is goin' to do *any* good at all lookin' out for them boys on the street, you've got to know their mamas and even where they live.'"

"You know where I lives?" Tyrone whined, his head cocked to one side.

"Yep. And it's not far from the church, neither. Get in, I'll ride you home."

Tyrone hesitated for a moment. He didn't know this man. He wasn't in uniform, although the car looked authentic enough. It even had a tiny aerial sticking out of the crack in the trunk door.

"Here," the man said, "take a look at this." He took a small imitation leather folder out of his shirt pocket and flipped it open. The badge was silver and said "Birmington Police Department." The identification card on the opposite side bore a picture of a man looking about the same, but a few years younger.

Tyrone squinted at the badge and nodded.

"That good enough?" the man asked. He was in his late thirties, clean-shaven, close haircut, good teeth. He wore a well-pressed blue suit and a starched white shirt open at the neck. His thick glasses slipped slightly on his large thin nose.

"I guess so," Tyrone said, "but I don't live very far off."

"That don't make no never-mind, boy. It's part of my job. I'm just doin' what the chief told me to." He leaned across the seat and opened the passenger-side door. "C'mon," he said.

In the light of the open door, Tyrone could see the man's face better. He looked like all the rest of them cops, Tyrone thought.

"I'll even buy one of them candy bars," the man said.

Tyrone's eyes doubled in size. That would make it six dollars! His mama would be *real* proud. "You will?" he asked, crossing in front of the car to come around to the passenger side.

"Sure will. Maybe two." The man leaned across the boy to help him pull the door closed. He smelled of some kind of after-shave Tyrone wasn't familiar with. It was the kind of smell you smell in big department stores where they have all those sample bottles open on the counter with little pumps sticking out of them just waiting to be squirted just once before the saleslady catches you. He and James had tried that at Rich's. James smelled funny for three whole days.

"This car don't have no radio," Tyrone said, adjusting himself to the passenger seat.

"Special unit," the man said almost secretively. "That way the bad guys don't know who we are." In fact, there was a radio, but it was installed in the glove compartment.

"Oh," Tyrone said, unconvinced.

"You may have to tell me which block to turn," the man said, speeding across the parking lot. "I can't remember every single street down here."

Tyrone said "Uh-huh" as he fumbled with the flaps on the cardboard box in anticipation of his double sale. The man said nothing more.

After two or three fast miles and several turns that screeched tires, Tyrone looked out of the window more intently. The neighborhood was sort of strange to him. It was not his usual route home.

It was not his route home at all.

On Monday, they would find his body.

2

Dr. Putnam seldom went to the apartment on Sunday. Sunday was a day he reserved for guilt over his absence from church. Frequently Putnam would repress the guilty feeling by inventing work at his office. But *this* Sunday he felt an uncontrollable urge to a simple desire. He had never picked up a child at noon, and vowed not to vary his routine this time either. But the feeling was there. A distress in the depths of his abdomen and an ache somewhere in his pelvis. A tremble of the hands and an unexplainable satisfaction in attempting to run over a cat crossing the street.

His heart was racing slightly as he entered the unguarded front door to the apartment house. The building was four stories high and sat alone at the end of a cul-de-sac in the eastern part of the city. The neighborhood was mixed, but predominantly black. There were eight apartments on each floor. Each door faced a long central hallway that was covered with ratty green carpet. There was a stairwell at each end of the building, and the land fell sharply away in back, giving the two upper-rear apartments a nighttime view of the city lights. Putnam's was one of these.

All of the apartments were occupied, but Dr. Putnam didn't know that or care. He had never spoken intimately to any of the neighbors, and only once had he been spoken to by the old woman who lived across the hall with her fat, yappy dog. The nameplate on her door said "McCroughough." Putnam had read the name several times but had never discovered how it was correctly pronounced. The dog was named

Murphy. He knew that because he had heard her call the damn thing all the way out and all the way back many evenings. There was no name on his own door. For a while he had allowed the nameplate of the previous occupant to stay there rather than post the pseudonym he had given the manager. Then, after several weeks, the manager, who lived somewhere else in the city, came by and posted new nameplates, a courtesy that delighted all occupants except Putnam. For several days thereafter, the name on his door said "Bernard Parsons." Putnam was careful to retain the same initials with his fake name. He considered leaving it there, but then took it down, preferring anonymity. He had explained to the manager that he had an out-of-town job and hinted that it had something to do with "the government." For that reason and for an extra fifty dollars, the manager had let Putnam remove the name, install his own lock, and "forget" to file a copy of the key. This nonaccess violated the fire laws, but the manager didn't care. He hated to go near the place anyway. "Filled with old people who cough a lot and pee on their carpets," he told his wife.

His description would have changed if he had seen the inside of Putnam's apartment. In the doctor's apartment there was an entrance foyer, a kitchen nook, a living room that opened to a tiny balcony, and a single bedroom. The living room was covered by a deep red shag carpet, and big white fuzzy pillows had been tossed around to serve as furniture. One of the boys had remarked that the pillow he was lying on reminded him of an angora cat his older sister kept in her bedroom.

The sliding door to the balcony had been covered by aluminum foil that was black on the inside. Putnam had altered the door-latch mechanism so that only he could open it. He was confident the mechanism was sufficiently difficult to baffle any young black boy for several minutes—long enough to be recaptured—but in fact, not one of them had ever attempted to escape by that route.

The bedroom was Putnam's pride. He had covered two walls and the ceiling with mirrors and had installed a television recording system that would have made small broadcasters envious. It was operated, as were the studio lights in the ceiling opposite the bed, by a panel of electronic buttons built into the headboard. The bed was king-size and covered with red satin sheets.

In the closet there was a variety of costumes in both adult and small-boy sizes. With them, a large number of roles could easily be assumed, depending on the mood of the players. The costumes ranged from classic Disney characters to pirates, baseball players, monsters, and spacemen. Each of the costumes was neatly hung, the adult and child sizes side by side. Makeup and masks for these roles were kept in the vanity area of the bathroom, where some builder had anticipated a housewife applying her cosmetics.

The bathroom itself was equipped with flashing colored lights and a variety of water nozzles along three walls of the combination shower and tub. Putnam had not dared to call in a plumber to install these spray heads and tubes. As a result, the room had an awkward do-it-yourself appearance only partially hidden by the flashing lights.

The apartment was Putnam's refuge. An oasis from the strain of his job at the state crime laboratory and an escape from his wife. To construct it, he had smuggled the supplies into the building at odd hours, and always deceptively wrapped. Even Mrs. McCroughough and her dog were unaware of his remodeling.

This noontime he had parked on a side street several blocks away. He made it a point not to park in the same spot too often, thereby avoiding recognition by neighbors who had nothing to do but stare out their windows and claim the empty spaces in front of their houses as their own. Even when Putnam brought a boy to the apartment, he followed the same plan. The difference was that he never brought a "guest" until after dark. On those nights, he and the boy would enter quietly through the rear entrance and mount the back stairs. The boy, convinced he had been hired to help remove packages from the apartment to the car, would not complain. The generous payment he was invariably promised saw to that. One intelligent lad did inquire why Putnam had chosen such a distant parking place when they were going to carry several packages to it. Putnam had replied that the packages were surprise gifts for some people that lived in the apartment house and that they had to be taken downtown for last-minute adjustments at a local store. A small boy's curiosity is often satisfied by any plausible explanation as long as it is glib and imaginative. To remain convincng, Putnam kept a dozen or so shoe-box-size empty packages wrapped in plain brown paper in one of the cabinets in the kitchenette. So far, he had never been required to show them.

Although it was midafternoon and Putnam had not had lunch, he was not hungry. Yet there was an anxious hollow feeling in his stomach. He had come to the apartment because he was nervous. He had come to inspect the red satin sheets and collect the two soiled bath towels. He had also come to return the medium-size oriental rug. The one he had used to wrap the body of Tyrone Lewis. Putnam was confident that no one would question his bringing an oriental rug into his apartment in the afternoon. It was tightly rolled and fit easily over his shoulder. He brought it in through the front door without so much as a hello from any of the other occupants and carried it up the front stairs to the fourth floor. Even in the top-floor corridor he went unchallenged all the way to his door. Inside the apartment, Putnam stood the rolled carpet in the far corner of the bedroom closet behind the Popeye suit. His wife had received the rug as a gift from her mother shortly after they were married. For this reason and because TD, his wife, hated the pattern, they had agreed one weekend to throw it out. As far as TD knew, Barry had taken care of it.

Putnam then began to examine the red satin sheets on the bed. There was an irregular ring-shaped stain in the middle of the bottom sheet, and Putnam knew they might have to be destroyed. He was able to wash the towels at home without attracting any attention. The towels were plain blue and stock items for any department store. The sheets were a different story. Putnam had purchased the sheets by mail, using an advertisement out of the back pages of a men's magazine. He had had them sent to the laboratory marked "personal and confidential." Putnam had reasoned that if anyone at the crime lab opened the package, he would simply state that he needed the sheets for comparison. However, the package had arrived intact and his cover story had not been required.

Now the sheets were badly stained. Putnam bent over the dried ring in the middle of the bed and scratched at the mark. Without lab tests, he was unable to decide whether the stain was urine, semen, or perspiration. He had given Tyrone a Coke, but the boy had not spilled any. At least, not that Putnam could recall.

Then, with a trembling hand, Putnam rolled onto his left side and fumbled for the switches to his television recorder. Replaying the tape would identify the origin of the stain. And with that discovery, Putnam could decide whether to launder the shiny slick sheets, send them to a dry cleaner and risk discovery by some teenage counter girl, or throw them out completely. The latter choice was the safest, and Putnam had considered it from the beginning. The problem was that he not only liked the color and the feel of red satin sheets but also wanted to retain *this* pair and all of the visions and memories that came with them.

Putnam unlocked the panel of the headboard and selected the proper combination of buttons. The room began to darken. Simultaneously the television screen began to flicker and Tyrone zigzagged into view. He was wearing a diminutive police sergeant's uniform that fit surprisingly well. It was cut of typical blue, and authentic for any big city, except for the modified short pants. An oval had been cut out in back, exposing both cheeks of his smooth black buttocks. The boy was obviously pleased with the uniform and sat cross-legged in the middle of the bed sipping from a six-ounce Coke bottle and smiling at someone or something off-camera. The tape had its own soundtrack, and when the boy spoke, his lips flapped rapidly and his eyes sparkled excitedly. He did not seem to be afraid.

Then, with only a mute warning furnished by the boy's look of anticipation, Dr. Putnam came into view. He was dressed as a Hollywood stereotype of a Southern convict. Striped shirt, striped pants, striped cap perched high on his head, and a ball and chain shackled to his right ankle. The ball and chain were apparently made of styrofoam and were tossed around effortlessly by the prisoner.

"I surrender, officer," the Putnam on the screen said, holding his hands over his head. "You've got me."

Tyrone Lewis, the cop, giggled with delight.

The prisoner sat on the edge of the bed and extended his wrists. "You can put the cuffs on me," he said.

The boyish policeman took a pair of toy handcuffs from his leather belt and put the first one around Putnam's left wrist. Then he paused to look at his half-captured prisoner. "What did you do?" he asked.

"I was bad," Putnam said in a sad, childish voice.

"Real bad?"

"Real bad."

The boy nodded somberly, as if he understood. "I was bad once too."

"But you're a cop," Putnam said.

The boy shook his head. "No I ain't," he said. "I'm just playing I'm a cop."

"No you're not," Putnam insisted. "You *are* a cop. And I'm the prisoner. You've even got a badge."

"Cops are bad," the boy said simply.

"Some of them are," Putnam agreed.

"They pick on kids."

"Do they pick on you?"

"Sometimes," the boy said.

"Like what?"

"Like picking me up when I ain't done nothing. Like making me get out of a store when all I was doing was looking."

"Did they ever touch you?" Putnam asked.

"Sometimes." The boy looked at Putnam for kindness and understanding and seemed to find some.

"Like this?" Putnam asked. He reached for the boy's naked buttocks protruding from the abbreviated uniform and stroked the skin.

"Uh-huh," the boy said affirmatively. "Some of them did." He did not retreat from Putnam's gentle advance

"Did they touch you here too?" Putnam asked, running his handcuffed hand across the front of the boy's pants.

"Sometimes."

"I'm going to touch you there too, and you mustn't be afraid. I'm your prisoner. You're the cop. Right?"

"Right," the boy said cautiously.

Putnam felt himself being aroused by the television scene. On other days he had enjoyed the apartment alone, sometimes watching the cassettes, sometimes dressing up in a costume, but always ending up with prolonged erotic posing nude in front of the full-length mirror. Some of the games he played alone were stored on tape too. Those tapes pleased him the least, because when he replayed them he could not recall the exact fantasy that had raced through his mind during his masturbation. Instead, he appeared on the screen as a writhing, tortured man flogging himself to achieve satisfaction and simultaneous destruction of his mental movie.

There was a prolonged pause on the TV as Dr. Putnam made fumbling movements with Tyrone's clothing.

"You going to pay me?" the street-wise boy said, breaking the silence.

"I'm going to give you a dollar," Putnam moaned.

"Five," the boy said. He had actually never participated in a homosexual act before, except as mutual entertainment with his brothers and a few of the other adolescent boys in the neighborhood. But they had all talked about it, the older ones instructing the younger on how much they could charge a desperate man and how not to be afraid. A lot of the advice was pure bullshit, and both the teller and the listener more or less knew it. But all of them wanted to believe. It was part of the heroism of becoming an adolescent. It was part of growing up. Tyrone had known that, more than the experience and more than his five dollars, he wanted to be able to report back to his group, "I done it. I let this dude have it and I made five bucks." He wanted to be able to say, "I know something personally that you assholes are still just talking about."

Impatient with the brief wrangling which occurred before the boy agreed to the fee, Putnam pushed the fast-forward button and calculated how far ahead he wanted to go before allowing the machine to resume play. This time the screen was filled with another kind of activity. The players were still Tyrone Lewis and Dr. Putnam, but the costumes were gone. For the boy, the activity was no longer sexual. For the doctor, the excitement was intense. He was rigid and explosive. He held the boy's neck in his hands and smiled strangely as he watched the boy's eyes flash a last desperate message. On the screen, small hands on bigger hands tried to break the death grip. Small feet thrashed and twisted and then lay still. The half-naked convict continued to hold the neck tightly.

This was the part of the tape he wanted to see again. As the moment approached, Putnam slowed the tape until a single frame was frozen on the screen. There, in midair, he had captured his own orgasm. He knew again how the sheet had been soiled. He had always known. But now he had relived the moment anew.

Outside the door, there was a muffled yapping. A small, fat yellow dog sniffed at the threshold and then reluctantly entered the apartment across the hall in response to its owner's demand. As she closed her door, Mrs. McCroughough paused at the last crack and studied the apartment across the way. She had seen the occupant only a couple of times and her curiosity gnawed at her like a hungry rat.

3

Chief of Police Gayle Wesley Sullivan had not come up through the ranks. The older men resented that. He had a Ph.D. in criminology from the University of Michigan. The younger men resented that. He was also black and only thirty-eight. The white cops said he was chief only because he had been a classmate of the mayor, Cleland Wilson, at an all-black college. They said that with or without his doctorate, he had never been chief anywhere. They reasoned that if an outsider had to be brought in and appointed chief, he should bring with him an impressive history of success in other cities. To his closest friends the mayor admitted he had never been mayor anywhere else either. As a result, he had appointed his own man and vowed to stand behind him come hell or high water.

Chief Sullivan had a boyish face, a slight build, and a refreshing smile—not exactly the stereotype of a big-city police chief. He zealously believed in sociology, crime prevention, and community relations. That, he was convinced, was the key to peace in a racially mixed Southern city. To reach that goal, he and the mayor had initiated a progam to hire hundreds of black policemen and to make them highly visible in *all* of the neighborhoods. The reception in old-line well-to-do white sections of the city was, to say the least, mixed. To these people the mayor explained that he was striving to make the *whole* city safe. Some of them responded (to each other, of course) that he was also making the whole city black. Many of them moved to the suburbs. But as the program progressed, and seemed to succeed, some moved back. As a result, the racial mix hovered at sixty percent, with a worried white minority.

Mayor Wilson and Chief Sullivan were not satisfied with their individual successes. They knew they needed another strong black personality on the team to hammer the program home. A city does not live by police alone, Mayor Wilson told his police chief one evening. There were also firemen, sanitation workers, schoolteachers, and parks employees. The sanitation jobs were secure enough, he pointed out, if only by default. But the fire department was another matter.

"Which racist is going to kick a black ass off his property when the flames are licking through the upstairs windows?" he had asked Sullivan.

"W. T. Stoner?" Sullivan had asked.

"Luckily, Gayle, old W.T. doesn't live *in* Birmington. Only too damned close to it."

"Who you got in mind for fire chief?" Sullivan had asked, enjoying the mayor's remark.

"Not fire chief, Gayle. The fire department is owned by rednecks with seniority. What I had in mind was commissioner of public safety."

"Commissioner of . . . ?" Chief Sullivan knew the position was held by an elderly cracker with more political pull than George Wallace.

Wilson had nodded slyly. "Lancaster's going to resign and I'm going to push Peter Greene into the vacuum."

Sullivan had been taken aback by both announcements. As far as he knew, Clay Lancaster had no intention of resigning as commissioner of public safety, even though it was common knowledge he resented a black police chief under him, and Peter Greene seemed too happy serving the United States as a token black college cop for the LEAA. What Sullivan hadn't figured on was Greene's inside information that the Law Enforcement Assistance Administration was scheduled to fold and that Lancaster had cancer of the lungs. As a result, Peter snapped up the Birmington offer and joined his two buddies in the Deep South. Together they had more postgraduate criminal-justice education than the rest of the police force combined, but two Ph.D.'s and a lawyer was more than the old-timers could tolerate. Some resigned immediately, while others simply eased back to serve out their twenty.

But that had been a couple of years earlier. *This* bright Monday morning, interdepartmental jealousy and bickering over assignments were the farthest thing from Chief Sullivan's mind. Once more he had been shattered out of sleep at dawn by a phone call from homicide announcing the discovery of another dead black male child. Homicide had used telephones exclusively to slow down the news hawks, but paid tipsters within the department had alerted Channel Three even before Sullivan arrived at the scene.

The body had been left in a vacant lot long overgrown by brush. A frequent dump for household trash in big green plastic bags, the lot had once held a house. Now only the block foundation existed. The neighborhood was also gone, creating an air of desolate peace. The area had been isolated by the throughway, pushing it over the brink from poverty to despair and then nonexistence. Now only occasional bums stayed in the few windowless houses that remained before they too moved on. Rousting one of them out into the cold after his small fire had half-destroyed an abandoned, leaning house, a BPD officer had asked him if he weren't afraid of ghosts.

"Black folks don't leave no ghosts," the tramp had informed him.

When Sullivan arrived, the scene was in high progress. The medical examiner's investigator was already there, squatting among the homicide men to get a closer look at the body. Sullivan was not a homicide man. He depended on his homicide chief, Henry Willis, to take charge of murder scenes. At forty-eight, Willis already had more than twenty years invested in the police department. He had come up through the ranks to command the homicide squad, and everything about him said so. He wore his hair in a short gray crew cut and was oblivious of his scuffed shoes and his out-of-date blue suit. For press relations, Willis could be counted on to tell the nearest TV reporter to fuck off, especially if the reporter were female. He was the old-line, redneck, a-woman's-place-is-in-the-kitchen type of white Southern plainclothes cop. Channel Three's girl on the scene, Joan Burke, was a tall, lanky, good-looking single blond from Milwaukee moving up by moving South. She was twenty-eight, and as dedicated to getting the story as Willis was to solving the crime.

Sullivan ducked under the yellow nylon rope that described the edge of the scene and accepted a snappy salute from the young black rookie serving as sentry. He raised one finger toward Joan Burke to tell her he'd get back to her. Chief Sullivan was in full uniform because he was scheduled to appear at some civic dedication with His Honor the mayor later that day. It was the opening of another neighborhood center for the elderly or some such nonsense, but Mayor Wilson never missed an opportunity to show off his two Ph.D. colleagues, Sullivan and Greene. The mayor's motto was: "Be seen and be reelected." If that theory were true, he would have already banked enough personal-appearance time to keep him in some public office for at least a hundred years.

"He's about thirteen, Chief," Willis said through clenched teeth as Sullivan picked his way toward the small knot of men in the middle of the clearing.

"Any identification?" Sullivan said, looking down at the boy. God, he thought, they really *do* all look alike. It had been suggested by the medical examiner that several of the murdered black children bore striking resemblances to each other.

"No paper," Willis said, "but we already done made him."
"How?"
"His mama's been squawking about how he didn't come home from the shopping center Saturday night. I sent a car over to her house with a Polaroid of his face. She said that's him." Willis made it sound easy and all so matter-of-fact. He had been on homicide for fourteen years and had a reputation for tough thoroughness and gut instinct. God, how Sullivan wished Willis were black.

"She take it pretty hard?" the chief asked.

"Oh, God, yes. A lot of yellin' and screamin' and carryin' on, but you know how . . ." Willis caught himself just in time and stared at the chief, waiting for his reply.

"Yes, Henry," Sullivan said, smiling ever so slightly, "I know how *they* are."

"He's been out here awhile," the medical examiner's investigator said. His name was Jerry Carson and he too had had fifteen years' experience with homicides. He had put his time in with the county police rather than the city, and had moved over to the medical examiner's office when it had first been organized. The county P.D. had replaced a corrupt Sheriff's Department to police everything outside the city limits, and the M.E. had taken over from an inept coroner's system.

"You think he's been here since last Saturday night?" Chief Sullivan asked. He really needed to sound knowledgeable.

Carson bent the boy's leg at the knee again, mentally gauging the remaining rigor. "Could be," he said, standing and dusting his hands together. "There's almost no stiffness left, except from the cold. Saturday night's as good as any."

"Cause of death?" Sullivan asked, looking from Carson to Willis and back again.

"Just like the others," Carson said flatly. "Some kind of strangulation."

"But no marks," Willis added.

Sullivan nodded slowly. "Was this how he was found?"

"Just like you see him, Chief," Willis said. "Lying on his back, arms folded across his chest, his pants pulled down around his ankles. Don't look like nobody dumped him here."

Carson shook his head in agreement.

"He's been carefully laid out for us to find," Willis continued. "Just like the others."

Sullivan looked at the boy again. There were a few pubic hairs trying to grow around his shriveled penis, but he was still just a kid. "You going to take him downtown?" he asked Detective Willis.

"That's up to Sergeant Carson," Willis said, bowing to protocol and acknowledging the investigator's old rank with the county P.D.

"It's okay with me," Carson said. "I've done all I need to out here. We've both got our pictures, and I've already called for an ambulance."

"Well, do what you've got to do, gentlemen," Sullivan said, straightening his uniform jacket. "I'll see what I can do about satisfying the press for you." He looked over at the nylon rope where Joan Burke was arranging her cameraman and microphone for the interview he had silently promised her.

"Get 'em to hell off my back," Henry Willis said. "I don't want nothin' to do with them TV bastards."

"They *can* be tiresome," Sullivan said, feigning slight boredom.

"A pain in the ass," Carson added. He was white, well-groomed, good-looking, and friendly with all the ladies. Since he had quit smoking, he tended to be a little overweight. He liked his job with the medical examiner. It gave him repeated opportunities to show the cops on the scene how little they knew about rigor mortis, trace evidence, and various prescription drugs. For a self-made cop with no formal college training other than forensic seminars, it was a damned good job and Carson intended to keep it.

"I'll check with you downtown, Henry," Sullivan said. He turned and started toward Joan Burke.

"Are you coming to the morgue, Chief?" Willis asked. He was careful not to sound taunting. He knew there wasn't a snowball's chance in hell of Sullivan's showing up at the morgue.

"No, I'll see you in your office," the chief called over his shoulder. He had already begun to exhibit his meet-the-press personality.

"Roll on everything," Joan told her cameraman as the chief approached. "Don't wait for a setup. We might not get one."

Sullivan made a move to duck under the yellow rope. He had carefully chosen the spot for his exit to right in front of Joan Burke. On the other side of the roped-off area, Charlie Thompson, the man on the scene for Channel Seven, began to scramble toward Joan and the chief.

"Is it like the others, Chief?" Joan asked, thrusting her mike into Sullivan's face.

"There are certain similarities."

"Has the boy been identified?"

Sullivan wondered why Joan Burke had said "boy" instead of "child," but let it pass as an obvious guess. Only another teenage boy could have evoked such a knee-jerk response from the police department. "The child has been tentatively identified," Sullivan said to the reporter. Then, slowly turning his head to look directly into the camera, he added, "We are withholding the name at this time to allow proper notification of the next of kin."

Academy Award, Joan thought. Still, if she was going to get anything at all for the six-o'clock, she would have to give the chief his moment on the tube. She knew she could edit out all the hokey crap downtown, but she also knew Sullivan would tape it at home and would resent every inch they didn't show.

"Chief Sullivan, the last several cases were found in wooded lots such as this one. The bodies were all neatly arranged. Did this body show the same characteristics?"

"There were similarities," Sullivan said, instantly regretting that he was repeating himself. He quickly decided to give the editor another chance. "I will, of course, wait for the official report from the medical examiner," he said somberly, "but I was struck by how the arms and hands were arranged in this case."

Joan Burke caught Channel Seven's approach out of the corner of her eye. She wanted her timing to be exact. "How *were* the hands and arms arranged, Chief Sullivan?"

"The arms were neatly folded across the chest, the hands grasping each other."

"And that indicates that the boy was not simply dumped here, right?" Seven's Charlie Thompson was getting into range now. He had his microphone out and was waving instructions to his own camera and sound men.

"Chief Sullivan," Joan Burke said expansively, "we know you will do everything you possibly can to catch this killer before he can kill again." She pushed the microphone into his face and stepped sharply to her left, blocking Thompson's view.

"Thank you, Miss Burke," Chief Sullivan said, picking up the unspoken cue.

Joan stepped closer to the camera and intoned: "From Southwest Birmington at still another child-murder scene, this is Joan Burke, Channel Three News." With that, she half-turned, smiled at the chief, and almost begged him to get the hell out of there. She gave a quick cut sign to her cameraman, leaving the chief in the awkward position of either moving on about his business or obviously waiting for Charlie Thompson. Even Sullivan couldn't stand that kind of pressure. He hurried off in the direction of his car, hoping Thompson would chase him. Instead, Thompson stopped to quiz Joan Burke.

"Want to pool?" he asked.

"Why, Charlie, you know I can't agree to that without my editor's permission."

Thompson smiled sweetly at his rival. "Bitch."

"Careful," she said, returning the smile. "My sound is still running."

"So's your mouth." Thompson turned toward the scene to see what was left. "Come on, Milton," he said to his camera-man, "let's go film Henry Willis scratching his ass and listen to him tell us to go fuck ourselves."

"Have fun," Joan chirped.

Downtown, the mayor's office was gearing up for the inevitable attack. As soon as the word went out that another black child's body had been found, Mayor Wilson knew the pressure groups would arrive. Some of these had been made up of well-intentioned and painfully frustrated parents and relatives of the murdered and missing children. Later, the pros began to come out of the woodwork. One of the pros was the Reverend Jessie Cadillac. That, of course, was not his real name. He had been baptized Jessie Weed, but changed it when he opened his Chapel of Prosperity. He preached that if the Good and the Faithful were persistent enough to ask—and generous enough to contribute to their minister's own welfare—everything would come to them. After all, he argued, it wouldn't look right for the leader of the Chapel of Prosperity to look poor.

The Reverend Cadillac had camped outside the mayor's office ever since his source inside the police department had tipped him off that another body had been found. At earlier scenes, Jessie had discovered that no matter how he ranted or waved his arms, the television people ignored him. At City Hall, on the other hand, he was news. Apparently badgering the mayor was more acceptable than interfering with the police.

"I *demand* to know when the mayor will see me," Reverend Cadillac shouted at the receptionist. There were no TV cameras there yet, but Jessie was warming up.

"The mayor is *very* busy, Reverend Cadillac. He has to make a speech this afternoon."

"But another black child has been murdered. Doesn't he care about that?"

"I'm certain the mayor is *very* concerned about that, Reverend. He has already been on the phone with Chief Sullivan." The mayor's receptionist was thirty-five and totally dedicated to her boss. She had majored in psychology at Cookman College and had taught school for a while before she married a local black attorney. He had been a year behind the mayor at law school and would have risen to a prominent position in Wilson's administration had he not been stabbed to death outside the courthouse by an enraged client. After the funeral, Mayor Wilson had offered the receptionist's position to his widow, Florence, and she had readily accepted. The elderly white woman she replaced resented being fired, but since the mayor's immediate staff was exempt from Civil Service, she offered no resistance. To the victors belong the spoils.

"And just what does the mayor intend to do about the child?" Cadillac said, waving his arms to a room empty except for his two assistants. The gesture threw open his ankle-length fur coat and exposed his pink velvet jacket and red silk tie. His hair had been carefully straightened, oiled, and set, and he smelled strongly of Aramis.

"I *intend*," a deep voice boomed from behind him, "to use every means at my disposal to get to the bottom of this." Cleland Wilson, hearing the commotion in his outer office, had chosen to take on the reverend face to face and get it over with.

"*My* flock, *Mister* Mayor," Cadillac began, "is—"

"Your *flock*, Reverend Cadillac," the mayor said, interrupting him, "has been a continuous disturbance in these investigations."

The two assistants stepped closer to their spiritual leader. Each of them was dressed in a black suit, white shirt, and black tie. Like a pair of matching bookends, they had their heads shaved perfectly bald to match their smooth, pampered faces.

"My people are volunteers, sir," Cadillac said. "They are inspired by the Lord himself to join in the search for them poor missing children."

"There are hundreds of volunteers, Cadillac," the mayor said. "But most of them cooperate with Captain Bayberry. Most of them, that is, except your *flock*." Cleland Wilson was six-feet-three and weighed two hundred and ten pounds. He had played mediocre football for State and looked like a man who could handle himself. The presence of the Reverend Cadillac and his two goons posed no real threat to him, and he knew it, although there was no doubt in his mind that the goons were armed.

"Almighty God speaks to *me*," Cadillac said, thumping himself on the chest with his thumb, "and *I* direct my flock. I don't need any Captain Bayberry to tell us where to search."

Wilson took a step closer and put his face directly into the reverend's. "You screw up one crime scene, Mr. Weed, and I'll have your ass thrown in jail."

"The television cameras are downstairs, *Mister* Wilson,"

24

Cadillac said. "I'm going to disclose your true attitude." His jaw stuck out defiantly, matching the mayor's.

"The public has heard all of your shit before, Weed," Wilson said. "You've stirred them up so often they've got nothing left."

"Yes they do, Wilson," Cadillac said. "They've got one more dead kid to worry about. They've got a madman loose somewhere, an insensitive lawyer-politician for a mayor, and an asshole Ph.D. for a police chief. They know they're not safe."

"That kind of talk doesn't help anyone," Wilson said. "You know there's no proof that all the murdered and missing children are linked. And there's even less evidence it's the work of one man."

"*Evidence!*" Cadillac sneered. "That's lawyer talk. What we need, *Mister* Mayor, is for somebody to solve these cases. We need an arrest."

"Who do you want, Weed? A Ku Kluxer in a bloody sheet?" The mayor looked at each of the bald henchmen for facial response that never came.

"The people are fed up, Wilson. They want a head. If you and *Doctor* Sullivan can't find them one, I'll hand them yours."

The Reverend Cadillac turned to leave, his ankle-length coat twirling against the mayor's trousers. The two henchmen fell in behind their leader.

Mayor Wilson looked at his receptionist and gave her a theatrical shrug. "I guess I'm mayor of *all* the people, Florence," he said loud enough for the departing Reverend Cadillac to hear. "Even kooks like that."

"Not for long, baby," Cadillac shouted without turning around. The second bodyguard closed the door with a force just under a slam.

"I think I would have punched him in the mouth," Florence said.

"And he would have shown his bloody nose to every TV camera he could find downstairs. He'd love to be a martyr—as long as it didn't kill him."

Florence gave him a little smile. She admired her boss for

his ability to take it all from so many divergent groups and still keep his head above the political waters. What his critics called compromise, she called flexibility. With a little encouragement, she knew she could easily love him. But encouragement seldom came. Since his divorce he had been a loner, and only a few years had passed. He was still too sensitive to touch openly.

"Call Chief Sullivan for me, please," he said, reaching for the door to his private office. "And get the name of the mother of the latest child. I want to send her a letter of condolence."

"Yes sir," Florence said. "Would you like me to have her brought in so you could speak to her privately?"

The mayor shook his head. He did not look back. He had two teenage boys of his own, although they were with their mother in Carolina. "No, thanks." He sighed. "I don't think I could take that just now."

Florence didn't see the tears in his eyes.

4

At the medical examiner's office, things were busy. Carson had authorized the removal of the body and had beaten the ambulance to the morgue. He knew his boss, Tom Langdon, M.D., the chief medical examiner, would not stand for any slipups on this, the latest child murder. Langdon had built the place, and Carson had been with him from the beginning. The previous morgue had been a rathole attached to the basement of the city hospital and intermittently directed by one of the pathologists on staff. All of them had hated court and considered forensic pathology to be beneath them.

Tom Langdon had gone to Yale Medical School. His father, who'd been a general practitioner, had hoped young Dr. Langdon would go into a clinical specialty, but Tom had found internal medicine and surgery boring. For his pathology residency he chose Houston, and after a few weeks of bullet holes and homicide investigations with the police, he knew he wanted to be a medical examiner.

The body of Tyrone Lewis had been brought in through the rear double doors and placed on the scale, ambulance cart and all. There, an overhead camera snapped a wide-angle photograph for the records. The picture included the scale weight (corrected for the cart), the date, an assigned serial number, and the child's length.

The clothing remained untouched. Carson saw to that. Dr. Langdon would want to see it exactly as it was found. In some cities, a pathologist was often dispatched to the scene of a homicide. Miami was one of those. But Langdon saw that as an intrusion on his own investigators. He said that a man could never grow until he had been given real responsibility and many opportunities to make mistakes. This attitude made some of the younger investigators nervous, but Carson liked it. He knew he was good on crime scenes and appreciated Langdon's faith in him.

"You'd better tell Jeff to get a full set of Polaroids and thirty-five-milimeters," Carson said to the outer morgue attendant. "One from every angle. Langdon will eat him alive if the police photographer picks up a scratch that's not in one of our pictures."

"Yes sir, I surely will," Billy said. He had worked the back door to the morgue for eight years, mostly the day shift after he got married. Officially it was his job to receive the bodies, set up the weigh-in, shoot the log picture, and move the body into the walk-in cooler. But over the years, he had become liaison to the local funeral directors and resident psychologist to the next of kin who showed up to identify bodies. There was an attendant for each shift around the clock, but Langdon acknowledged Billy Cashman as the best. Billy had wanted to complete his studies at State and qualify as an EMT on the city ambulance crew, but an infirm mother, a big family, and an early marriage had prevented that. Soon after he started to work at the morgue, Billy knew he had made the right choice.

"You want those pictures shot in the dissection room or out here, Sergeant Carson?" Billy asked.

"Take him straight on in, Billy. I've got the feeling the boss is going to get right at him. The press will be all over us on this one." With that, Carson turned to leave the outer morgue area by cutting through the cooler. It led directly into the dissection room, where three or four autopsies could be handled at once, depending on which pathologist was on first call and how many cases there were to be done. The medical examiner's office carried three senior-pathologist positions and slots for two residents in forensic. Dr. Langdon and the number-two pathologist, Burton Davis, preferred to do their cases all at once. Langdon referred to that as "the horizontal approach." The other senior pathologist, Kaleb Mazouk, a British-trained Lebanese, preferred to do his cases one at a time, even pausing several times to dictate the monotonous details of the dissection as the autopsy progressed. His style tied up the morgue assistants for many more hours than the simultaneous system, but they never complained. At least, not to Mazouk.

Inside the cooler, there were seven other bodies. One was a fresh traffic ("off the road at high speed in the north part of the county," the preliminary report read). Another was a domestic stabbing in a card game (his brother, aged twenty-six, got him when he discovered two jacks of hearts). There was an old geezer from behind the union mission (sixty-eight, with three hundred thousand miles and a half-empty pint of muscatel in his urine-soaked pants pocket). The other four were leftovers waiting for relatives to make claims or for the county to buy graves.

All of them would have to wait until Dr. Langdon had taken care of the newest child. Carson was certain of that.

"Don't get up, you guys," Carson said to the dead bodies as he walked across the cooler. "I'm just passing through."

"They ain't goin' to pay no attention to you, Sergeant," Billy called after him.

"They might if I was the Reverend Cadillac," Carson shouted back just before the heavy door clacked shut. He found himself in the dissection room. A stainless-steel table occupied one end of the room. It was seldom used for an autopsy. All of the pathologists preferred to use portable carts backed up feetfirst over low flush sinks. This arrangement allowed them to work without moving the body off the cart onto the table and back to the cart again after the dissection was completed. With a thousand autopsies to do every year, every streamlined technique was appreciated.

The attendants were busy setting out the instruments on Mayo stands. It was like a low-key operating room without anesthesia or sterile green drapes. Dead bodies, after all, did not contract diseases. At worst, they transmitted them. But only when the pathologist or his attendant made a mistake and cut himself during the autopsy.

"I hear they found another kid," Bubba Hutcheson, the senior attendant, said to Carson as he entered the room. He had been with the county morgue even longer than Billy and considered himself in charge of the nontechnical personnel. Bubba Hutcheson was six-one and two hundred and forty pounds. In his apron, he looked like an enormous black storekeeper.

"You heard right," Carson said. He glanced around the room, making sure that everything was about ready. He knew Langdon would ask him that when he got upstairs.

"That's bad," Hutcheson said, shaking his head sadly. "I got kids of my own."

" 'Cept you don't know all their names," the other attendant quipped. The little jokes in the morgue were almost automatic, a relief from the daily parade of tragedy.

"He don't even remember all their mamas, Hampton," Carson said to Hampton Jones, the second attendant, who was older than Bubba and had gravitated to the morgue from an unsuccessful attempt at managing a local black funeral home. "Now, you boys pull up your sox, 'cuz I expect that the boss is going to come down right away after I make my report to him." Sergeant Carson had enough seniority both as a member of the M.E. staff and as a native-born Southerner to get away with calling them boys. He meant no offense, and none was taken. Particularly when there were no outsiders present.

Upstairs, Tom Langdon was on the phone. Since the child murders had begun, the phone rang off the wall and the crayon letters poured in daily. Langdon was in his early forties and had the lean athletic look of a runner about him. He had married a nurse at Houston, but when she ran off with a plastic surgeon, he remarried forensic pathology, his first love.

"Of course I'm going to *do* him this morning," Langdon said into the phone as Carson appeared in the doorway to his office. He cupped his hand over the phone and mouthed

"Chief Sullivan." Carson rolled his eyes and nodded, agreeing with the apparent frustration of the call.

"No one will find out any details until you do personally, Chief Sullivan." Langdon was standing now. He was dressed in gray flannels, genuine Clark's desert boots, and an oversized green scrub shirt. "Right. You have my word on it." He leaned toward the base of the phone, still on his desk, as if to hurry the call to completion. "Send them over, Chief. Send anybody you please, but do us a favor. Make sure one of them is in charge." He threw a glance at Carson and shrugged helplessly.

"Tell him to send Henry Willis," Carson added in a stage whisper.

Dr. Langdon nodded complete agreement. "Chief, you could . . ." He paused, waiting his turn to get a word in. ". . . you could . . ." He held the phone away from his ear and made a face at it. Then with feigned patience he put it close to his mouth and said, "Send Henry Willis over here. We need all the help we can get." The compliment apparently worked. Langdon winked at Carson and gave a little smile. "Good-bye, Chief. I'll call you."

"He's sending Willis?" Carson asked.

"Uh-huh. He wanted to send a whole squad. One detective for each of the prior cases. It took me twenty minutes to convince him that was a hokey idea."

"More than three cops in the morgue is close to worthless," Carson said. "One pays attention. Two discuss the case all during the autopsy. Three begin to argue, and four or more talk about their girlfriends and the ball game. Henry Willis was out at the scene."

"Good," Langdon said, coming from behind his desk. "What did *you* see out there?"

"Crowds," Carson said. "And TV."

"Clothes on the kid?"

"The usual. I had him carried in 'as is.' "

"He's downstairs now?" Langdon threw a glance at his watch.

"Billy's got him for the weigh-in."

"Any known connection with the other kids?"

"About the same age. Black. Pants down. Hands folded across the chest. That's about it."

"How 'bout location of house?"

"He's from Southwest. One of the other kids was too, but they're too far apart to go to the same school. Henry's going to run that and give me a call."

"Location of body?"

"Vacant lot, wooded. A new address, if you go by streets and numbers. But this makes three if you call it Southwest."

"We'll let the press call it Southwest," Langdon said. "I don't want a connection until *we* see a connection."

As he left his office and brushed by his secretary's desk, she waved several pink call-back slips. "Joan Burke, Channel Three," she said.

"Later." Langdon kept walking, with Carson one step behind. On the way to the dissection room, Carson kept up his steady barrage of facts calculated to satisfy Langdon's every question on the latest child case. Carson's written report would follow, but the essentials would be transmitted to his chief directly. As Langdon put it, reports were only for the file and for preparation for court, if in fact a court case ever followed.

Tyrone Lewis, still half-clothed and still on his cart, had made it to dissection slot number one by the time Dr. Langdon walked into the room. The tiled floor shone spotlessly, reflecting the overhead lights. Bubba took pride in the cleanliness of the morgue and often ate lunch there. He claimed it was cleaner than the cafeteria at the hospital across the street. No one argued with him about that, but no one joined him for lunch, either.

Dr. Langdon approached the boy's body and studied it silently. "The first thing to do in a forensic autopsy," he lectured the medical students annually, "is to do nothing. If you show a specimen to a surgeon, the first thing he'll do is grab it. Offer it to a forensic pathologist and he'll *look* at it." The medical students got the idea, but invariably reached out to touch the specimen he offered for their observations.

"They not only don't know how to look," he'd lament later, "but they don't know how to listen, either."

Langdon moved around the body like a cat ready to pounce. In the boy's hair he observed the weeds still trapped between the wiry strands and subconsciously estimated how recently the hair had been cut. He looked at the face, searching for minute scratches and tiny bruises. At one point he adjusted the overhead light to send the beam *across* the throat, hoping to catch a slight abrasion. Then he moved to the arms, the hands, the clothing, and the sneakers.

"Give me a pair of pickups," he said to Hutcheson without looking up. Bubba, well trained and used to Langdon's methods, responded with a clean pair of forceps and a small plastic bag. Every eye strained as the pathologist picked a single black hair from the boy's shirt and placed it in the bag.

"It's probably one of ours," he said, "but who knows?"

"You want to see his back now, Doctor?" Hutcheson asked as he carefully folded the tabbed end of the plastic bag and placed it on a clean sheet of paper.

"Carefully," Langdon said.

Jones and Hutcheson stationed themselves on the same side of the table opposite Langdon and carefully placed their gloved hands on the shoulders and hips. Then with a coordinated movement usually reserved for the most delicate of neck injuries, they rolled the body upward, exposing the back. They held the body motionless as Langdon continued his observations. Behind them, Jeff, the medical examiner's photographer, stood ready, his thirty-five-millimeter in hand.

"Okay," Langdon sighed. "Give Jeff a chance to shoot a set, and then undress him onto a sheet."

Hutcheson responded by unfolding a freshly laundered sheet and spreading it on the floor a few feet away. The technique was to undress the body without cutting or tearing the clothes and to place them on a sheet so that trace evidence would not be picked up from the floor to later mislead some enthusiastic criminalist at the crime lab. Theoretically, the case could be solved by the identification of an incriminating hair or a fleck of paint. The chances of that happening, they all knew, were slim, but at least they didn't need to add material from the floor. Later Langdon would mark the clothes with the case's I.D. number and his initials so that he could identify them in court.

"Did Chief Sullivan say homicide would be right over?" Carson asked.

"Who knows?" Langdon said flatly. "If we wait for them, they'll never come. If we go on, they'll show up and look hurt. What's the difference? They don't come to look at the pathology. They come to hear me tell them what I found."

"And what it means," Carson added.

Langdon opened a sterile pack of latex gloves and slipped them on his hands with a technique precise enough to please the toughest surgeon. Then, with a body diagram attached to a clipboard, he began to sketch his observations, or, in this case, the absence of observations. On this form he would include the name, case number, date, the height and weight, the color of the hair and eyes, and a list of the clothing.

Dr. Langdon paid particular attention to the boy's underpants once they were removed. He looked for extraneous hairs or unexplained stains, but found none. The boy had a few pubic hairs of his own, but not even any of these had stuck to the underpants.

"I'm going to want a full set of toxicology tubes, hair bags, nail-scraping slides, a urine bottle, and a tissue jar on this one," Langdon said. He needn't have mentioned these items, since Bubba had set them up even before the body had been moved into the room. With these tubes, Langdon would be able to send blood to the crime lab for routine toxicology and typing. The hair bags would be used to save head and pubic hair for later microscopic comparison if an opportunity presented itself. Years before, in a rape-murder case, hairs thought to be those of the victim were found on a pillow in the suspect's hotel room, but the pathology resident had forgotten to save any pubic hairs for comparison. A brief interruption at her burial had saved the day and the resident's career.

Scrapings from the victim's fingernails had been a part of

Langdon's routine from the beginning. He admitted he had never seen anything incriminating retrieved by that laborious technique, but he did it anyway.

"I want a full set of oral and rectal sex swabs, too, Bubba." These too had already been laid out for him.

A few minutes later, as Langdon inserted his first swab into the boy's mouth, Henry Willis walked in alone. "Fishing for sperm?" he asked.

"Well, hello, Henry," Langdon said, recognizing the detective's voice. "I understand you got your fresh-air exercises in this morning."

"Got me out of bed at dawn," Willis said. "Somebody walking his dog found this kid in the bushes."

"Better check your shoes," the pathologist said. He removed the swab from the boy's mouth and smeared it on several alcohol-cleaned glass slides. Later they would be stained and searched for sperm by an aged but patient female technician at the crime lab. Word had it that she could find a single sperm on a slide as big as a department-store window. Some of the detectives said it was because she had spent a lifetime waiting to receive some personally.

After he had made the slides, Langdon broke off the wooden stick and placed the head of the swab in a small test tube. This would be tested for acid phosphatase, an enzyme produced in abundance by the prostate gland and ejaculated with semen. Even if no sperm were found, a high level of acid phosphatase would prove that semen had been present. The test could be used to prove rape cases even when the assailant had had a vasectomy.

"Got anything working?" Langdon asked as he repeated the swab technique on the rectum.

"Not much," Willis said. "The mother says he was out selling candy for her church Saturday afternoon and didn't come home. Of course, she didn't report him missing until late Sunday."

Langdon paused in his slide-making. "Didn't she get concerned sometime Saturday night?"

"She said she was busy with her church. She said she

thought he was home somewhere. The kids sort of take care of each other." Willis was repeating her story, but it was clear he was not convinced.

"Half of these kids sneak out after they get home anyway," Carson added. "You can find them on the street all hours of the night."

"Well, there won't be much more of that," Willis said. "The mayor's going to ask the City Council for a curfew."

"And patrol can spend the whole night riding them home," Carson said.

"Well, he's got to do something," Willis said. "I understand some of the family and church groups are after the mayor's ass."

"And they can have it for all I care," Carson said. "I can't see how he's done any good for the city."

"You're just mad because he hired so many black officers," Langdon said. He started on the fingernail scrapings, with Bubba holding the slides to catch the fragments.

Henry Willis was not in the mood to get involved in that sort of discussion. Certainly not in front of the two black morgue assistants. Willis' own division had remained whiter than some of the others, but that was due primarily to seniority. He knew that eventually Sullivan would replace his group too. None of his detectives were getting any younger.

"Any marks on the kid?" Willis asked.

Dr. Langdon shook his head. "Nothing definite," he said. He pulled the lower eyelids down and motioned to Bubba to adjust the light. "Except these."

Willis and Carson took a step closer to the table. Both of them were experienced enough to recognize what they saw.

"God damn," Willis said. "Petechiae."

"Strangled?" Carson asked. He too had seen these little bleeding spots on many occasions. They were telltale signs of asphyxia.

"Probably," Langdon said. "The outside of the neck is clean. But there might be marks on the structures of the throat inside."

"You get those in hangings too, don't you, Doc?" Willis asked.

"Hangings, strangulations, cave-ins—anything that shuts off the airway. They really blossom if you can increase the venous pressure in the head at the same time."

"Like something around the neck," Willis suggested.

"Yeah, Henry," Langdon said, "but you can even get a few of them in drownings or a plastic bag over the head."

"Or a penis down the throat," Carson added.

Langdon and Willis turned to look at the chief investigator. They both knew he was right. Again.

5

In his office, Henry Willis pushed three more pins into his map on the wall. The solid blue showed where Tyrone Lewis lived, blue with white dot where the body was found, and blue with white stripe where the boy was last seen.

The "press," as Henry liked to call the media at large, had insisted that there were twelve boys in what *they* called "the series." Somehow they had selected the murder of a black male child in the Southwest section of the city as the first case, and had reported each additional death as another in the series, even when the cause of death was markedly different.

Willis and Langdon had agreed, for example, that Myron Diggs, child murder number three in "the series," had been lured from his mother's apartment by the disputed but probable natural father of the child, and had been held captive for two days before he was killed by a blow with a baseball bat after he had defecated in his pants. The old man had been drunk again, and the boy was petrified of his father's violent mood changes.

Myron's body had been left in a storage closet of an abandoned apartment house scheduled for demolition in the path of the new rapid-transit line. The construction workers used the rooms as inconspicuous places to relieve themselves, and after a few days noticed an odor stronger than their own urine. The stink was oozing from Myron's bloated, maggot-ridden body.

Dr. Langdon had discovered the fractured skull with ease. The rest of the body was too rotten for him to see soft-tissue injury, although there did not seem to be any bleeding into deep muscle masses to indicate a beating. Myron's mother had reported him missing after two or three days. ("He often stayed out all night," Joan Burke had reported, narrowing her eyes to convey unspoken criticism to the television audience.) Willis had picked up the kid's old man the same afternoon the body was found, but lengthy questioning by teams of experts had failed to produce a confession. He was released, and Willis had assigned two men as a twenty-four-hour surveillance on him. Later, when it was recognized that the man was obviously not going to go anywhere except to work, to a beer joint on his block, and to bed in his unheated room in the back of a bummy rooming house, the watch was reduced to daily spot checks. By then, Willis needed his men elsewhere. "The series" had grown by one, and the press had begun to apply pressure.

One rainy night, months after Myron's burial, one of the detectives got pissed off, stormed into the man's room, and beat the living shit out of him. Willis had accepted the detective's explanation that the suspect had resisted arrest after confessing the murder, but had transferred the man to burglary for three weeks anyway. "You can't let these things get out of hand," Henry had said.

Henry Willis looked at Myron's pins on the map and sighed deeply. An arrest would certainly solve the Myron Diggs case in a hurry. The problem, he had tried to explain to Chief Sullivan, was that the TV people would swarm all over the case, demanding the man's head for *all* of the child murders, even though they weren't related. Willis knew the Diggs case was really a "domestic"—a garden-variety child murder showing little or no variation from the dozen or so similar cases that can be found in any big city every year. "The rule of thumb," Willis had lectured to his squad, "is whenever you get a dead kid, look inside the family. If the marriage is on the rocks and it ain't one of the parents, go pick up Mama's new boyfriend. Stepdaddies don't take any crap from any pain-in-the-ass kids that ain't their own," he added through clenched teeth. "Bogeymen that jump out of the bushes to kill other people's kids only come along once in a lifetime."

This time, he thought to himself as he stared at the site-found pin for Tyrone Lewis, the bogeyman might be with us.

Bobby Dempsey, one of Willis' younger and more excitable detectives, entered the office without knocking. He was twenty-nine and liked to wear his gun under the shoulder, upside down. He held the holster in place with a series of belts, straps, and buckles that creased his well-pressed white shirt and made faint but telltale lines appear on the back of his jacket.

"I checked out the minister of the Lewises' church, Chief," Dempsey said, almost slamming the door. "He's a fag. Vice had him twice. I'm running his prints through the Bureau just in case."

"Anything recent?" Willis asked absently, still staring at his pins.

"None, uh-uh," Dempsey said. "Last known offense was fifteen years ago."

"*Before* he got religion, I presume," Willis said.

"I dunno. I—"

"If he hasn't had an arrest since he took over that church, he's probably cured," Willis said. "Now he's sucking on the left hind tit of God instead of something else." Willis turned from the map to look at Dempsey. "Get a haircut," he said.

Dempsey touched the hair combed straight down over his ears and winced slightly. "It's part of my cover," he said.

"My ass," Willis whined. "They know you're a cop. You might as well look like one."

"Look like what *you* think one looks like, you mean," Dempsey said.

"Whatever John Q expects," Willis said. "He pays the bill." His own crew cut had long since quit standing up. Now it circled his head like a thinning halo, accenting his bald spot, a tonsure to his years of service. It had been years since he had put on a police uniform, but habit had effected a new one for him: he either wore a blue suit or a single-breasted blue blazer with brass buttons and the pocket flaps tucked in. His trousers were seldom pressed and his right-front pocket had a hole in it from the keys he carried. He wore brown loafers or cordovan wingtips, depending on whether it was

41

an odd or an even day. "Change your shoes every day, Henry, or they'll stink and everybody but you will notice them," his father had told him. He had followed the advice, but only to change from one pair to the other. At five-feet-ten-and-a-half, he was well-built and free from the potbelly that affected the others of his age and rank. His face had become craggy and his strong hands wrinkled and veined, but his eyes remained as bright as they had been when he first cried out in the delivery room of old St. Joseph's Hospital. His parents, like most of their neighbors, were Baptists, but due to his mother's sudden and slightly premature labor while shopping downtown, he had been born at the city's only Catholic hospital. Years later, due to the discovery of the log kept by a devout but faintly demented nun at the hospital, it was revealed that he, like many of his contemporaries, had been baptized "Catholic" shortly after his birth. This revelation had caused him no embarrassment or religious concern, since as an adult he had attended no particular church. The precinct had become his parish, and the bums along the street his congregation.

"What about the kid's old man?" Willis asked Bobby Dempsey.

"Nothing special," the detective said, chewing his gum. "Two strikes for drunk, one arrest for a fight in a bar. Pleaded self-defense. Let off on probation. Nothing since."

"Recent?"

"Naw. Six years ago."

"Job?"

"Nothing steady. Mostly furniture-truck-unloading for some rental house that caters to cheap apartments."

"Big guy?"

Dempsey nodded. "Ain't they all? Six-foot, two hundred twenty-two pounds. Sixth grade. Arms like an ape."

"How about juvenile or children's services? Anything between him and his kids?"

"Juvenile says he's clean," Dempsey said. "And I give up asking children's services for anything. Those state sob sisters won't tell you shit."

Willis knew that the last remark was true enough. Even

after they had released a beaten and cigarette-burned little girl to the custody of her "rehabilitated" and "extended" family, only to have her drowned in the bathtub by the stepfather, welfare had refused to turn over their entire file to homicide. "Not in the best interests of departmental objectives," the matronly director had said. Willis had screamed bloody murder to the old chief and the district attorney's office, but to no avail. The state statute was impregnable. Thereafter, the chasm between the two departments had grown wider and wider until Willis had unofficially designated them as "uncooperative." "Whatever information they may have," Willis had instructed his men, "treat it as unavailable and let them choke on it when the next kid gets killed." Even "the series" had failed to make a significant change in their attitudes.

"How 'bout the mama?" Willis asked.

"Day work when she can find it, and a lot of whoopin' and hollerin' at her church Wednesday nights and Sundays."

Willis touched the pin for the Lewis house with a gnarled finger. "Put a man on him. But no muscle."

"Round the clock?" Dempsey continued to chew incessantly.

"Only until he gets home at night. He's probably not the type to come out again once he gets his shoes off and his belly full of pork chops."

"Shit, neither am I," Dempsey said, smiling broadly. He had straight white teeth and a dimple in his chin that convinced him he was good-looking. In fact, he was.

"That's not the report I get from the airport, Bobby," Willis said softly.

"Well, hell, boss, even an airline stewardess has the right to be taken home safely."

"They'd be safer if you took them to their own motel than to your place, Bobby."

"Can I help it if I'm devoted to my duty?" Dempsey asked. He adjusted his jacket and shrugged his gun into a more comfortable position. Willis knew that Dempsey had been married at eighteen, divorced at twenty-two, and hell on wheels ever since. Even so, he was a good homicide detective and, somehow, always available. Murders were solved by knowing a lot of people and by being in the right place at the right time when the tips were being passed. A nine-to-fiver with a pipe and slippers was almost worthless. If he had his druthers, Willis would have filled his department with three dozen Dempseys and let all the old farts out to pasture. Unfortunately, the druthers belonged to Sullivan, and he didn't go in for cowboys.

"I want a full work-up," Willis said. "Just like the others. School, classmates, odd jobs, clubs, boy scouts. All that happy horseshit."

"The Lewis kid went to Clarence Fallon Elementary. That's the first one we've had from there," Dempsey said.

"So?" Willis sounded unusually impatient. Why was everyone so reluctant to plow new ground? "Work it up anyway. Get me a list of the entire faculty, including substitute teachers and the whole damned student body. Who's working this case with you?"

"McDonald. He's down in the file room."

"Out for coffee is more like it," Willis snapped. "Look, I don't mind you guys hopping around, fucking the duck. Do it your way—when it works. But when we get a new one, go by the book, will you?"

"The system doesn't seem to be working on this one, Captain," Dempsey said softly. Willis seemed unusually strained.

Henry Willis could tolerate racial slurs, open attacks on political views, contempt of traditional religious values, and even an off-color remark about motherhood if it were said with a smile. But he would *not* tolerate criticism of or lack of faith in *the system.* Without it, a police force becomes a hodgepodge of prima donnas and fat-assed pensioners at each end of the scale, separated only by bureaucrats and administrators. Willis was committed to the principle that solid investigative police work always paid off. He admitted it might take a while, but was confident that in the end, the truth would come out and justice would be served. As a result, there were no unsolved cases in the closed files. On some, the trail was as cold as the annual dogsled race from

Anchorage to Nome, but Willis insisted the cases stay officially open.

Old-fashioned as Willis' system seemed, it had actually anticipated computers. The department had a few of those gadgets, but they were mainly used in traffic, administrative, and supply. The police journals said they were coming. But for now, "the method" would continue to be "tedium according to Willis."

"And when you get all those names, addresses, and living habits compiled, Bobby, I want you and McDonald to get with the men on the other cases and compare notes. Look for similarities, coincidences, anything out of the ordinary."

"You always said there *ain't* no coincidences, Captain," Dempsey said. He had heard Willis' pep talk on a new homicide many times before, but he knew he'd have to go through it again.

"There are as long as we're looking for them," Willis said, stabbing his finger in the air at Dempsey. "There ain't when we *find* them."

Dempsey nodded silently. There was more than a new homicide case gnawing at Willis. Dempsey was sure of that. "Can I apply for secretarial help?"

"You can apply for a trip to the moon if you want." Willis snorted. "You know what it's like to pull secretarial help around here. Send your stuff through the typing pool. That's as good as it's going to get."

Dempsey shrugged and sighed simultaneously. He defined a police typist as an unmarried job-core dropout trying to learn the alphabet between pregnancies.

"You know, Captain, that I've got four other hot homicides I'm working besides the Lewis kid," Dempsey said, spreading his arms wide to show that his task was almost hopeless.

Willis allowed a cynical grin. "One of them is Myron Diggs, so stop crying."

Dempsey nodded, letting his arms drop again.

"What else have you got?" Willis demanded.

"A domestic shooting, a stabbing in a bar, and a whore strangled in a motel."

"So? The shooting is a member of the family, the stabbing

is the dead guy's best drinking buddy, and the whore bought it from her last customer." Willis ticked off his theories on appropriate fingers, leaving the prostitute dangling in midair on his middle one.

"It ain't that easy, Captain. We think the girlfriend shot the domestic, but the guy's *wife* swears it was self-defense. The bar was solid black and nobody—I mean, *nobody*—saw *nothin'*, even though it was a Friday night and the place was jammed. And naturally the whore didn't keep any business records."

"Okay, so the wife is a lesy and you got the scene backwards. One of the females shot the guy because he interfered with *them*, for Christ's sake."

Dempsey raised his eyebrows and puckered his lips. He hadn't thought of that angle.

"And in the stabbing," Willis continued, "go out and pick up the bartender and bring in the liquor license. That'll sharpen somebody's memory in a hurry. You just let all those niggers line up in the rain for a week waiting for their favorite booze joint to reopen and see what happens. Tell the bartender the state liquor commission is looking into the case."

"Are they?" Dempsey seemed surprised.

"How the hell do I know?"

Dempsey nodded again. He was catching on. When Willis felt there was time for careful and traditional police work, he let the pieces fall into place by pure gravity. But when he was pressed, he had better ways. Some of them were left over from the old days when, as he put it, victims had rights and suspects often wound up with broken fingers. Willis had called that "persuasive interrogation."

"What about the whore?" Dempsey asked. He figured he might as well get a tip from the master on all of his cases.

"Stick her pimp in the drunk tank with a bunch of Saturday-night pukers. And make sure he's wearing his fine fur coat and alligator shoes. See if that don't remind him who he rented his last rowboat to."

Dempsey pushed his lips together and nodded appreciatively. "I've got to hand it to you, Captain. You sure do know how to get to the bottom of things."

Willis walked around to his desk chair and sat at his cluttered desk. "Kiss my ass, Bobby. You and McDonald would have tried all of those tricks and more if you were sure I wouldn't chew you out for it." He threw a hand toward the door and began to scan the first memo on the desk. "Now, get your ass out of here and put in some time on this latest kid. Sullivan and the mayor and Peter Greene are going to turn lily white and eat us alive if we don't show some progress. Understood?"

"Understood," Dempsey said, opening the door.

"And listen, asshole," Willis said, narrowing his eyes and pointing a gnarled finger at the younger detective. "Don't you hotfoot it out there and collar some Alabama Klansman with a big mouth and a belly full of Jack Daniel's. I don't care what he says about the fair city of Birmington, black kids, or our beloved mayor. And I don't care how many outraged citizens in that bar heard him say he killed them all with his bare hands. It ain't him, you understand?"

"Yes sir."

" 'Cuz if it was, he'd be off somewhere by himself telling his girlfriend or maybe his closest buddy. But not no goddamn bar full of rednecks." Willis leaned up from his desk and lowered his voice for emphasis. "You bring in some loud-mouthed racist bragging about them kids, and this whole town will explode. You copy?"

"Yes sir, Captain," Dempsey said in an equally hushed tone.

"They'll make Detroit and Watts look like a Fourth of July picnic. You just better say your prayers that when we catch this son of a bitch, he's blacker than your shoes."

"I understand, Captain Willis," Dempsey said. "I'll pass this along to McDonald." Suddenly he felt a little uneasy about "the series." The shoes he was wearing were white.

Willis watched the younger detective leave and wondered how long *he* would be able to take it. An unsolved homicide was hard enough to live with, but a string of child murders was a different ball game entirely.

47

Willis had tried to hide the frustration, but his men could read it in his attitude. Always relentless and unforgiving, he had become sarcastic and increasingly critical with his men. There was a strangler out there, and he was goddamned smart. Willis knew it, and it made him angry inside. He was angry with the department and angry with the new chief, but above all he was angry with himself.

"I'm going to get you," he said aloud to the unknown assailant. "You're smarter than me, but sooner or later you're going to fuck up." He made a fist so tight his nails made creases in his palm.

The phone rang to interrupt his threats.

"Captain Willis," he said grimly.

"Captain Willis, this is Joan Burke, Channel Three . . . ?"

Willis glanced at the ceiling and silently said "Jesus."

"I was wondering if you had a statement to make concerning the Lewis case," she said. "I'm taping."

"Tape this," Willis snapped. "We've got a kid killer out there and we're closing the net on him."

"You haven't got a clue, have you, Captain?" She sounded too confident. Too right.

"Yes, we've got a clue, goddammit," Willis said. "We've got a shitload of clues. Big ones, little ones, red ones, and even blue ones." He glanced at the pins in the map and threw his pencil across the room at it.

"So I can expect an announcement from your office shortly, right?" She was almost taunting him.

"You can expect whatever you goddamned please. Just stay the hell out of our way."

"It's not just *your* way, Captain," she said. "We're looking into these cases too. The public has a right to know."

"And when you screw it up, Miss Burke, I hope you'll have the balls to admit it to the public." He said "the public" as if it were a new name for a group of undesirables.

"Cooperate with me and I'll share everything I've got with you," she said.

"Whatever you've got, you can keep," he said angrily. He slammed the phone down and stared at it for a moment. "Reporters," he said aloud. "There ought to be a law."

6

Although the mayor was *not* wearing white bucks (and probably never had, even during his college days), he too was concerned about the increasingly ominous mood smoldering within the black community. He had come into office well after the riots of the sixties and had so far presided over a relatively peaceful city. Differences between the white and black communities had been mostly talk after he was elected, and Cleland Wilson intended that things would stay that way. He had contacts on both sides of town feeding him confidential information. "Mood indicators," he called them. When feathers got ruffled over hiring policies or taxi territories, Wilson's contacts let him know before things got out of hand. He didn't pay much attention to the professional loudmouths like the Reverend Jessie Cadillac. Wilson knew that Cadillac and his kind were only concerned about themselves. The sources Wilson believed in were quiet, reliable, and too often deadly. Based on his latest information, the mayor had invited his police chief and his commissioner of public safety for a late supper at his apartment.

Following his divorce, Wilson had moved into a three-bedroom apartment in a downtown high-rise. He had announced to the public that he had done so to demonstrate that downtown Birmington was safe at night and to be closer to the people. Some of that may have been true, but an equally compelling reason was to get out of the neighborhood in which he had been a "married man." Wilson was not much for extramarital or even postmarital affairs, but on the other hand, he had not taken vows of celibacy either. From time to time a woman, usually from out of town, would join him for an evening or a weekend, but hardly ever two times in a row. Wilson knew the press would find scandal where none existed, and spaced his affairs very carefully. On such occasions, only Sullivan would know and police guards would be carefully juggled at the service entrance to the mayor's apartment house so that no one man, no matter how trusted he might be, would know it all.

Florence Potter was another matter. As the mayor's receptionist and private secretary, she was expected to come and go from the apartment, but only during daylight hours and always so obviously that any suspicion would be defeated from the start. She brought briefcases and papers and said hello to everyone in the lobby, but Sullivan knew she had pajamas and a toothbrush hidden in a corner of the mayor's dresser. Florence was quite willing to be more than a private secretary whenever Cleland wanted, and hoped for a lot more, even though she knew about the others.

For the mayor's secret meeting with his police officials, she had prepared a large pot of chicken and dumplings with a side dish of greens and cornbread. Such very private meetings demanded ethnic cuisine. Publicly, the mayor avoided fried chicken, watermelon, and any other easily photographed food item that might land him on the front page of some national magazine.

Chief Sullivan had arrived before Greene. He had entered the back way after his driver and confidential assistant, Lieutenant Howard, had distracted the police guard in the parking lot. The guard had surmised what the distraction was for but had openly cooperated so that he could be one of the "see-nothings" on whom Sullivan relied.

"That certainly smells good," Sullivan said, uncapping a beer.

"Down-home cooking is one of my hidden talents, Gayle," Wilson said, carefully lifting the lid on the chicken with a potholder.

Sullivan assumed that Florence Potter had prepared the food that afternoon, but if Cleland wanted to claim credit for it, there was no reason to be impolite. "You'll have to teach me sometime," he said.

"You have to learn *that* at your mama's knee," Wilson said. He poked at the chicken and made a frown that told his guest his cooking skills were minimal.

"*My* mama was from Ann Arbor, my dear mayor. I'm afraid she knew more about white rats and abnormal psychology than she did about kitchens. And as far as Southern cooking goes, she thought that grits were better suited for wallpaper paste."

"With a psychologist for a mother and a surgeon for a father, how did you ever wind up in police work, Gayle?"

"Just bad luck, I guess," Sullivan quipped. "Somewhere along the line, I decided that the campus life was not for me. I wanted to do something about our cities and criminal behavior."

"You should have gone to law school," Wilson said, replacing the lid and opening the refrigerator. The entire two bottom shelves were packed with bottles of Michelob, stacked like artillery shells. The mayor never drank in public. He even toasted visiting dignitaries with water. But at home, it was a different matter. Either he or Florence took the bottles out in a specially designated briefcase to be quietly disposed of somewhere between the apartment and City Hall.

"No, thank you, your Honor. Law school is not for me," Sullivan said, using the title lightly. "I'm not that kind of a crusader. Black lawyers either end up angry criminal-defense counsels or politicians. I want to make my contribution from a different stump."

"Well, Gayle," Wilson said, gulping half his beer nonstop, "whatever your motives, I'm glad you're here. I really mean that."

"I never thought I'd end up in Birmington, Cle, but I'm glad you asked me to come down."

Wilson held up his beer bottle in an unspoken toast, and Sullivan responded with his.

"I promised you when we were classmates at the university that if I made it, you'd be right there with me, Gayle."

"Considering the fact that I was offered the second-in-command slot in St. Louis, I'm not sure if you did me any favors, Cle."

"In St. Louis you'd be the token black, and you know it," Wilson said. "I gave you a job with challenge."

"And a chance to be tarred, feathered, and run out of town the first time I fall on my black ass." Sullivan finished his beer and put the bottle on the countertop. As a beer drinker, he was not in the mayor's league.

"Well, when they run you out of town, get to the front of the line and make them think you're leading the parade. And look over your shoulder. I'll be right behind you."

"Wearing a sheet?"

"Nope. Handing out campaign buttons for my next election. In a different town, of course." The two men clasped each other on the shoulder with their free hands and laughed loudly as the doorbell rang.

"That must be Peter," Wilson said.

"Yo' tend to yo' cookin'," Sullivan said. "I'll show Mastah Greene right on in here." His Southern accent was unpracticed and unconvincing. He did an exaggerated cake walk to the door and opened it widely.

"Good evening to you, Mr. *Chief* of Police," Greene said, extending his hand. Like Sullivan, he had come alone, but had entered through the front door. By nature, Peter Greene was less secretive.

"And good evening to you, Mr. Commissioner. Won't you come in?" Sullivan continued to shake Greene's hand as he led him into the apartment and closed the door.

"Hello, Peter," Wilson called from the kitchen. "Come in and have a cold beer."

" 'Evening, Cle," Greene said, walking across the living room. "May I have a Scotch instead?"

"Help yourself," the mayor called. "You know where it is."

Greene headed for the little rolltop bar that Wilson kept well stocked in the corner of the living room. Closed, the bar looked like an old-fashioned desk. Wilson didn't like the sight of liquor bottles and glasses dominating the main room of his apartment. Florence had said that was a subconscious hang-up from his Methodist childhood, but Wilson had worried that someone would bribe the apartment manager and photograph his place while he was gone.

"How was your day?" Wilson called. Anticipating the commissioner's needs, he had stocked the little bar with ice.

"Today the firemen's union was on my back," Greene said, making himself a drink.

"The black union?" Wilson asked. He came out of the kitchen wiping his hands on his apron. The apron said "Barbecue King" on the front of it. It was a joke gift from his old campaign manager.

"Who else?" Greene said. "They don't want equal rights. They want preferential treatment." He took half of his drink in one long swallow and closed his eyes as it went down pleasantly. "The mayor stocks damned good Scotch," he said to Chief Sullivan.

"He can afford it," Sullivan said.

"If you want water with that stuff, you can get it in the kitchen," Wilson said, joining his friends. "I broke the little pitcher."

"I'll take it like it is, thanks," Greene said. "It took them too long to make it to water it down." He finished the drink and poured another on the rocks. Peter Greene was ten years older than the other two. He was taller, grayer, and thinner than the mayor and lacked Sullivan's youthful face. He had been raised in Washington, D.C., where his father had served twenty-five years as a minor official in the Postal Department. He had gone to Howard University and like Sullivan had obtained a Ph.D. in criminal justice. Unlike Sullivan, his interests had been in criminology rather than police administration, and he had taught for a few years at Georgetown before a Kennedy aide had offered him a position with the Law Enforcement Assistance Administration. From the beginning, he had seen the LEAA as a stopgap measure slated to run out of gas as soon as the riots of the sixties cooled, but had also seen the position as a stepping-stone to some other federal job. That ambition had been temporarily put aside when Cleland Wilson had offered him his present position. Wilson had come to Washington to give him the commissioner's job, and after a bottle of Chevas Regal and an all-night discussion about the future of America, its cities, and its blacks, Peter had accepted. The move to Birmington had not pleased his wife, who felt that anything that was worthwhile could be found in Washington and not in the South. She was the daughter and the granddaughter of judges and had come to know a gentle and influential Washington that most blacks never saw. With a solemn promise from Peter that they would return to the capital the day after his Birmington job phased out, she had located a house in a fashionable white neighborhood in the city and had packed the china. Contrary to her preconceived ideas, the neighborhood had quickly accepted them both.

"I hear the firemen like you, Peter," Wilson said. "I mean *all* the firemen."

"I don't know why," Greene said. "I'm certainly no sugar daddy to them."

"But you treat them fair, and that's what counts," Wilson said. "You've got a good head for administration."

"Beats me," Greene said. "I'm a criminologist. Hell, they didn't tell me about any fire departments when I was at Howard."

"Policemen . . . firemen—they're all the same," Wilson said.

"Huh," Sullivan snorted. "You'd better not say that in public, Cle."

"Well, you know what I mean. They're just doing a job. A lot of hanging around punctuated by brief periods of excitement. They're cut out of the same mold."

Sullivan threw his eyes at the ceiling and turned to look out the window at the lights of the city. He hadn't come to the mayor's apartment for a trivial argument.

"They sound a hell of a lot different when they come to my office, Cle," Greene said. He made a practiced circular motion that twirled the ice in his new drink without spilling a drop.

"You just listen to them, Peter," Wilson said. "They talk about pensions, benefits, equal pay for equal time, and increased allowances for their uniforms. They bitch to me too, you know. Only I've got them *all* to listen to. Parks and recreation, sanitation, health department, dogcatchers, you name it."

"Cheers," Greene said, lifting his glass and changing the subject.

"Right," Wilson said, lifting his Michelob. "That's not why I asked you both to come over. We've got worse things to discuss."

"The kids?" Greene asked. He took a longer, slower sip of his Scotch without taking his eyes off the mayor.

"That's where it starts," Wilson said. He glanced at Sullivan. The police chief was still looking out the window, his hands clasped behind his back. "I've got a couple of ears to the ground out there, and I don't like what they're hearing." There was still no response from Sullivan.

"What *are* you getting from them, Cle?" Greene asked.

"Early discontent," the mayor said. "They want some action."

"Action my foot," Sullivan said, turning suddenly from the window. "They want a head."

"Well, you can't blame them, Gayle," Wilson said. "Who-ever's doing this isn't picking up white kids."

"We're running the same number of kids missing and murdered this year as we did the last," Sullivan snapped.

"But last year they were white *and* black. And they weren't all boys," Wilson said. He didn't like to see Sullivan warming up so early. He knew he would have worse things to say when he got a chance.

"They're not all boys, for Christ's sake," Sullivan said. "There have been a couple of girls missing too."

"Gayle," Wilson said firmly, "*I* know that and *you* know that, but the media make it sound like it's all little black boys. And the public's upset."

"The public," Sullivan said contemptuously. "You mean the black community is upset. The whites don't give a damn."

"That's not so, Gayle," Greene said. "We get a lot of comments from white folks about the problem."

"Sure," Sullivan said. "You and your wife get sympathetic comments from your la-di-da neighbors up there in the

Northwest. But they are not your average white citizen around here."

"They're good people, Gayle," Greene said.

"No argument about that, Peter," Sullivan said. "But your neighbors are lawyers and doctors and businessmen with Cadillacs and country clubs and cigars. Talk to the working-class whites and see how concerned they are."

"I talk to them, Gayle," Wilson said. "I get to talk to lots of them. And a lot of them are as concerned as our black brethren." He paused to eyeball his chief of police. "But you're right. A lot of them aren't."

"Huh," Sullivan snorted again. He turned to look out the window again. "To me, every one of those lights down there represents a problem. I may not know the details about them yet, but every goddamned one of them is a problem. You know it and I know it."

"And you're doing a good job, Gayle," Wilson said. "Nobody says you're not."

"Nobody but the entire white police force," Sullivan said.

"For some of them, you'll never do anything right," Wilson said. "But that doesn't surprise you, does it?"

"Nothing surprises me," Sullivan said. He put his hands behind his back again and began to tap his right foot on the mayor's thick oriental-style carpet.

Wilson looked at Greene and shrugged. It was obvious that Sullivan was edgy, but Wilson was determined to go on. "It may surprise you, Gayle. My people tell me there may be trouble over this mess before it's finished."

"Street trouble?" Greene asked, finishing his Scotch.

"Just like Miami, if we're not careful," Wilson said.

"And what do they want from my men?" Sullivan asked, turning from the window again. "Some kind of miracle?"

"We'll leave the miracles to the Reverend Cadillac," Wilson said.

"That asshole," Sullivan said. He headed for the refrigerator, his face flushed with anger. "I need another beer," he said.

"My *black* contacts tell me that they're not satisfied with

56

homicide's investigations," Wilson said, watching the chief twist the cap off his new Michelob.

"They wouldn't be happy with Dick Tracy," Sullivan said. The beer foamed from the bottle and ran down over the back of his hand before he got it to his mouth.

"They would if he were black," Wilson said.

Sullivan paused, the beer bottle barely touching his lip. He looked at Wilson and then at Greene without moving.

"That's right, Gayle," Wilson continued. "They are worried about Henry Willis."

Sullivan lowered the bottle without taking a sip. "Henry Willis is the best we have to offer," he said. "I haven't got another man that even comes close."

"So what?" Wilson said.

"So *what?*" Sullivan asked. "So, do you want to break this case or not? Willis *knows* homicide. Willis *is* homicide, for Christ's sake." He looked at the beer in his hand as if it had just appeared, and took a long swallow.

"Now, Gayle, you know as well as I do that the people out there capable of starting a riot and burning down half of the city aren't exactly mental giants," Wilson said.

"Amen to that," Commissioner Greene said.

"Some of them have been spreading the idea that there may be white cops involved in this," Wilson said.

"Involved?" Sullivan said. "What do you mean, involved?"

"White cops pissed off about the reorganization of the police department," Wilson said. "Pissed off about the numbers of black officers we've hired lately. Some of the people think these kids are being knocked off by a group of white cops that are out to get back at you."

"Oh, bullshit," Sullivan said.

"Oh, bullshit, my ass," Wilson said. "That's what I'm getting from my contacts. They figure that with all the publicity these cases have been getting, it would take somebody like a cop in uniform to get a kid in a car."

"These are street kids, Cle," Sullivan said. "The last car they'd get into would be one with a white cop in it."

"You're probably right," Wilson said. "But they think the

57

man has to look so trustworthy to these kids that they get right into the car with him, no questions asked."

"Sounds to me like a black cop would generate greater trust," Greene offered.

"I agree with you, Peter," Wilson said. "But a lot of blacks don't see it that way. I don't think they can conceive of a black cop doing it."

"Well, I can," Sullivan said. "Don't you think we've considered those angles? Henry Willis and I have talked about that many a time. Hell, we've also thought about it being a black minister or a nurse. Anybody with a uniform that adds up to instant trust. But we haven't gotten anywhere with that kind of thinking."

"But it makes sense, Gayle," Greene said. "These kids are getting into a car for some reason."

"Look," Sullivan said. "We sent out several of the shadiest-looking plainclothesmen on the force to try to pick up kids just to see what would happen."

"And?" Wilson asked.

"And all they had to do was offer the kid five bucks to watch the car while some 'salesman' unloaded a couple of boxes for a convention at a hotel. At least, that's all they had to tell the kid. Show them the five, and bam, they're right in the car. The door's closed, you give them a cock-and-bull story about having to run out to the airport to pick up something else, and the kid's delighted to earn another buck. The guy doesn't have to have a badge or a Roman collar. These kids are hungry. They don't have nobody to give them a couple of bucks when they want to go to the movies. They've got to get out there and hustle." Sullivan looked at the ceiling in disgust at his colleagues' naiveté.

"I can't imagine a child of mine getting into a stranger's car," Greene said, making himself another drink.

"First of all," Sullivan said, counting on his fingers, "you haven't got any kids, and second, if you did, you'd pack them off to private schools up North where they could play golf and hobnob with some doctor's kids and smoke pot."

"I beg your pardon," Greene said indignantly.

"You beg my pardon all you want, Commissioner," Sullivan said. "But I'm telling it like it is. The kids we're dealing with here are street-wise. They know what's up. They've got nothing and they know if they're going to get something, it will have to be by their own doing. Don't take offense. I didn't mean to get personal."

"And I'm not out to step on your toes, either, Gayle," Wilson said. "You know you have my complete confidence as chief of police. For that matter, so does Henry Willis."

"But you want me to dump him and turn the investigation over to a black detective," Sullivan said.

"Not exactly," Wilson said. "I just want to suggest a reorganization."

"Uh-huh," Sullivan said, sipping his beer suspiciously.

"What have you got in mind, Cle?" Greene asked.

"Get your plates and help yourself to some of my famous chicken and dumplings and I'll tell you about it," Wilson said. "What I've got in mind is a task force."

"Now, if that doesn't sound like a lot of political horseshit," Sullivan said.

"Horseshit or not," Wilson said, "it's got two big advantages. It will take the total responsibility for the investigation out of Henry Willis' hands, and that will sit better with the black community. Plus, I think I can use it to get some federal money to finance the whole thing."

"Now, *that* part I like," Greene said. He put his arm around the mayor's shoulder and turned him toward Sullivan and the kitchen. "Let's see about your world-famous chicken and dumplings, shall we?"

7

The state crime lab was housed in one of the brick buildings sprawled across an irregular nonacademic campus on Thurmond Avenue. Keeping it company were the main offices of the state highway patrol, the maintenance depot for the bureaucratic motor pool, and the administrative complex for the state national guard. Nearby, the neighborhood had degenerated into a salt-and-pepper remnant of a once grand Victorian district. All of the houses needed painting, and several displayed plywood windows where expensive stained glass had once gleamed.

In the Northeastern United States, where American forensic science (and some say everything else) began, crime labs were born Siamese—always attached to medical examiners' offices. A few evolved from the ballistics laboratories inevitably established by metropolitan police departments. Once these labs got going, routine examinations of victims' clothing, paint fragments, and trace evidence led to more sophisticated chemical testing and larger facilities.

In the South, however, the state crime labs were developed to assist the sheriffs, whom nobody fully trusted, and the lay coroners, whose lack of medical expertise was legendary. Since the rural coroner was unlikely to be a physician, it did not violate anyone's sense of logic that the "expert" sent down from the state crime lab to do the autopsy not be one either. As a result, the autopsy expert was often a Ph.D. who had received only basic instruction in pathology at the local medical school. Since he was already comfortable with the title "doctor," only minimal deception was required to convince the local police that the man from the state crime lab was skilled in forensic pathology. Later, some Southern states gave in and hired M.D.'s with board certification in pathology.

The state crime lab automatically offered services in criminalistics and forensic pathology and toxicology to every county except Birmington. The traveling teams of scapel-wielding chemists and pharmacologists performed reasonably well wherever the grass grew in the streets, but were professionally snubbed in the state's largest city. Tom Langdon's arrival had seen to that. Once the police and the prosecutors in Birmington had experienced his real training in forensic pathology, the imitation variety became unacceptable. When invited by Langdon to participate in a Birmington homicide, the experts from the state crime lab were confined to photography, fingerprints, toxicology, and the analysis of trace evidence. Some of these services were repeated independently by the Birmington P.D. and by Langdon's technicians. Too often their prints and photos were better than the state's, but sheer volume made Langdon turn to the state crime lab for help in criminalistics.

When things were quiet and news was scarce, the local newspaper thrived by fanning the flames of this interdepartmental rivalry, extracting derogatory quotes from the principals involved and highlighting any inadequacies. But the deaths of the black children had changed all that. At least for the time being. There was work enough for all the experts and news enough for all the media. Rivalries and jealousies would have to wait. Most of the technicians at both labs were happy to be rid of the bickering over jurisdiction and free to get on with their cases. But Barry Putnam felt left out entirely.

Dr. Putnam had backed into forensic work after three failed attempts to get into medical school and a successful postgraduate program in veterinary biochemistry at Auburn. He had done outstanding work investigating a series of cattle poisonings and had accepted a position with the crime lab in Memphis before coming to Birmington. With a Ph.D. in animal biochemistry, he handled the switch to human toxicology with ease, but within himself he knew he wanted more. In Birmington, as one of "the doctors," he was allowed to do human autopsies in remote areas of the state, and the thrill never had left him. He could easily trace a bullet hole in a dead body and could catalog massive trauma in traffic cases better than many hospital pathologists, but when it came to identifying a tumor, he was almost illiterate. His pathology training had been limited to the first-year course given to medical students, and as a result, he understood only the basics of inflammation, degeneration, neoplasm, and metabolic disease.

Putnam's boss, old Cyrus Atwood, had his Ph.D. in pharmacology. He was also self-taught in forensic pathology, but over the years he had developed a reputation in small towns as a formidable expert witness. But Atwood was nearing retirement and had become deeply involved with the administrative duties of the office. Attention to these burdens and the demands of the legislative committees, from whom all funds flow, forced Dr. Atwood to push Putnam into the number-two position at the state crime lab and to give him senior responsibility for the autopsy service. This gave Dr. Putnam virtual command of all homicide scenes around the state, except those in metropolitan Birmington. In the boondocks, his expertise was awesome and went unchallenged. He was also frequently wrong, but no one ever knew. Not even the police.

Dr. Putnam was thirty-six and delicately built. He had deep-set brown eyes that seemed much larger behind his thick glasses. The heavy lenses frequently sat low on his thin hatchetlike nose and pulled his ears forward on their tight wire frames. His hair was short and expertly cut. In fact, no one at the crime lab could ever remember Barry Putnam needing a haircut or appearing on a scene in a wrinkled shirt or needing a shine.

In contrast to Dr. Atwood's clutter of undone work and useless memorabilia, Putnam's desk was a model of compulsive organization. He had an in-box where work paused briefly, an out-box where nothing was allowed to remain for more than fifteen minutes—and, if Putnam had control over the matter, nothing in between. Other than the pen-and-pencil set which occupied the center of the desk and which always worked, other adornments were limited to a small block of marble presented to him by an obscure branch of the Kiwanis in exchange for a noontime talk about drug abuse, and to a photograph of his wife, TD. Putnam had found TD in a research laboratory at Auburn. She was doing independent research on a virus that seemed to attack only male pigs and reduce their fertility. Putnam had no interest in the pigs, their reproductive habits, or their germs, but was instantly captured by their researcher's eyes and mouth; especially her mouth. She had a thin upper lip with a lower one which turned downward fully, causing her to suck in slightly on her cheeks to cover her perfect white teeth. The perpetual pout was more than Putnam could stand. Despite her wheelchair, Barry Putnam quickly fell deeply in love. The fact that he was light black and she was pure Alabama white didn't seem to matter.

Terry Dee Young became Mrs. Barry Putnam the day after he obtained his Ph.D. and six months before she got her own. She had been known as TD since childhood. Her father, an ex-tackle for the Crimson Tide, wanted to name her "Bear" or "Bryant," but had settled for "Terry Dee" when he discovered what the initials would be. From that day, he had never allowed her to be called anything else.

When she contracted childhood polio and came home from the hospital in a wheelchair, her father was heartbroken, defeated, and bitter. His family physician, a college classmate and lifelong friend, had become a chiropractor when he could not get into medical school. He had kept Big Bill Young properly adjusted and aligned, free of antibiotics and other harmful drugs, and full of vitamins and advice. He had also convinced Bill that polio vaccine was just one more of the poisons invented by M.D.'s to disrupt the natural harmony of the body. As a result of this charismatic chiropractic crap, TD was never immunized. The chief of the infectious-disease section at Children's had been sympathetic when he explained the diagnosis to Bill and Bonnie Young. But he was outraged when Bill told him that TD had never received her shots. Dr. Burnside had pointed a finger at Big Bill Young and said, "You and your chiropractic quack are the reasons that TD will never walk again." Six months later, when Big Bill Young had convinced himself that Dr. Burnside was right, he sat in his big red Cadillac with the Crimson Tide decal on the rear bumper and put a bullet through his brain.

TD's fascination with viruses and their effect on nervous tissue flowed compulsively from her throughout her undergraduate days at Alabama and later during her postgraduate work in veterinary-medicine research at Auburn. For experimenters, the virus was easier to track and defeat in animals than it was in humans. For TD, it was retribution.

TD's marriage to Barry Putnam came only after she had convinced herself that it could work. Recurrent bladder, bowel, and vaginal infections from her paraplegia had rendered her scarred and probably sterile. There was little she could offer a man, she thought, but Barry had said he didn't care. She took that as so much talk at first, but later she began to believe him. While she didn't feel capable of real intercourse, she wasn't asexual. And when she offered him other things, he wasn't interested. Instead, he seemed only sympathetic and kind. But frequently he was gone.

Dr. Putnam wasn't gone on this particular day in Birmington. He was at his desk at the crime lab staring into space, his hands folded on his clean, shiny desk. His work, as usual, was done. He had spent all morning in his laboratory completing his dissections, and the first half of the afternoon in his office rereading the newspaper about Tyrone Lewis. The articles were riddled with errors, and finding them made Putnam feel superior. As he clipped the articles for his collection, his mind wandered to the little apartment and what frequently went on there. Dr. Putnam and his wife lived in a modest house modified for her handicap in a quiet neighborhood near the federal laboratory where she was employed. The laboratory and research complex was administered by the Public Health Service for the investigation of communicable diseases.

Many of the neighbors were on the undergraduate teaching staff at the university and saw the Putnams as highly educated people who never caused trouble and preferred to keep to themselves. Their interracial marriage posed no problem in that neighborhood. University people claimed to be above such things. Some of the women dropped in to visit with TD at home, but few of the neighbors knew Barry. He was too quiet to communicate with socially and appeared too distant or preoccupied to care about them.

He never told any of them, including TD, about the apartment or the things he kept there.

Dr. Putnam looked at the clock on the wall of his office. It was almost three-thirty. He felt bored and vaguely discontented. It was a feeling he had experienced many times before. Beneath his desk, his left foot tapped nervously. His hands were moist and his pulse ran slightly ahead of normal. He had often experienced this sensation and knew what it meant. He got up from his desk, picked up his soft leather briefcase, and headed for the door, pausing at the opening to the adjacent office.

"Checking out," he told his secretary. She was a career employee, with few interests beyond her own retirement. In her seventeen years of faithful but almost perfectly nonproductive service, she had never before been asked to work for a Negro. When assigned to Dr. Putnam, she had voiced her objections privately to Dr. Atwood, but had gotten nowhere. "Times have changed," Atwood had told her. She could either take the assignment or put in for transfer. "Besides," Atwood had said, "Dr. Putnam is a quiet, unassuming man to work for. You'll hardly even know he's around." That prophecy had been true enough. Putnam had never caused trouble or made demands on her at any time. He did his work in the lab, completed his autopsy field assignments, and dictated his reports in a soft articulate voice that belied his Alabama background. Not sounding Southern was one of Putnam's fetishes. He had been offended by Kennedy's New England twang and Johnson's Texan accent. A Ph.D., he vowed, should sound educated, not regional. And with practice his speech had become as unidentifiable as a Californian's.

"You may have court tomorrow, Doctor," his secretary said without looking up. She placed her hand on a short stack of routine subpoenas, each paper-clipped to its corresponding file.

"Where?" he asked, unconcerned. The crime lab received a routine subpoena in almost every case it handled, but more often than not, the district attorney and the defense stipulated to the official report.

"Leesburg," she said, biting the inside of her cheek and opening the folder. "A vehicular homicide. You typed the blood from the right-front fender. The DA says that the car and the victim are no longer in dispute. I don't think he'll use you."

"Good," Putnam said softly. He hated court appearances in places like Leesburg. He knew that in isolated towns of that size, old Southern prejudices were still very much alive. When he testified in *those* courthouses, he could actually taste the resentment. The local police resented his testimony and hated his authority despite the fact he was appearing for the state. There was no doubt in his mind that all of the police in those small towns were active members of the KKK and considered themselves the last line of defense against the liberal erosion of the American way of life. In their eyes, he wasn't white enough to be a real forensic expert. He quietly hated them for that.

Putnam turned from his secretary's office door and walked down the main corridor of the crime lab to the rear exit. The corridor was lined by glass showcases with hundreds of confiscated handguns hanging upside down on their trigger guards. Saving murder weapons for public display was one of Dr. Atwood's private passions. Secretly, he wished he could also preserve the parts of the victims' bodies that showed typical wounds, the way they did in some of the South American countries, but he knew that the sensitive Middle American ethic would not permit it. "In the United States," Atwood would lecture the rural police departments, "the surviving next of kin has a quasi-property right in the dead body. When the investigation is over, we are obliged to return it to them for burial." Then he would add with a sigh, "Such a waste of good teaching material."

Putnam's car, a plain-looking Ford, was parked in an official space behind the main building of the crime lab. It was assigned to him as a modest perk to his salary. He was paid in the mid-forties and resented the fact that the pathologists in the Birmington medical examiner's office made over sixty. Even Dr. Atwood's salary was less than the senior members of Langdon's pathology staff. His explanation was that Langdon's people were county employees, while he and his staff were state. This fiction was more acceptable to him than an admission that Birmington employed only M.D.'s with full training in forensic pathology.

Dr. Putnam's unmarked Ford swung out of the parking lot and onto Thurmond Avenue, apparently unnoticed by any of the other drivers in the afternoon traffic. His internal ache urged him to go straight to the apartment, but the schools were letting out. On most of the corners there were huddled groups of children laughing and playing their way home. The sight of them excited Putnam, and sweat appeared on his upper lip and below his eyes the way it did when he ate spicy food. Stirrings within him made him feel nervously alive, but the excitement was melancholy.

Putnam maneuvered the Ford through a series of turns that carefully avoided covering any block more than once. Groups of small black girls laughed and giggled as they walked along, their books held tightly to their diminutive breasts. The girls did not interest the doctor. Beyond them in swaggering, jostling knots that pushed and bumped along the sidewalk were the boys. They had neither books nor concern for the world. Ahead of them lay the future of confident, ignorant expectation. At age twelve or thirteen, everything was theirs for the taking.

Putnam took another left and entered a once grand neighborhood, now begging for restoration. Turrets and gables cried out for attention and mourned for missing spindles. The steep lawns were overgrown and the verandas sagged under the weight of time and neglect.

This street was virtually deserted, and Dr. Putnam regretted having turned away from the after-school activities of the previous avenue. Suddenly his heart skipped a beat and his throat refused to swallow. A boy was standing alone in the middle of the block, his back to a low wall, his head held high as he watched a busy squirrel in the tree across the street. The resemblance was uncanny. Putnam's mouth grew drier and his heart continued to pound in his chest. It couldn't be! he told himself. It was Tyrone Lewis. It was the same long pale face, the drooping lip, the sad, sagging eyes.

The doctor's memory rushed to the night he had spent with the boy, and he became excited again. He remembered the boy's unconscious naked body bathed in the soft lights of the apartment. He remembered stroking Tyrone's soft brown skin and the sensation of the boy's warm body next to his own. He stopped the car a few houses away from the boy and slumped down unseen in the seat to watch him. There were no other cars or people on the short cluttered street. For the moment, he was alone with Tyrone Lewis again and he caressed himself.

"Captain Marvel," Tyrone was saying. "I want to be Captain Marvel."

"But the Captain Marvel suit is too big for you, Tyrone." *It was Putnam's voice, but the tone was distant and singsong.* *"Try the Robin cape."*

"I hate Batman and Robin," Tyrone whined.

"You be the pirate," Putnam was saying. "You get to have a cutlass and shiny black boots with silver buckles."

Suddenly a stone rattled through the branches and dropped harmlessly on the hood of the Ford. The noise brought Dr. Putnam back from his dream. He sat upright behind the wheel, startled to see the boy staring at the car from across the street. For a moment Putnam too was stunned and immobile, panicked by the fear that the boy would suddenly run. He knew he couldn't let him escape and be lost to him forever.

Putnam quickly rolled down the window of the car and waved pleasantly at the boy. The boy stood motionless, staring at the car. The boy knew that trouble was probably coming, but yet the waving hand seemed so friendly.

"It's all right, Tyrone," Putnam called. "There's no harm done." His hand continued to beckon the boy.

"I'm awful sorry, mister," the boy called. "I was shooting

at the squirrel." He pointed into the tree but didn't look to see that the squirrel was gone.

"Come on over here, Tyrone," Putnam pleaded, the tone of his voice sweetening the invitation.

The boy shook his head quickly and looked up and down the empty street.

"I've got five dollars for you," Putnam said in a singsong. He took a five-dollar bill from his pocket and held it out the window. "I need you to help me with something."

The boy put his index finger on his chest and assumed a "Who, me?" pose.

"It's all for you, Tyrone. Don't be afraid."

The boy hesitated for a moment and then slowly crossed the street, his eyes transfixed on the five-dollar bill. He was dressed in jeans and a thin nylon jacket and worn sneakers with mismatched socks. His step was light but cautious. The smooth movement of his body was like a ballet to the doctor, who studied his every motion. The boy stopped in the middle of the street about six feet from the open window and looked at the man behind the wheel. He saw no threat in the man's appearance. For an instant the boy thought the man might be a cop. The car was plain enough. But he had never known a cop that offered money and looked so friendly.

"What do I have to do?" he asked.

"I've got some packages to deliver to a house down the street, Tyrone. You can help me carry them in. It'll only take a couple of minutes." Putnam held the five-dollar bill closer to the boy.

The boy considered snatching the money and running, but he knew the man would be faster, and he was afraid. "Which house you talkin' about, mister?" He took a step or two closer.

"One of the ones in the next block. I'll have to read the numbers."

"I've got to be right home," the boy said. "My mama said so."

"You'll be right home, Tyrone. It'll only take us a few minutes." Putnam felt himself bulging against the bottom of the steering wheel. "Come on around and get in."

The boy extended his hand cautiously and took the money in his fingers. It was a marvelous feeling. He hadn't had any real money for a week or so. "My name's not Tyrone," he said softly.

With the denial came an instant recognition. Putnam knew the boy was right, and he instantly remembered why. Tyrone was on the bed, his body growing cold and stiff and then redressed and rolled in a spare oriental rug and carried over the shoulder to the backseat of the car and then unrolled in a vacant lot, neatly arranged, his hands folded at peace across his lifeless chest.

"Tyrone is my name for all good-looking little boys," Putnam said, recovering his composure.

"I knowed a boy name Tyrone once," the boy said, "but he dead."

Dr. Putnam felt a sudden chill. Had he come to the well once too often? Was it true that all the little black boys in Birmington knew each other? Would he have to grab this one right off of the street in broad daylight and pull him, struggling and screaming, into the car? With unseen neighbors watching at every window? Was it suddenly over?

"His bike got hit by the bus," the boy added.

Putnam sighed and offered a little smile. "That's too bad," he said. "A boy has got to be careful."

The boy stuffed the five into his pocket and came around to the passenger side. "How big are them packages?" he asked. He got into the car and adjusted himself in the seat, his short legs barely touching the floor.

"We'll be able to handle them," Putnam said. "They're in the trunk."

The boy nodded and continued to inspect the clean, plain car.

"You live around here?" Putnam asked.

"No. Uh-uh."

"I can bring you back here or take you home when we're finished. Whatever you want." Putnam started the car and slipped it into drive. He moved ahead slowly, giving the boy no cause for alarm.

"I lives a couple of blocks over. I can show you where." The boy pointed vaguely to the right. "It's on Ash Street."

"I know where Ash Street is," Putnam said, increasing the speed slightly. "What's your name?"

"Martin Luther Peale." The rhythm of his reply implied that it was always "Martin Luther" and never "Marty."

"You're named after a famous preacher," Putnam said. "Maybe two." The Ford took a series of quick left turns and reentered Thurmond Avenue.

"My granddaddy is a preacher," the boy said, looking at the houses as they passed.

"And your daddy?"

"Daddy's gone," the boy said without looking back.

"You live alone with your mama?"

The boy shook his head. "Got a sister."

Putnam put his hand on the boy's thigh and patted it gently. The boy did not flinch. "My daddy went away when I was a boy too."

The boy turned to look at Dr. Putnam. "Is you a cop?" he asked casually.

"Me?" Putnam laughed. "Not me. I'm a doctor. From the government." The car was moving faster now. Too fast for anyone to safely jump out. Without warning, Putnam squealed onto the interstate and moved up to a comfortable seventy, heading east. He took his hand off the boy's leg and held the steering wheel with a tense, stiff-armed grasp.

"Where are we going?" the boy asked, still not alarmed.

"To unload the packages," Putnam said, staring ahead. "At my apartment."

"Mama gets mad at me when I'm late. She yells at me sometimes."

. . . Putnam's mother's shrill voice echoed in his mind. "You is going straight to hell, boy," she screamed, slashing at him with a leather belt. "You and those other boys. Straight to hell."

"But he made us do it, Mama," the boy Putnam screamed, ducking and rolling to avoid the belt.

"That man is a reverend. You boys and the devil made him

get into trouble." She scored with a blow his flailing arms had not managed to ward off.

"Reverend Rooney said it was part of learning about life, Mama!"

"The deputy say you and those other boys was there in his house—the one the church gave him to live in—and you all had your clothes off and—"

"He took them off us, Mama. Honest. Don't hit me no more. He took them off, Mama. He made us do it." He scrambled for the space behind the sofa, but it wasn't big enough for his eleven-year-old frame.

"A man of God?" she shrieked, the belt still active in her hand. "It was you. You and the devil." The belt found the lower edge of his buttocks and the backs of his thighs. There were welts there now, raising and blackening his skin.

"The reverend say we had to do it, Mama," the boy screamed. He wriggled farther under the couch. "I won't do it no more."

"You won't, because he is gone," she yelled. Her fat hypertensive face ran with sweat. Her bulbous eyes seemed enormous and on fire. "The deputy took him away. And it's all your fault. You and them other boys."

Then, as it always did, the vivid memory ended with his mother staggering to the old brown overstuffed chair and collapsing as she struggled for breath as he ran from the house. He later learned the gray station wagon he saw from beneath the neighbor's porch was the coroner's.

The aunt they sent him to live with said it was a shame. His daddy, the only black pharmacist in town, a heart attack, and his mother taken with a stroke.

The aunt said he'd have to make something of himself to even things up. The boy Putnam had promised her he'd use the insurance money to become a doctor and make people well. He never knew where they sent the minister.

8

Joan Burke knew that it was definitely not her neighborhood. She had called Bessie Lewis at home, hoping only for a little background color, a one line quote—at best, a comment she could paraphrase and use on the six-o'clock news. Both she and her editor knew she needed something fresh. The reruns of the vacant lot and the hospital ambulance being loaded again were growing stale. New titles and fresh voice-overs weren't enough. Unless she could come up with something else, the story and her clips would die. There was a motor-cycle accident in an adjacent county that was good enough to take over. Joan had pleaded with Arlo Jacobs, her news director, to let the Lewis case play once more. He had given her a minute and twenty seconds at six on the second day and even less on the third. But to air a fourth day, she would have to come up with new material.

The funeral had been covered well, but every channel had more or less the same shots: the outside of the church (with titles, five seconds), the minister's eulogy (five seconds); the ladies up front, including Bessie wailing on the edge of hysteria (fifteen seconds); the pallbearers carrying the casket down the front steps of the church (voice-over throughout, ten seconds); the hearse pulling away (three seconds); the on-camera tag by the reporter: ". . . at still another funeral of a murdered black child in Birmington, this is Whoever, Channel Whatever News." The coverage was so similar that one out-of-town salesman, flipping channels in his hotel room while trying to tie his tie and catch the score of a ball game at the same time, complained to the girl in the room with him that "they could at least put all that shit on at the same time and get it over with." The local stations were about three minutes apart with the story, and by chance he had caught it no matter which way he turned the dial. The girl with him was from Birmington, but she was young, white, and bored. She not only didn't care about the story but also was eager to get back on the street before some black hooker took her corner.

Tom and Bessie's house was in the middle of the block. The neighborhood had once been white, but that was before Pearl Harbor. It had never been wealthy, but it was by no means a slum. Tom Lewis and sometimes his brother had worked nights and weekends to paint and rebuild, but working with scrap lumber or whatever was on sale at a flea market. The result was an incredible assortment of styles and colors, making the house a caricature of its former self. The neighbors did more or less the same. In the end, the Lewis house, with its lavender-and-white porch and kelly-green front door and red trim around the windows, didn't look out-of-place.

It was almost dusk as Joan Burke got out of her Channel Three car and walked up the slanted concrete walkway to the Lewis house. She brought a cameraman and a soundman along, partly to be prepared for a story and partly to satisfy the nagging insecurity she felt (but would never admit) about being in a totally black neighborhood.

"Watch the front door," she told the cameraman. "I'll give you a wave if it looks like she'll talk to the lens."

"I'll bet she don't," the cameraman said. He was also black, but had drawn this assignment by pure chance. He did not believe that, of course, but kept his doubts to himself.

"I never bet against myself," Joan said. She had chosen a well-tailored brown suit for the visit. Arlo Jacobs had reminded her right after Bessie Lewis had invited her over that black people dress for important meetings. Jeans, an Ivy League shirt, and Top-Siders would definitely not do, he had said. Begrudgingly she had admitted he was right and had gone home to change.

Avoiding the flaking paint, Joan tapped lightly on one of the small windowpanes at the top half of the door. Joan had the feeling she was being closely inspected through tightly drawn curtains. After a few minutes the door opened an inch or two.

"What you want?" a mature black male voice asked.

"Bessie Lewis asked me to come over. I'm Joan Burke from Channel Three."

The man said nothing and closed the door again. Instinctively Joan looked over her shoulder at the car. Her cameraman and soundman were watching some kids play across the street.

Then the door opened again a little wider. In the doorway stood Bessie Lewis. She was older and shorter than Joan Burke had imagined her. So far, she had seen the woman only from a distance or in news clips.

"Mrs. Lewis?" Joan asked.

The woman nodded her head. She did not step back out of the doorway. She was dressed in a clean black dress and scuffed black shoes. Her face looked tired and drawn and it was obvious she had been crying.

"I'm Joan Burke. From Channel Three. We spoke on the phone." She put out her hand, and the black woman accepted it limply.

"Does you want to come in?" Bessie said awkwardly. Not many white people had been inside the Lewis house. The few that had come to the door on business had preferred to talk on the porch.

Joan started to glance at her car again but caught herself in time. "Yes, Mrs. Lewis," she said warmly, "I would like to come in if I may."

"It ain't much," Bessie said, stepping aside.

"It seems *very* comfortable," Joan said, entering the living room just inside the door. The black male who had answered the door was nowhere in sight. Neither were any of the children. Somehow Joan had expected a more emotional scene, with relatives and children comforting each other. Perhaps that was going on in some other part of the house, she thought to herself.

"We raised all our children here, Tom and me," Bessie said. "The house is small, but it's enough if you're careful."

"I'm awfully sorry about Tyrone," Joan said. She sat on the edge of a clean but battered sofa opposite Bessie, who had taken a chair.

The sound of the boy's name caused Bessie to stifle a small sob. She put a crumpled handkerchief to her nose and dabbed gently. Joan correctly assumed it was sore.

"He was a good boy, Miz Burke."

"I'm sure he was. And it's Joan."

"But he's gone," Bessie said with a heavy sigh.

"And we want to help you find who did it, Mrs. Lewis." Joan reached across the low coffee table between them and patted Bessie on her other hand.

"The police, they say they don't know nothin' 'bout who did it."

"All that takes time, Mrs. Lewis. May I call you Bessie?" She didn't wait for the permissive nod of the head but continued on. "That's where we can help. The police need all the help we can give them. The more information the public has, the easier it will be to catch the man."

"God will help us," Bessie said. "Tyrone was working for our church."

"Your church? What was he doing for your church?" Joan felt an urge to reach for her long narrow notebook, but knew that taking notes too early in an interview tended to shut off the flow of information.

"He was selling candy. We are collecting money to fix the organ."

Joan nodded encouragingly. "And that's what he was doing out at the shopping mall last Saturday?"

"Uh-huh."

"What time was he expected home?"

"For supper. He weren't never late for supper before. 'Cept once or twice."

Joan knew that was hardly true. Twelve-year-old boys were often late coming home, supper or not, but Tyrone's death had the expected effect of causing his mother and others who knew him to forget his minor faults. Psychologists called that idealism.

"Was he out there alone?" Joan asked.

"Uh-huh. Sometimes his brother James went with him, but not this time."

"Where is James now?"

"He stay with my sister till all this is over."

"Does he know what happened to Tyrone?"

"He knows he's dead. We told him that much. He went to the funeral. But we didn't tell him no more."

"I can understand that, Bessie. There's no need to scare him."

"James ain't scared none, Miz Burke. He's only ten, but he knows how to take care of himself."

Joan was a little surprised at the display of bravado. "But you're not going to let *him* go out and sell candy alone, are you?"

Bessie shrugged. "We is all in God's hands. He won't let nothin' happen to nobody unless *he* wants it to happen."

"I admire your faith," Joan said. In fact she thought it was a lot of foolishness to tempt fate. "But you'll have to tell James to be careful of strangers."

"Our Lord tell us to *help* strangers," Bessie said flatly.

Joan Burke had no intention of letting Bessie change her interview into a theological debate. She had been unexpectedly invited into this woman's house and wanted to capture the best of it for a clip that Arlo would accept. She had expected an almost incoherent woman broken by emotion and the loss of her child. To that she would have added a sympathetic voice-over and close-out on-camera in front of the house. But here was this strong female personality expressing faith in God. It might not sell with her news director, but Joan was determined to get some of it on tape.

"You've got to share your faith with the rest of the people, Bessie," she said softly.

"I does. I tells them wherever I meets them."

"You could tell many, many more on television." Joan paused to let her suggestion sink in. She hoped she had not

79

been too abrupt. She stole a glance at her watch. There still was time.

"I don't know nothin' about television," Bessie said. "Ours is broke."

"It's just like talking to me, Bessie. Just like we're doing now. Only a man would stand over here behind me with a camera. That's all there is to it."

Bessie began to shake her head but continued to stare at Joan Burke. "Right here?" she asked.

"Right here in your own home. Or maybe out on the porch. Could you do that?"

Bessie shook her head again, but not as forcefully.

"My cameraman is right outside," Joan said quickly. "Let me call him in. You'll see there's nothing to be afraid of." She got up and took a few steps toward the door before turning back to Bessie. "It will be all right," she said smoothly.

Bessie got up and stood in the doorway as Joan returned to the car. After a moment, two men began to lift equipment out of the trunk. Bessie was relieved to see that one of them was black.

"What are they going to do?" a male voice said behind her. It was her husband, Tom.

"They is going to bring in a television camera," Bessie said, her eyes glued on the activity in front of the house.

"Television camera?" Tom asked. "What for?" He moved closer to the door and squinted over his wife's shoulder. He was balding now, and beads of perspiration stood out on his exaggerated brow.

"The television lady say she wants me to tell people about our faith in God," Bessie said.

"You mean *your* faith in God. I got no time for any God that would let somebody kill Tyrone," Tom said loudly.

"Now, don't start again," Bessie scolded without looking back.

"If they wants you on television, they can pay for it," Tom said.

Bessie flopped her hand in front of her ample bosom as if to discourage a pesky fly. Over the years she had heard all of Tom's growls and knew that his protests and inflexible complaints were just noise offered against frustration.

In the street, Joan Burke had started to return, the two men behind her filming as she came up the walk. She was delighted that now both Bessie and her husband were waiting in the doorway. In her mind she could already hear the voice-over: ". . . there is nothing pretentious about the house where Tyrone Lewis lived with his mother and father . . ."

"Are you Mr. Lewis?" Joan asked as she stepped onto the porch. She offered her hand simultaneously.

"This is Tom," Bessie supplied.

"All right," Tom said as if Joan had asked about his health. He took the reporter's hand carefully and gently, as if he had been given a bird to hold. The cameraman got it all, zooming in from the far end of the walkway. The soundman behind him was still too far away to pick up anything useful.

"I'd like to ask both of you some questions on-camera," Joan said. She glanced over her shoulder and motioned the cameraman forward with a slight grimace. She knew he was watching on close-up.

"You going to show my picture on Channel Three?" Tom asked. He watched the two men mount the porch and stared into the lens as if to discover something secret hidden inside.

"Yes sir," Joan said proudly, "on the six-o'clock news." When Tom began to shake his head, she quickly regretted her enthusiasm.

"For nothin'?" Tom asked.

"What do you mean?" Joan asked. She looked at Bessie for an instant and then back at Tom. Bessie had begun to tug on her husband's shirt sleeve.

"He don't mean nothin'," Bessie said.

"Now, don't *tell* me I don't mean nothin', Bessie Lewis," he said. "This lady knows what I'm talkin' about." As usual, the intensity of his scolding was far beyond what was required to make the point, but Joan Burke took it as real anger.

"I'm not sure that I do," Joan said icily. She found herself coming to Bessie's aid and regretted her momentary lapse in objectivity. A journalist, she told herself, records and interprets and reports, but *never* participates.

"You pay Walter Cronkite, don't you?" Tom said. He turned both palms upward and shrugged. The cameraman got it all, including a quick zoom into the empty hand.

"He's not on our network," Joan snapped, "but are you suggesting that Channel Three pay *you* for appearing on the news?"

"You got it," Tom said firmly.

"And do you agree with that, Bessie?" Joan asked, her voice softening.

"Well, I . . ."

"Sure she do," Tom said. "You just look around this place. We ain't got nothin' and now somebody steals our little boy right out of a parking lot in broad daylight and kills him dead and we have to bury him and we has to look out for all our other children and we has to answer all kinds of questions to the police and now you come around and want to take pictures of us while we is grievin' and show them to the whole wide world on television and . . ." He was becoming even more excited. Bessie's tugging did little to slow him down.

"Hush, Tom," she pleaded.

He yanked his arm from her grasp and began to wave it at the cameraman. "You shut that thing off. You got no right to take *my* picture on *my* front porch without *my* permission and . . ."

"We can't offer you payment for being on the news," Joan said. Her tone implied that the conclusion was obvious.

"Then you can pack all this stuff up and put it back in your car and drive right on out of here, too," Tom said. He glared again at the cameraman, who had never stopped taping for a moment.

"But, Bessie . . . I mean Mrs. Lewis, had agreed to talk to me about Tyrone and how God . . ." Joan explained.

"Ain't nothin' in all of this about no God," Tom shouted. "What we're talkin' about is money, pure and simple."

"Lord have mercy," Bessie said softly. "He don't know what he's sayin'."

The thought of totally losing the interview rushed through Joan's mind. She needed this spot. And more than anything else, she dreaded the thought of Arlo Jacobs' cynical laugh and male remarks when she came back empty-handed.

"Bessie . . ." Joan began. She discreetly motioned to her men to come in closer. "Is this what you want too? Is this what Tyrone would want you to do?"

Bessie threw a quick glance at her husband, and as Tom began to speak, she raised her hand. "My Tyrone was a child of love and a child of God," she intoned. "He's with Him now. Lord, have mercy." Her voice trembled as she spoke.

"Now, Bessie . . ." Tom said. He'd seen her before when she had lifted her face to the sky and closed her eyes and called out to God. He'd seen her with her face streaked with tears and her voice hoarse from shouted prayer, her dress soaked with perspiration. He did not need that kind of a display on his own front porch in front of white strangers. As far as Tom was concerned, that sort of carryin'-on should be confined to church, where others did the same and young black ladies in white starched uniforms stood vigilant with smelling salts.

"He's *gwine* to look out for us," Bessie moaned loudly. He's *gwine* to to lead us home. He's *gwine* to come for us all on the last day." She spaced her promises for choruses of "amens" that were present only in her mind.

The TV people filmed every inch of it. Being careful enough not to stick the microphone too close to the woman's face and look pushy, Joan Burke stood next to Bessie and cut Tom out behind her right shoulder. She was confident her cameraman would frame just the two of them.

"What can you tell the other mothers, Mrs. Lewis?" Joan asked, milking the scene shamelessly. "What about other little boys who might be in danger?"

"They' got to trust in the *Lord*," Bessie shouted. No "hallelujah" came back.

"And then keep them off the streets?" Joan asked.

"Then keep them *all* off the streets," Bessie wailed.

At that Tom turned on his heel and stormed into the house, convinced that Bessie had just let a golden opportunity slip through her fingers.

"Should they get into cars with strange men, Bessie?" Joan

continued. She knew she could edit out the questions and dub new ones to fit the answers. That was considered ethical if the new question was framed as a narrative: ". . . I then asked Mrs. Lewis about the danger of accepting rides with strangers . . ." and dealt with the same subject matter. It was up to the news director to evaluate the fairness of her rewording. And for Arlo Jacobs, ethics was a stepchild of production and demand.

"Those children got to be told *never* to go nowhere with no strangers," Bessie announced. Sweat had begun to bead on Bessie's flushed, puffy face. With the slightest turn of a knob, unseen by all, the cameraman moved in on a tear emerging from the woman's left eye and then backed out slowly to frame her face and the edge of Joan Burke's hair. He knew it might be too maudlin for Jacobs, but what the hell, he thought, Arlo had accepted a close-up of a cop in uniform crying at the funeral of another cop killed on duty. Arlo had given him a bonus for that shot.

"What kind of a terrible person would do something like this to Tyrone, Bessie? Wouldn't you think he'd have to be some kind of a criminal? An animal? A sex deviate?" Joan had already decided that series of questions would be replaced with: ". . . when asked to characterize the assailant . . ."

"A man like that is the worst," Bessie said, her eyes narrowing slightly. She couldn't hear Joan Burke's unspoken cheerleading urging her to pour it on. "He's got to be some kind of a sick person."

Careful, Joan thought, don't get too technical. No psychiatric defense. That won't look right for a simple, bereaved black mother on her own front porch.

"He's got to be out of his head," Bessie continued, warming to the subject. "Whoever he is, he's got to turn to God and confess his sins."

That's it, Joan thought. She flashed her eyes encouragingly. That's good stuff. Pour it on, Bessie, pour it on.

"He's got to get down on his knees and *beg* the Lord for forgiveness." She raised her crumpled handkerchief and shook it ceremoniously.

"And . . . can *you* forgive him, Bessie?" Joan asked softly.

God, she thought, what an ending. This distraught woman offering her simple forgiveness to an unknown man who has abducted and murdered her son. Arlo will play it at six and eleven and again in the morning. Maybe even network.

"I wants him to be thrown into prison," Bessie growled through her teeth.

The shock almost registered on Joan's stony face. The reply would be great for *Sixty Minutes* or some magazine that thrived on cynical answers and open rejection. But not here. Joan knew that Bessie was blowing the spot. Still, the question was a good one, and she hoped Bessie would come through.

"Bessie, do you hope that Tom and the other children will keep on loving Tyrone even though he's gone?"

"Oh"—Bessie began softening instantly—"you know I do. With all my heart."

Joan turned to face the camera and said, "That's enough. Let's do a couple of shots from the street and get back to the studio. We'll skip the reverses." She never liked reverses. All she got to do was to mouth words and nod as the person being interviewed appeared to be answering. With Bessie Lewis, it probably wouldn't work anyway.

"Thank you, Bessie," Joan said, coiling her microphone cord. "I'll be back in touch with you." She leaned in a little closer and said softly, "Tell Tom I'll see what I can do for him downtown."

Bessie nodded, somewhat surprised.

"No money, you understand," Joan continued, "but maybe a little something somewhere. Like a new TV?"

Bessie smiled and put her hands on Joan's shoulders. When Joan didn't come closer, Bessie aborted the embrace.

"When will this be on?" Bessie asked.

"That's hard to say," Joan replied. She was assisting the two men in gathering their equipment. More than anything else she wanted to get the hell out of the neighborhood. "I'll give you a call and let you know."

" 'Cuz we'll have to go next door and watch it with the Armstrongs. They got color," Bessie said. Her emphasis on "color" was unmistakable.

Bessie stayed on the porch as the TV people went down

the front walk toward the street. Near the car, the cameraman shot a couple of scenes of Joan speaking into the lens and nodding her head toward the house. At one point she turned to face the porch as the cameraman panned slowly to the right, framing the house and coming in closer on Bessie at the front door.

"When we get back downtown, boys, I want the field cassette," Joan said, gathering her cord again. "I'm going to do my own editing on this."

The two men nodded in agreement. Neither of them could have cared any less. As far as they were concerned, Joan could edit this mess into an interview with Ronald Reagan at his California retreat.

On the way to studio, Joan sat quiet and alone in the backseat. She was pleased but not happy with the Lewis interview. She had hoped to come back with a clean tape. Something Arlo could clip for the six-o'clock without even thinking about it. But the scenes with Tom Lewis were more than Joan had expected, and Bessie's responses were somehow less. Joan liked some of Bessie's pious remarks and she knew Arlo would buy a few of them, but the contrast between Bessie and Tom was too abrupt. She knew she had to either cut and paste or junk the whole cassette.

Arlo Jacobs had been good to her over the years. He had given her an occasional on-the-street spot when they both knew she wasn't ready and had let her sit in at the anchor desk to give a live lead for some clip about the dog show or the clown at the hospital Christmas party. "Got to get experience somewhere," he had said. And she had loved him for it, but not physically.

Joan thought about Arlo and his inflexible ways as the car roared along the bumpy city street. All in all, she didn't feel insecure at Channel Three, but she didn't feel out of danger either. She knew that she could be there one day and suddenly gone the next. That, she was repeatedly told, was the nature of the business. No hangers on. No screw-ups. No no-shows.

It was already five o'clock when they reached the door to the newsroom. "Let me have the tape," she said to her field crew. "I'll find Arlo and see what we can make out of this crap."

"Okay, Miss Burke," the soundman said. He paused in the hallway and snapped the cassette out of his recording machine. "You need us anymore?"

"You're free as far as I'm concerned," she said. "Check with the assignment desk. And, Harry," she added as her cameraman turned to leave, "I may not show all of this to Arlo right now. Keep it between us, okay?"

"Right on," the cameraman said. He was convinced that all of the reporters were a little crazy anyway. Especially the women.

Joan opened the door to the newsroom but did not enter. Jacobs and one of the anchormen were hunched over a cluttered desk on the far side of the busy room. Arlo had a pencil crosswise in his mouth and several tear sheets from the teletype in his hand. The two of them were completely engrossed in the last-hour preparation of the six-o'clock text. Joan took the field cassette and stuffed it into her leather over-the-shoulder bag. Then, assuming a casual, half-smiling attitude, she entered the room and crossed it with a light springy step that exuded confidence. She went straight to the corner where Arlo was working and paused in front of the desk.

"Can you save me three minutes?" she asked.

Jacobs looked up for a moment before resuming his work with the papers in front of him. "What have you got?" he asked. He was one of that kind who can read one subject, talk about a second, and think about a third without strain or confusion.

"I'm not sure," Joan said. "Mostly easy stuff and tears. Bessie Lewis was kind of broken up."

"I haven't got time to wade through an hour of shit to find your three minutes," Arlo said.

"I know where it is, Arlo. I'll cut it myself." Joan held her breath but continued to smile. Stay busy, she told him silently, stay goddamned busy.

Jacobs glanced up at her and then at his anchorman, Myles

Van Horn. Arlo was dressed in designer jeans and wore a tattered Yale sweatshirt, although he had gone to the University of Cincinnati. He was thin and athletic, but pale and tired-looking. At thirty-eight he was overworked, a success among his peers, and already approaching total exhaustion. By contrast, Van Horn, an erect middle-aged, authoritative white male with a strong jaw and steady blue eyes, had a well-rested face and a steady voice. In a three-piece blue suit, he could announce that there was no state of North Dakota and everyone would believe it. As a field reporter he was hopeless, and as a news writer he was a complete failure. But God, could he read!

"Show me your final clip no later than five-thirty-five," Arlo said, glancing at his watch. "We'll save her three minutes at the top of the second segment, Myles, but keep the spot about the apartment fire as a backup."

"Got it," Van Horn said, marking his format with a blue pencil.

"If it doesn't fly, it's out," Jacobs warned Joan. "No buts, no arguments. Agreed?"

"I'm already on it," she said, rushing away excitedly.

"And I don't mean five-thirty-six," Jacobs called after her without looking up.

The main editing room was halfway down the corridor, but someone was working in there. Carrying her field cassette in her hand, Joan rushed to the end of the hall, where there was a small editing complex usually reserved for work on local commercials and Sunday public-service shots. As expected, the door was unlocked. Joan switched on the desk lights, snapped her field cassette into the editing pair, and put a blank on the other side. Her interview with Bessie Lewis was still fresh enough in her mind that a full review was unnecessary. She rushed to the top of the field cassette and picked out a street view of the house which led to her walking up the front steps. It was a natural as an "establisher."

Joan reversed the lead-in and set the blank. Then with a simultaneous beginning she copied her establisher and dubbed in the lead: "The neighborhood is not exactly prosperous . . . but it's full of love . . . and lately full of sorrow as well. . . ."

She paused to let herself mount a couple of steps and approach the door before she added: "Bessie Lewis, the mother of Tyrone Lewis, one of Birmington's latest missing and murdered children, knows a lot about both, as we shall see in this exclusive interview."

The street cameraman had zoomed in on Bessie when she opened the door. The long-distance microphone, a little windy and therefore quite authentic, had picked her up saying, "Does you want to come in?"

Joan reversed the field cassette, stopped it at the door opening, and carefully lifted the sequence onto her copy. The segue and the door greeting were a perfect match. But Joan knew she had no footage from inside the house. From the scenes showing the two of them about to enter, Joan cut to Tom's appearance in the doorway. She sat quietly and studied the dialogue and lip movements. The close-ups were of Bessie and Tom, with her own head angling from time to time, establishing her presence but not locking her into lip movements. The cameraman was a real pro, she complimented silently.

Carefully and selectively Joan added to her copy Tom's angered statement: ". . . you can pack all this stuff up and put it back in your car and drive right on out of here, too." At the end, Tom's eyes were wide and his jaw was set tight. Joan froze the face for a voice-over.

"As you can see, the strain of all this has had its effect on Tyrone's father, Tom Lewis. But his wife, Bessie, did not agree at all with his position."

Joan advanced to another of Bessie's answers and copied "He's got to be out of his head" before she reversed and lifted the scene of Tom turning on his heel and storming into the house. With Tom out of the way and logically accounted for, she began to review Bessie's answers again. She stole a glance at her watch. There was still plenty of time.

As Tom closed the door behind him, Joan added, "We asked Bessie how she felt about her son Tyrone."

Selectively for the copy cassette Bessie replied, "My Tyrone was a child of love and a child of God. He's with Him now. Lord, have mercy."

That, Joan reasoned to herself, ought to be a grabber for the Baptists just finishing their suppers. She then found a sequence where Bessie's face filled the screen while Joan asked an off-camera question. The question was replaced with "What if the mayor said that we had nothing to worry about? What would you think, Mrs. Lewis?"

Immediately Bessie replied, "He don't know what he's sayin'." From this frame Joan spliced a zoomed close-up of the woman's face, accentuating the beads of sweat on the brow and the tear at the corner of the eye.

From there she cut to the wrap-up scenes shot in front of the house after the interview. She knew there were a couple of goodies in there and she now only had to find them and add them to her copy cassette.

"Bessie Lewis is concerned with the effectiveness of the investigation," Joan said, facing the cameras. "She seemed somewhat bitter when I reminded her that budget restrictions would not allow the chief of police to add more patrol cars to the street surveillance."

"Then keep them *all* off the streets," Bessie wailed.

"And what if the mayor cannot add any more policemen to this case?" Joan's dubbed question asked.

"I wants him to be thrown into prison," Bessie replied.

Then, back on the closing scenes on the street, "This is Joan Burke, Channel Three News, Birmington."

She glanced at her watch again. She had five minutes to erase her field cassette and deliver the edited copy to Arlo. The field cassette was on inventory, but only as a blank. Erasing it was a safe-enough move. At network level, field tapes were kept as backup to prove the aired edition if challenged. But local stations still erased and recycled field cassettes, if only in the interest of production economy. And above all, Arlo Jacobs' point of view was local, not network. Joan Burke was confident her edited tape would get by, especially so close to air time.

She made it back to the newsroom with minutes to spare on Arlo's five-thirty-five deadline. He was still in last-minute conference with Van Horn. Too savvy to butt in and spoil it all, Joan stood to one side, edited cassette under her arm, occasionally glancing at her watch but carefully not tapping her foot.

"Got it?" Arlo asked.

"Right here," Joan said, patting the cassette.

Arlo nodded and looked at his watch. "Punch it up on number four."

The words were hardly out of his mouth before Joan had the cassette in the machine. The starting mechanism was agonizingly slow as Joan stood there tapping her lower teeth with her ball-point pen. Finally there was a speckled blank lead and then Joan's street intro. Jacobs leaned into the tiny monitor, listening to every word and watching inflections. Simultaneously, his practiced eye scanned the background for inappropriate gestures from passersby or commercial signs that were not essential to the story. News privilege or not, Jacobs was not one to give away freebies.

As the tape rolled, Joan studied Jacobs rather than the interview. She knew it was smooth, and under the circumstances, a masterpiece. Still, Arlo was an expert and not to be underestimated.

When the tape had ended, he said, "Roll it back to that remark about the mayor."

Joan suddenly found it hard to swallow silently as she pushed the button and calculated about how far back it was. "You mean this?" she asked.

"Shhh," Arlo said, holding his hand in the air.

"What if the mayor said that we had nothing to worry about? What would you think, Mrs. Lewis?" Joan's voice asked on the monitor.

"He don't know what he's sayin'," Bessie replied.

"That's tough stuff," Jacobs said as the tape rolled on. He was suddenly oblivious of the rest of it.

"Wilson has said that kind of thing repeatedly," Joan said.

"Wouldn't you say he has been generally reassuring?" Arlo asked.

"We've got him on file tape every day from a week from Tuesday saying something like that, Arlo."

"Could you back it with a quote if you had to?"

"The statement isn't a quote, Arlo, its—"

"Yeah, Joanie, I heard the 'that.' Just the same, if he goes bananas, could you back it with a substantive quote?"

"I'm sure I could," she said, her heart racing. He's concerned about the *mayor's* remark, she thought. There were a thousand remarks from ole Cleland telling everybody not to worry. Arlo wasn't even concerned about Bessie's reply. He bought it hook, line, and sinker. She almost leaped for joy.

Jacobs stood quietly for a moment, his hooked forefinger cradled between his chin and lower lip.

"This is Joan Burke, Channel Three News, Birmington."

"Well?" Joan asked, live.

"Run it," Jacobs said, turning away from the monitor to glance at the clock and his air-time staff.

"Thanks, Arlo," Joan said.

"But, Joanie," he added, "next time, come in earlier and get one of the news editors to help you. This one's a little rough. Oh, it'll air all right, but as an expert, I can tell you did it yourself."

"I'll work on that," Joan said.

"Crap," Arlo said pleasantly. "Stick to being a good reporter. The interview is good. I don't need you to waste your time trying to be an editor. I can get plenty of that kind of house animal. I need guys like you on the street."

"Thanks, Arlo," Joan said again. She was beginning to fly on his low-key compliments. "I'll try to bring you the kind of stuff you expect."

Jacobs turned and looked at the reporter. Suddenly he didn't seem as tough as he really was. "Okay," he said, "now get your pretty little ass out of the newsroom so we can pollute the airways on time."

Joan nodded silently and half-smiled for him.

"Van Horn?" Jacobs shouted, turning away.

"Yo!" Van Horn replied military-style from across the room.

"Get a look at this tape Joan Burke shot with one of the kids' mothers. I want a soft intro and a straight face. Got it?"

"Got it."

Jacobs turned back to say something else to Joan Burke, but she was already out the door.

9

"How many blocks are we from where we found the other kid, Tyrone Lewis?" Jerry Carson, the medical examiner's investigator, asked. He gently flexed the newest little boy's forearm to test for rigor. It was nine-thirty on a Saturday morning and a bright sun was warming the sky.

"About twenty-six," Henry Willis said.

"Connected?" Carson asked.

"Everything's connected," Willis said. " 'Cept we ain't always privy as to exactly how they are connected."

Carson nodded and stood up, arching his back to get rid of an impending kink. "I make it no later than late last night."

Willis nodded at the reasonable estimation of the time of death. He had already come to the same conclusion but wanted to hear it officially from the medical examiner's man. Several years before, the two departments had agreed to let the body studies fall exclusively to the M.E. and the rest of the scene to homicide. That entailed constant cross-training as men came and went from each department, but even those who stayed on and who knew each other's jobs as well as their own followed the rule.

"One degree centigrade per hour?" Bobby Dempsey asked. His question received a scowl from Henry Willis.

"Keep that in your crime-stoppers' notebook," Carson said. "You know that sort of horseshit is not reliable."

"That's what Dr. Langdon told us at the academy," Dempsey persisted. "He said a dead person's body temperature drops about one degree centigrade per hour."

"Sure," Carson said cynically. "And he also said we don't really know what a victim's temperature is when he is killed and how fast the body heat drops when he is wet."

"Or when the wind is blowing on him," Willis added.

"Or if he is partially undressed," Carson said. He glanced at the boy again. He was dressed but his pants were pulled down exposing his abdomen, protuberant navel and penis.

"So that's why you guys don't run around with a rectal thermometer," Dempsey said. "They did that at a seminar I attended a couple of years ago."

"The final indignity," Willis said. "It's not enough that you get killed, but somebody has to come by after they find your body and stick a thermometer up your ass."

"To say nothing about what a good defense attorney could do to you in court when you tried to talk about contamination of rectal sperm or acid phosphatase," Carson said. "The best thing is to slip a hand under some protected area and see how warm it feels to you. Same thing for rigor. You feel it gently. Wiggle a couple of fingers, maybe an eyelid or the jaw, and then move on to a bigger limb. If it's stiff, there's rigor. If it isn't, you've either got no rigor developed yet or you're too late and it's gone by. It's all a matter of time."

"Yeah, but how much time?" Dempsey asked.

"Sometimes more, sometimes less," Willis said. "That's why we call the M.E. When he's wrong, it's no skin off our ass." He smiled at Carson as he finished his remark.

"At least this time we don't have to wait for the autopsy to come up with the cause of death," Dempsey said.

"You're going to stake your international reputation as a homicide detective on those scratches on the neck?" Carson teased. The marks of manual strangulation were obvious for anyone to see.

"His reputation," Willis said, "only extends to the county line."

"Or maybe only to the city limits," Dempsey added with a shrug.

"Whatever your fame, Bobby, you're probably right this time," Carson said. "I don't know when I've seen a better set of finger abrasions on a neck."

"Right-handed or left?" Dempsey asked.

"From the front or the back?" Willis added with a little smile. He knew the questions were almost impossible to answer accurately.

"Come on, you guys," Carson said, "this isn't a Hollywood production. How do you know the marks weren't inflicted by more than one person?"

"How about two amputees?" Willis quipped. "One with a right hand and one with a left?"

"At least the body arrangement is the same as the other kid," Dempsey said. "Looks to me like he's been laid out for us to find again. The arms are folded across the chest and the pants are pulled down."

"Coincidence?" Carson asked lightly.

Willis shook his head. "You know what I think about coincidence."

"He's about the same age as the other kid, too," Dempsey added.

"They even *look* alike," Carson said.

"Maybe they're related," Willis said. "We don't have any I.D. on this one."

"Nobody missing?" Carson asked.

"Not yet," Willis said. "Somebody will come out of the woodwork as soon as this hits the news, Saturday or not."

"McDonald's checking with the Lewis woman right now," Dempsey said.

"You don't think it's another one of hers, do you?" Carson asked.

"Well, look at it this way, Jerry," Willis said. "Most child murders are done by someone close to home. A stepfather. An uncle. So if he was spotted by one of the other kids in the family, he'd have to take care of him, too. We're checking it out."

"The best we could hope for is a cousin," Dempsey said. "The Lewis kid's brother was too young and they didn't look that much alike."

"Well, if it's a family affair, it'll be a lot easier to crack," Carson said, closing his notebook. He glanced around the vacant lot. The scene could easily be mistaken for the place where Tyrone Lewis had been found. There was even a remnant of an old foundation, and a broken walkway led to the street. The lawn was overgrown with weeds, and abandoned cans littered the area.

"You need anything more here?" Willis asked. The ambulance had arrived and the crew was waiting patiently in the street beyond the yellow rope that defined the limits of the crime scene.

"Just a couple more thirty-fives," Carson said, swinging his camera to his eye. "I know your men shot a shitload of film, but Dr. Langdon always wants us to get a few of our own."

"Help yourself," Willis said.

"And then I want to have him wrapped in a clean sheet," Carson said. "If we come up with anything on him that matches the Lewis case, I want to be sure we didn't pick it up from the ambulance or the crew."

"Like what?" Dempsey asked, squinting to look at the body again.

"Who knows?" Carson said. "How 'bout black hairs?"

"Yeah," Dempsey said appreciatively.

"Like feathers in a hen house," Willis added. He knew that hair comparison was based on exclusion and dissimilar characteristics rather than common points of identity. Black hairs on a black victim would be of minimal value.

"Are you waiting for the chief on this one, Henry?" Carson asked. He had already shot a half-dozen slides from different angles.

"Not this time, thank you," Willis said, glancing over his shoulder. "He's in a closed-door meeting with the mayor and Peter Greene. Nobody knows what they're up to, but they've been holed up in the chief's office for an hour or so. Whatever it is, the mayor's office leaked it to the news. The cameras are already lined up downtown."

"I thought they seemed kind of light out here," Carson said. Beyond the yellow rope there were a reporter from the newspaper and a still cameraman working with a long-range lens. The TV crews were conspicuously absent.

"I thought we needed a break," Willis said quietly. "I put a phony scene address on the air."

"They'll eat you alive when they find out," Carson said, smiling appreciatively.

"So what's new?" Willis said, hunching his shoulders and stuffing his hands into his pockets. The homicide chief was unable to repress his self-satisfied smile.

"In that case, I'll have him transported immediately," Carson said, beckoning to the ambulance crew.

———

Downtown, in a conference room near the office of the chief of police, the cameras had been set up in an orderly semicircle that gave no channel an advantageous angle. The microphones had been taped to a small tripod in front of the middle seat behind a long empty table. Three chairs had been provided for the anticipated speakers. Joan Burke, Charlie Thompson, and the others representing all the local channels, several of the radio stations, and the two major newspapers huddled in small groups, smoking cigarettes and chatting with a nonchalance that belied their keyed-up interest and anxiety. They had been told that Chief Sullivan would appear jointly with the mayor and Commissioner Greene and that there would be an announcement of major importance. The subject matter had been left to their imaginations.

Joan had suggested that they were going to announce Peter Greene's resignation and his return to some high-level federal job. She said that that was about what his performance in Birmington deserved.

Not so, Charlie Thompson had said. An announcement like that would have been staged in the commissioner's office. Breaking the story anywhere else, he had added, would make it look like Greene was being fired. "No," Thompson theorized, "it has to be something coming directly out of Sullivan's office. Probably a plan to hire more cops."

"Or to announce the location of the annual NAACP costume ball," a reporter from an all-news radio station suggested dryly. Joan gave a little laugh, but Thompson remained deadpan. He had his eye on Homer Lavine, the veteran police reporter for the morning paper. Homer pronounced it "La-vine" to rhyme with "sign" but Thompson made it "La-veen" whenever he could, even to Homer's face. Privately he called him the inky kike and trusted him not at all. With inches to fill each day, Homer was not above reporting the "attitudes" of the television crews on the scene, and more than one management memo telling them to shape up had been based on one of Lavine's filler paragraphs. Homer covered his beat in a worn three-piece gray suit and detested the jeans and long hair of the camera crew.

"They're ten minutes late," Joan remarked.

"Cleland's sense of theater," Thompson said. "He wants to make sure we're all here."

"Bullshit," Joan said softly as the side door to the conference room opened. "He just wants to show us that he can keep us waiting on a Saturday."

As the side door opened, Thompson gave a low whistle and moved away to assume his appointed position.

Commissioner Greene entered first, glanced at the three chairs, and paused to receive a subtle direction from Chief Sullivan, next in line. The mayor came in last and took the center chair. He sat with his hands folded and appreciatively surveyed the crowd. It was said he could spot an absent reporter from twenty yards and neither forgot nor forgave.

When all movement and throat-clearing had ceased, the mayor glanced to his right and to his left before leaning forward to say good morning. The audiomen, used to his leaning in on opening, had already adjusted their sound levels. Some of them too neither forgot nor forgave.

"I intend," Wilson said ponderously, "to make a short opening statement." His diction in public announcements was annoyingly correct. "We will then be open to questions from the floor. You will kindly indicate to whom your question is directed *before* you ask it. It will be assumed that all non-indicated questions are directed at the chair. While we intend to be candid, all questions answered by 'No comment' are to be considered inappropriate and not pursued further. Everyone is to be given an equal chance. One follow-up question will be permitted before moving on to the next reporter."

Joan Burke caught Thompson's eye and carefully raised

one eyebrow. This asshole must be practicing to be president, her gesture said.

Wilson paused to allow the reporters and their crews a last-minute shuffling of feet and equipment before he continued.

"With me this morning are Commissioner of Public Safety *Doctor* Peter Greene and Chief of Police *Doctor* Gayle Sullivan." He waited for each of them to acknowledge the introduction with polite nods. It was impossible to tell if either of them blushed, although the veteran reporters knew how much Sullivan disliked having his academic title added to his police rank. There was enough crap about his Ph.D. in the squad room as it was.

"As the whole nation is aware," he continued, "we have been experiencing an unfortunate series of apparent murders in the Birmington area. The investigation of these cases has been a frustrating experience for Chief Sullivan and for all of us. The homicide division has been unrelenting in its efforts to track down the person or persons responsible for these killings. The men of that division deserve every praise. In particular, our gratitude goes out to Captain Henry Willis, the chief of the homicide division."

"Oh-oh," Joan Burke said almost inaudibly. "There goes Henry Willis."

"Captain Willis has been the director of the homicide division for many years. His devotion to duty and his generosity with his own time mark him as a man dedicated to his chosen profession. None of us has anything but the highest regard for Captain Willis' integrity and experience."

"Cut the crap and get to the bloodletting," Charlie Thompson said under his breath.

"But in times like these," the mayor continued, "alternative and sometimes novel methods are called for." He paused to glance at Chief Sullivan, hoping for a nod of agreement, but Sullivan was studying the palms of his hands. "The traditional approach to homicide investigations has been to assign a detective or perhaps two to each case on a more or less permanent basis. These men would then stay with that case

99

until it was completed or until transferred to other duties. Under ordinary circumstances, this traditional method has proved to be successful and satisfactory. But these are *not* ordinary circumstances. The cases involving our children call for a different approach.

"Chief Sullivan and Commissioner Greene and I have given this problem a great deal of our attention. We have searched our hearts and we have racked our brains in an effort to find an organizational solution. We have consulted with other law-enforcement experts in other cities and with agents of the federal government.

"Our solution, ladies and gentlemen, is a task force." He paused to let the title sink in, but not long enough to suggest that he had finished.

"Chief Sullivan will fill you in on the details. Chief?"

The press corps stirred slightly, adjusted lights, and cleared throats as the mayor sat back heavily and the chief of police leaned forward into the microphones.

"The concept of a task force is not entirely new," Sullivan began. He glanced quickly at the mayor, realizing he had suggested an apparent contradiction. "That is, not an entirely new concept for the science of law enforcement. Its employment in multiple homicides will, however, be *very* new for Birmington. I intend to collectivize all the detective personnel assigned to the various child cases and to add to that group a large backup force to supply routine information, to check out routine leads, and to monitor telephone calls. These isolated bits of apparently unrelated information will be fed into computers or otherwise displayed in a large common area within the department, where all similarities or differences can be identified and studied by *all* assigned personnel. Through this method, it is anticipated that every man assigned to the cases will reach a common understanding regarding the *modus operandi* and the circumstances. This sharing of information or pooling of knowledge, if you will, will greatly enhance the investigation and should lead to a prompt resolution of the problem."

Joan Burke could stand it no longer. The mayor had, after all, said that *he* would make an opening statement, after which there would be questions. He hadn't said anything about Sullivan. And now Sullivan had paused. "Who will head up this task force, Chief Sullivan?" she asked quickly and sharply.

The chief looked at the mayor, and the mayor looked at Commissioner Greene. The mayor's plan for asking and answering questions had already gone down the tube.

"After considerable discussion with the mayor and with Chief Sullivan," Peter Greene said slowly, "it has been decided that I will administer the task force. And I have asked Captain David Bayberry to assist me."

Several hands shot into the air, but everyone knew Joan Burke was entitled to her followup question. She waited only half a second, sifting through the several questions that had just leaped into her mind. She knew the routine questions would be asked over and over by the various reporters taking their turns. What Joan wanted was to capitalize on the moment.

"Has Henry Willis been informed?" Joan asked suspiciously.

At this, Greene looked at the mayor, and the mayor looked at the chief.

"Routine information has been sent through channels to all personnel concerned with this reorganization," Sullivan said.

That didn't sound like a yes to Joan Burke, but she had shot her two questions. She hoped that someone else would pursue the point.

"How many men will be assigned to the task force, Chief Sullivan," a young radio reporter asked.

"We have not set any absolute number at this time, but I anticipate the total will be in the neighborhood of one hundred officers and ancillary staff."

Joan Burke looked at her watch and glanced at Charlie Thompson. His hand was still in the air. She moved her head sharply to catch his eye.

"Pool?" she mouthed silently, the questions and answers droning on in the background.

Thompson frowned, squinted, and made a face usually reserved for sour foods. It was obvious that he thought Joan Burke had lost her mind.

"Please?" Joan said with her lips and her hands.

Thompson raised his other hand halfway to indicate there was nothing he could do but agree with her request.

She winked and nodded in return. Then she turned to her cameraman and the audio assistant. "Keep shooting," she whispered. "I'll be right back."

The two men looked at each other but repressed their amazement. She was, after all, senior to both of them. In fact, she knew neither of them gave a shit whether the assignment was to scoop the nation or cover a cat show at the county fair.

Joan moved slowly through the crowd of reporters, taking care not to cross in front of a lens or to jostle a light. Her route brought her close to Charlie Thompson. His hand was still in the air, his question still unasked.

"Have you gone bananas?" he whispered.

"Diarrhea," she said softly.

"Oh, I'm sorry, Joanie. I'll cover for you."

"Thanks, Charlie. I'll pay you back sometime."

"Right. Mr. Mayor!" Thompson shouted into the lull. The previous questioner had finished something about where the task force would be housed and how much the estimated budget was.

"Mr. Thompson?" Wilson said, acknowledging him.

"Captain Bayberry has been pretty much assigned to administrative tasks over the years," Thompson said. "How is it that he was selected to be number two on the task force?"

"I'll speak to that," Commissioner Greene said. He sensed Charlie Thompson knew that Bayberry had been selected because he was black. "Captain Bayberry has been one of the principal organizers in the volunteer citizen searches for bodies and clues. It's true that he has not had a great deal of hands-on experience in homicide, but there will be a sufficient amount of that kind of expertise elsewhere in the task force. What I need is a top-notch administrative assistant, and I am pleased that David Bayberry was available to me." As he spoke, he watched Joan Burke thread her way to the door and leave. He knew her departure was more than unusual.

Outside the conference room, Joan headed down the corridor toward the stairs. She raced to the third floor and homicide. Henry Willis' office was identified by simple lettering on the frosted-glass door. A nonuniformed secretary sat at a worn and scarred desk in front of his office typing on an ancient Underwood with her index fingers.

"Is Captain Willis in?" Joan asked, slightly out of breath from the climb.

"No, he's not," the secretary said. She did not look up. She was white, fortyish, overweight, and concerned only with her present inability to line up a piece of type with a faint line on a pink card.

"Do you know where I can find him? It's rather urgent."

The woman shook her head and continued to fuss with the card and the half-struck letter. "He's out on that child murder. That's all I know."

"Child mur—" Joan began, before catching herself. "You mean the new one?" she asked casually.

"Uh-huh."

"I thought that case was all wrapped up hours ago," Joan said, her pulse racing with repressed excitement.

"Beats me," the woman said. "I haven't heard nothing since they all left."

"Then they're still out at the scene?"

The woman shrugged. "Check with radio. Damn these cards. Some genius printed them just wide enough so they won't space in the typewriter."

At least not one vintage 1935, Joan thought. "Can I use your phone?"

"Help yourself. It's city property."

Joan dialed a few numbers while her thumb held the button down. "Excuse me," she said to the secretary, "what's radio again? I don't get to call them very often from my section."

"Four-nine-seven-four," the woman said, unconcerned.

Joan quickly dialed the combination and a man answered. "I'm calling from Captain Willis' office. What's the twenty on that signal five?" She held her breath, hoping her recollection of the code was correct.

"Stand by," the voice said. Inside calls were never questioned.

Joan bit her lower lip softly as she waited, her foot nervously turned to the outside.

"Nineteen hundred block of Chapel Street. It's a vacant lot. No number."

"Ten-four," Joan said. "And thanks."

"No problem," the man on radio said.

Joan hung up quietly and looked up and down the corridor. It was virtually deserted. "Thanks for the help," she said to Willis' secretary.

"That's okay," the woman said.

"Push the type against the card with your fingers. It'll make a faint mark, and then you can line it up." Joan didn't wait for the dull woman to acknowledge the suggestion or to give it a try. She needed another phone in a hurry.

Downstairs, the conference room doors remained closed and the TV equipment in the hallway said the press meeting was still going on. Down the corridor there was a pay phone. She got her assignment desk without having to go through Arlo Jacobs. Sometimes everything works, she thought excitedly.

10

Joan met her second camera crew in a mini-shopping center at the corner of Chapel and Minton streets. She had abandoned the company car at the police station and taken a cab rather than listen to the first crew complain about being stranded with all their equipment. The cabdriver, an elderly white man from Alabama, hesitated to let her out alone in front of Big Joe's Barbecue and the Blue Note Bar, where six or seven young blacks were standing around drinking beers out of paper sacks. He warned her that this was a tough neighborhood, even though he had never been there before. Joan had pointed out to him that the dozen police cars half-way down the block on Chapel would be protection enough, but the cabdriver had not been convinced. To make his point, he had told her about a white woman who had been raped in broad daylight near the main post office downtown while the police stood by in the relative safety of one of the little glass booths. The cabdriver could not supply names or dates for the incident when Joan challenged him, but said that he would never let any woman of his walk around a black neighborhood under any circumstances. When she paid him off and gave him a modest tip for the ride and the advice, he simply shook his head and departed toward downtown.

None of the men in front of the Blue Note spoke to Joan Burke, and she asked them no questions. They assumed she had something to do with the police scene down the street. She did nothing to discourage that misconception when she took out her notebook and began to record the street numbers and names of the business establishments on the corner. Her new camera crew arrived in ten minutes or so and parked behind the last patrol car. That solved the mystery for the beer drinkers. One of them remarked, "I done tole you she was from the news." He really hadn't said any such thing.

She led the crew to the edge of the vacant lot nearest the street and paused at the yellow rope to study the assembled police personnel. As far as she could tell, the evidence team was combing the lot, picking up trash and stuffing it into large green plastic bags. The ambulance had come and gone, and so had Carson. A smaller rectangle of yellow rope on wooden stakes outlined the place where the body of Martin Luther Peale had been found.

Joan directed the cameraman to shoot some background on the police cars and the activity in the lot. Then her heart leaped for joy as an older man in a blue suit and a younger man in a beige leisure suit made their way toward the street from the far side of the lot. They were talking intently and did not notice Joan or her crew.

She bided her time like a sniper before she spoke to them. When it was too late for either of them to escape, she called, "Captain Willis!"

The man in the blue suit turned in her direction and frowned before bestowing an exasperated look on Bobby Dempsey, the younger man with him.

"Good morning, Miss Burke," Willis said heavily. "I'm surprised to see you out here." He glanced again at Dempsey but got only a shrug in return.

"We heard you found another body," she said, microphone in hand.

"That's correct," Willis said.

"Another young black male," Joan added confidently. It was always more profitable to sound like you had the whole story and were only looking for confirmation.

"Uh-huh," Willis said.

"Another strangulation, right?" she asked.

"We don't know for sure," Dempsey said. "We are waiting for the medical examiner's report." His reply earned another scornful glance from Willis.

"Has the next of kin been notified?" Joan asked. She knew Willis wouldn't give out the victim's name anyway.

"Not yet," Willis said.

"But he was from this neighborhood, wasn't he?"

"We're not sure," Willis said.

"And more or less the same age as the last black child?"

"More or less," Dempsey said, again receiving a heavy glance from Willis.

"And will this case be referred to the task force?" She held her microphone a little closer to Captain Willis and prayed her cameraman was framing only his face.

"The . . . task . . . force?" Willis said curiously. He added a little laugh.

"Captain Bayberry's task force," Joan said.

"You mean his volunteer searches?" Willis asked.

"No. I mean the task force Commissioner Greene is organizing." She knew her hunch had been correct. Willis knew nothing about it.

"I'm afraid I don't . . ." Willis looked to Dempsey for a clue, but none was there.

"Has there been any mention of your reassignment, Captain?" she persisted, holding her microphone close.

"My reassignment?"

"The child cases. The team effort," she said. "The computers."

Willis' expression changed from mild and polite confusion to an impending storm. "Each of the child cases has already been properly assigned," he said firmly.

"Including this most recent one?" she asked.

"Detective Dempsey and I are handling this one and most of the others."

"But Chief Sullivan said—"

"*What* did Chief Sullivan say?" Willis demanded, forgetting the camera and the microphone.

"Chief Sullivan and the mayor have announced a reorganization, Captain Willis," Joan said flatly. "I thought you knew."

"A reorganization of what?" Dempsey asked. This time his question did not draw a glance from Willis.

"Well, I haven't heard *all* of it, Detective Dempsey," Joan explained, moving the microphone imperceptibly toward him, "but I understand that individual assignments in the children's cases will no longer be made. Do you have a comment on that?"

"You bet I've got a comment," Dempsey blurted. "I don't know where you're getting your information from, Miss Burke, but as far as I'm concerned, that's a lot of foolishness."

"Bobby," Willis said gently.

"It goes against everything I've ever learned about homicide procedure," Dempsey continued.

"How so?" Joan asked.

"Bobby!" Willis said loudly.

Dempsey looked at Willis and stopped in the middle of his next word.

"There *may* be some sort of a partial reorganization, Miss Burke," Willis said, recovering his composure. "We may not have all the details yet. We've been out here all morning."

"Then Chief Sullivan hasn't discussed the task-force concept with you or with Detective Dempsey," Joan said.

"Not fully," Willis lied. "I expect to be filled in on any new plan as soon as I get downtown."

"And you are going there right away?" she asked.

"Right after I check in at the medical examiner's office," Willis said. "I promised Dr. Langdon I'd come over as soon as the body got to the morgue."

"And how about you, Dempsey? Are you going to the police department or to the morgue?"

"I'm . . . I'm going with Captain Willis."

"May I call you later, Captain," she asked, "after you've had a chance to talk to Chief Sullivan?"

"I'm sure that won't be necessary, but we are always happy to hear from the press."

About as happy as Nixon after Watergate, Joan thought.

"Now, if you'll excuse us," Willis said, brushing by the reporter. "We've still got a lot to do."

"Excuse me, Miss Burke," Dempsey added, ignoring the cameraman to join Willis in leaving.

Every step of their departure, including their unmarked

car leaving the curb, was carefully filmed. When they were gone, Joan selected a background scene and taped a couple of sign-offs. She wasn't sure what she would get from Thompson's pool tape at the police department and wanted to cover herself.

"When we asked Captain Willis about the task-force reorganization, he had the following to say:" . . .

"Chief Willis seemed surprised and uninformed when I asked him about the task force." . . .

"Apparently neither Chief Sullivan nor the mayor had briefed Captain Willis about the details of Commissioner Greene's reorganization plans." . . .

"Detective Dempsey, on the other hand, seemed far more concerned." . . .

"Detective Dempsey, a veteran of many years of homicide investigation, had the following comment:" . . .

"Detective Dempsey seemed to disagree with Commissioner Greene's evaluation of the task-force/computer concept." . . .

"From the scene of another child murder in Birmington, this is Joan Burke, Channel Three News. . . ."

She paused, wondering if she should shoot a few more options, as the cameraman stopped shooting.

"Keep that son of a bitch running until *I* tell you to turn it off, Hastings, or I'll have you filming beer cans floating down the river for an environmental special."

With everything running again, she added, "Channel Three was on the scene when Captain Willis got the news he was being replaced." . . .

"He was not pleased when I asked him about the task-force reorganization and seemed to keep Detective Dempsey from answering my questions." . . .

She held up her finger to notify her cameraman she had one more.

"Captain Willis has been in charge of homicide for the Birmington Police Department for many years. His *latest* murder scene was this one, in the nineteen hundred block of Chapel Street."

———

TD Putnam was already up and about. She had left Barry still asleep in his bed while she struggled into her chair and wheeled herself into the kitchen. She had made coffee and had retrieved the paper from the front porch. As usual, the weekend edition, a composite of stale wire reports and an insert claiming to be an entertainment guide, was virtually devoid of news. The body of Martin Luther Peale had been found a few hours too late to make the home edition.

She sat near a pleasantly lighted window filled with potted ferns and toyed with the remnants of her third cup of coffee as she reread the page devoted to household hints, inane advice, and horoscopes. She was embarrassed to appear interested in such drivel when she discovered Barry standing behind her.

"You startled me," she said, reaching out to touch his hand. "Want some coffee?"

"Caffeine and traces of other xanthenes?" Barry said, faking astonishment. "To abnormally stimulate my brain cells, cause a diuretic effect in my renal tubular epithelium, and increase my chances for a pancreatic tumor?"

"Even biochemists deserve some kind of poison in the morning," she said, smiling at her husband. "How did you sleep?"

"If you wouldn't identify me as being one of the well-known in a woodpile, I'd say 'like a log.'"

"You were very late coming in last night."

"We had a backup at the lab and I thought I was going to testify in a traffic case this morning. I didn't think I'd be *that* late, but one thing led to another. I'm sorry." He bent to kiss her on the side of her neck. "I hope I didn't wake you when I came in."

"I heard you sneaking around the bedroom, but I knew you were tired," she said lightly.

"You could have said hello," he said, heading for the kitchen. The tables and countertops had been lowered to accommodate TD's height in her chair. This caused her husband to stoop slightly as he poured his coffee, but he didn't seem to mind.

"And you would have wanted to talk all night," she said over her shoulder. "I know how you are when you come home late."

"How am I?" he called.

"Oh, keyed-up and exhausted."

"It's my job," he said, coming into the dining room again. "We're all under stress down there."

"Is it those child murders?" she asked, looking up from her paper.

"Atwood's all excited about those cases. He'd give anything to take them away from Langdon."

"Well, why can't he? He's the director of the state crime lab."

Barry sat on the edge of the windowsill stirring his coffee. "It's not that simple," he said. "Atwood's got control over the state, but Langdon maintains complete authority over autopsies for Birmington."

"But didn't Dr. Atwood appoint Langdon?" she asked.

"Technically, yes. As head of the crime lab, he signs the appointments for all the medical examiners in the state. But in Langdon's case, it's more or less a rubber-stamp authority. Langdon and his pathologists are all certified in forensic. They've got more credentials than we have."

"But you do autopsies all over the state," she protested.

"Uh-huh. And don't you think that every defense attorney knows I'm not an M.D." He took a long audible sip from the surface of his coffee.

"I thought that had all been settled."

"Oh, Atwood got it through the legislature. We've got all the legal authority we need, but when it comes down to actually doing the autopsies, you and I both know the sophomore courses in pathology we got at the university are not enough. There are lots of times I'm in way over my head."

"That's what Langdon and that Burton Davis say. But Dr. Atwood doesn't agree with that."

"Atwood says a bullet hole is a bullet hole and that we don't have to be experts in diseases or rare tumors to talk about powder burns."

TD reached out and took her husband's hand. She had heard him express his insecurity before. "You're going to direct that lab someday," she said confidently.

"And then I'll have *all* the worries," he said.

"At least it will be organized."

"When Atwood retires, I'll make it purr like a Swiss watch." He put his cup on the windowsill and ran his hand down the back of her head. She was proud of her hair. Scarred below, she made herself a woman with her hair and her face and her breasts.

"Take me back to the bedroom," she whispered.

Barry drew his hand away and felt a chill come over him. "But I . . ." he stammered. Lately her advances had been more often, his refusals more awkward.

TD had not sensed his growing rejection this time. She smiled devilishly and put her hand boldly through the slit in his pajamas.

"Don't do that, TD," he said sharply, stepping away from her. "It's Saturday morning."

"So?" she asked trying to keep everything light. "What are you? Orthodox Jewish?"

He turned away and recaptured his cup and saucer. "There are things I want to do this morning," he said.

"There are things *I* want to do this morning, too." She cranked her chair in a one-handed half-turn toward him.

"Maybe tonight," he said, looking out the window.

She almost spoke her feelings aloud as she studied the back of her husband's head. He had never been a great lover, even in the early days, but lately she recognized his growing lack of interest in her and tried to deny it. Her analytic mind, searching for reasons, had half-admitted that another woman had found him. TD had fought the idea, unwilling to admit to herself that from her chair she had little hope of competing. Sweetness and love were her only weapons, and neither of them could be effectively used with hostility.

"All right, Barry," she said lightly. "Why don't we change and go to the mall? There are a couple of things I want to buy."

Her pause had given him time to regain his composure. He turned and offered a forced smile. "What do you want to buy?" he asked with genuine interest.

"Running shoes," she quipped. Then, laughing with her head thrown back, she balanced her empty cup on her lap and sped off toward the bedroom to dress herself.

Barry Putnam's laugh followed her until he heard the bedroom door close. Then he turned to the window and studied the activities in the street. A boy of about thirteen was raking the front yard two houses down. The doctor looked at the boy for a moment and then turned away uninterested. The boy was white.

In the bedroom, TD ran the water loudly to cover the sounds of her sobs. In her imagination, her adversary was a tall, beautiful, and terribly graceful light-skinned black girl in her early twenties. A technician from the lab. A graduate student from the university. A stranger.

11

On the way to the morgue, Willis and Dempsey hardly spoke. Willis wanted to go downtown, kick in Sullivan's door, and ask the son of a bitch what was going on, but he knew his first obligation was to the latest child victim. His own protocol dictated a visit to the morgue and to the medical examiner as the next obligatory stop from a murder scene. His mind reviewed the alternative as he drove:

"And after releasing the body from the scene, Detective Willis," an arrogant defense attorney asked while strutting before the jury, his hands on his hips, his face upturned as if to steady the ceiling, "what did you do?"

"I went home," a younger, greener Willis stammered.

"You went home," the lawyer mocked. He made it sound like desertion under fire.

"Yessir."

"And so you cannot tell this jury the condition of the body upon arrival at the county morgue." The lawyer pointed to his right without looking, removing all doubt as to which jury he was talking about.

"Well, I . . ."

"Of your own knowledge, Detective Willis. Not what you presume. Not what you suppose. Not what some pathologist may have led you to believe."

"No."

"And so if there were any alterations—any changes in the appearance of the victim's body—any modifications of the appearances of the wounds after the body got to the morgue, you wouldn't be able to tell us about it, would you?"

"No, sir."

From the moment he had left the stand, Willis had vowed that the scene in the courtroom would never be repeated. Not by him as a junior detective and not by anyone under him if he ever rose in rank. So far, it hadn't.

Dempsey slouched in the right-front seat, his knees against the dash, working on a stubborn piece of sausage between his teeth with the edge of a book of matches. He knew when to bait, when to yell, bitch, kick, and scream to get the information he wanted. He also knew when to shut the hell up. He could tell from Willis' iron grip on the wheel and the flex of his jaw muscles that this was one of those times.

In the morgue, Langdon and Carson had already worked their way through the routine pictures and the removal of the clothes. The pathologist was examining the boy's neck when Willis and Dempsey walked in.

" 'Morning," Langdon said.

" 'Morning," Willis said flatly. Dempsey joined in with a nod.

"Skin marks this time," Langdon added. He seldom pointed to the obvious. Especially with Willis.

"At least that's somethin'," Willis said.

"Can you link it to the other ones?" Langdon asked. He measured the abrasion and made a careful notation on his body diagram. The outline of a head and neck had been printed on the form. Four views showed the front, the back, and the two sides.

"Parts of it, yes . . . parts of it, maybe," Willis said. He watched as the pathologist drew the abrasions on the diagram. It was an art form—a style in the pathologist's movements that another expert, like Willis, could appreciate. Horowitz watching Willie Masconi.

"If this turns out like the other cases, I'm only wasting county paper," Langdon said.

"It's still sex," Willis said.

Dr. Langdon wrinkled his nose and nodded. "Who's arguing with you? I just wish I could pull out a couple of polliwogs or a sky-high acid phosphatase to back you up. I even checked the reagents to make sure the tests worked."

"What the hell else is a guy going to pick up adolescent black boys for?" Willis said. He leaned in to get another look at the scratches on the neck. The light in the morgue was better than it had been in the vacant lot, but everything looked about the same.

"How do you link the black boys?" Langdon asked, examining the inside of the boy's lips. There were no bruises.

"Porno movies, sex for hire with old men in fleabag hotels, something like that," Willis said.

"You've been talking like that for quite a while, Henry," Langdon said. He noted the absence of dental work on his diagram.

"Where there's smoke . . ." Willis added.

"There's hoofbeats," Langdon added. Willis didn't follow that, but both of them knew it didn't matter.

"Yeah," Willis said without enthusiasm. He jiggled his keys and searched the pocket for the hole he knew was there somewhere. The pants were relatively new, but it never took the keys long to tunnel through to his thigh. Without a hole in the right-front pocket, the pants always felt like someone else's.

"How 'bout spit, Doc?" Dempsey said, suddenly blessed with a bright idea. "Can you check this kid's pecker for somebody else's spit? I mean, what if he is the blow*ee* instead of the blow*er*?"

Langdon paused, rested his gloved hands on the edge of the stainless-steel autopsy table, and stared at Dempsey as he thought over the idea. "Secreters put their blood type into their semen and saliva, and if you had enough of it there, it's theoretically possible you could pick up a major blood group. You know, like a dried semen stain on underwear. But a thin film of saliva dried on a penis that's been exposed to the elements all night . . . I'd say forget it."

Dempsey nodded. He'd chased a lot of geese before and was

still willing to turn down a dozen blind alleys if there was a chance that one of them led somewhere. But it was not his job to force the issue with the chief medical examiner.

"Want me to give it a try, Henry?" Langdon asked. It was as if he were asking the senior detective whether he'd be embarrassed to be part of such a wild-assed idea. Both of them knew the process would fail, leaving them only with more convoluted explanations after the press got hold of it.

"Do whatever you want, Doc," Willis said wearily. "I don't think I'll be involved with these cases much longer anyway."

Dr. Langdon looked from Willis to Dempsey and back to Willis. A remark like that demanded follow-up, but not in front of a junior detective and a morgue attendant. Langdon stayed quiet for a minute or two, hoping Willis would volunteer more, but the old detective simply studied the boy's fingernails, one by one.

"Get me a swab and a half a cc of normal saliva in a test tube," Langdon told Bubba Hutcheson, his morgue assistant. The big black man, nursing a world-record hangover, said nothing as he gathered the simple equipment and handed the swab to his boss. The pathologist tore open the sterile package, removed the swab, and dipped it gently in the tiny amount of saline from the tube in Bubba's massive hand. Then, elevating the penis by a slight pinch of the foreskin, he performed the ablutions, hoping that any foreign saliva and blood antigens would be washed free, trapped by the swab, and released into the saline in the tube for later testing. He knew that the chances of success, to borrow a Henry Willis phrase, were "slim to none."

Dr. Langdon's mind raced with Willis' remark. Here they were looking at the latest dead black boy, none in the series solved, with Willis coming out with veiled resignation remarks. Or *was* that a veiled resignation remark? Langdon asked himself. Maybe it was a personal health report. Maybe Henry had gone in for his annual physical and they had found a shadow on his lung. He stole another glance at the detective, knowing full well that lung cancer in its early stages cannot be detected externally, even by a pathologist. He suddenly recalled the athletic, tanned, blond-haired kid he had autopsied years before. The boy, a muscular kid about twenty, had been working on a steel girder in a highway overpass. He had been the picture of perfect health when he fell and fractured his skull. But inside, he was filled with metastatic sarcoma from a primary in his left leg. For a while after the autopsy, Langdon had wondered whether the kid knew about the cancer and jumped off the bridge to collect the worker's-comp benefits. The theory made sense, and Langdon had cultured the idea for a while without telling anyone else, before he suddenly decided to hell with it and let the kid's family collect the money. If the kid had known he had that much cancer, Langdon finally reasoned, he wouldn't have wasted any of his precious time walking around steel girders in the hot sun for fifteen bucks an hour.

On the other hand, Langdon knew Willis was a different kind of duck. If Henry had gotten that kind of diagnosis, he would certainly not be above setting up an accident on duty rather than rot away in some dimly lit hospital room. But Willis didn't ever talk about his health with Dr. Langdon or anyone else at the M.E.'s office. Sometimes Davis would write a script for an antibiotic for a cop with the clap, but Langdon and Mazouk never did. Langdon refused because he did not want to establish an interdepartmental clinical practice on the side. There were clinics at the city hospital and the health department for that. Dr. Mazouk didn't hand out pills because he lacked confidence in his knowledge of clinical medicine. He had gone directly from his Lebanese medical school to the research labs in London, where he experimented with white rats and unkempt Irish physiologists, before choosing to hide even longer in a pathology residency. As a result, if a disease could be identified at autopsy, Mazouk would do it with painstaking accuracy. But if it required intuitive common sense, he deferred to Langdon or to Burton Davis.

"I'm going to meet with the chief when I get downtown," Willis said heavily. He paused to meet eyeball to eyeball with Langdon.

"Bubba," Langdon said, "take off your gloves and that bloody apron and go upstairs to my office and find me a book called *Johnson's Guide to Pathology*."

"Right, Dr. Langdon," Hutcheson said. "What color is it?"

"Ah . . . blue," Langdon said.

"Okay." Bubba had the feeling he was being conned, but he lacked the professional standing to inquire further. If Dr. Langdon wanted him out of the room, an errand for a book that probably wouldn't be there was good enough.

When he had left, Langdon said, "Now, what's going on, Henry?" He looked at Dempsey, but the younger detective made no move toward leaving. Getting rid of Dempsey was up to Willis, if he cared to.

"I don't know, Doc," Willis said. "I heard the mayor and Sullivan and Greene were meeting in Sully's office, but we figured it was just a rehearsal for their next Amos and Andy show. We got called out on this kid and never gave it another thought. Then Joan Burke from Channel Three came out to the scene—we had ducked them all until she showed up—and she began to pump me about some task force that Bayberry is going to head up."

"Bayberry?" Langdon said incredulously.

Willis shrugged heavily. "That's what she said. Something about a reorganization into a task force, with Greene and Bayberry in charge."

"And six computers, I'll bet," the pathologist added.

"I suppose." Willis sighed.

"But what about you, Henry?" Langdon asked. "Did Sullivan say anything to you?"

Willis shook his head. "Not yet. I'm going to see him right after we get through here."

"It's not fair for him to replace you and not tell you about it in advance," Langdon said.

"That's Sullivan," Dempsey said without smiling.

"Did you know about the task force?" Langdon asked him.

"Me?" Dempsey said, sticking his thumb on his chest. "I'm the last to know anything. When you work for Captain Willis, the rest of the department doesn't tell you squat."

His remark drew a half-glance from Willis.

"Sorry, Captain," he continued, "but it's goddamn true. The rest of these ass-kissers down there think 'the organization' is the whole thing. Some of them can compute their comp time and retirement faster than vice can make a junkie spill his guts. But things ain't that way in homicide." He directed his argument toward Dr. Langdon. "Like, Captain Willis here gives a man his head and lets him follow up on his own leads. Develop his own contacts. He don't give a fuck whether you've been on the case two days straight or a month without a phone call. He says, 'When it comes, it comes.' Ain't that right, Captain?"

"Something like that," Willis admitted.

"Then what are Sullivan and Greene up to?" Langdon asked.

"It's probably Wilson," Henry said. "He wants a smart nigger in every job."

"And there hasn't been one made that can fit Captain Willis' shoes," Dempsey said loyally.

"It all goes back to organization," Willis said. "Homicide and vice don't fit the mold. All your cases have got to be made by hand. You can't just plug that shit into a big computer like you maybe can with traffic and burglary, and expect it to come up with the answers. When some dude blows away his old lady, he doesn't look up the statistics to find out how to do it. He does it when he has to and wherever they are at the time. And if we don't get a lead on him in the first twenty-four to forty-eight hours, we may just as well kiss his ass good-bye."

"But we stay on him," Dempsey said.

"Sure we do," Willis said. "First, because he expects us to, and then because the girl is still awfully dead, and then because her mama calls the office every other day and wants to know when we're going to arrest that son of a bitch, and also because the press hangs around dragging up old cases for the front page whenever there ain't nothing else to write about on a rainy Tuesday."

"And sooner or later the case breaks," Langdon said, trying to bolster the sagging homicide chief.

"Every now and then," Willis said. "But only because somebody comes forward and says he can't stand the pressure anymore. What pressure? Chances are after a couple of months we haven't had his file out on a desk or even added a phone memo to it. But you see? That's the secret." He held his finger in the air for clarity. "As long as that asshole thinks we're on his case every day, he feels the pressure. He gets a little nervous twinge every time he sees a cop. Any cop. But sooner or later, when he sees the *same* cop over and over, hanging around just looking smart, talking to his friends again, he wants to throw up his guts."

"That's the pressure," Dempsey said.

"And that's the game," Willis added.

"And you don't think a task-force approach can do as well?" Langdon asked, obviously playing straight man for Willis.

"With a task force, everybody knows everything about everybody's cases and consequently nobody does nothing about anything because they all know too much," Willis explained. "The primary case man doesn't have to go out and be seen in the neighborhood every day. The pressure is gone. Now he can stay in his own home and watch TV . . . or maybe, like Dempsey here, stay in *somebody's* home and watch TV"—Dempsey assumed a totally innocent pose—"because he figures that 'the team' will crack the case for him."

"Comes down to initiative," Langdon said.

"Comes down to covering your own ass," Willis corrected. "When I assign a man to a case, he has to answer to me every goddamned time I run into him. Or at least he worries that he might have to. So what's he going to do? Hang around the department waiting for me to chew his ass out for not knowing one fucking thing more about his case than he knew yesterday? No way. He's going to get his ass out there on the street and reinterview the dude's relatives and friends, if only to avoid *me*, for Christ's sake."

"You'd think that Commissioner Greene would see that," Langdon said.

"They don't teach hands-and-fanny police work in graduate school," Willis said. "Remember, the guys who *teach* that stuff are the ones who are not on the street doing the job."

"You can say the same thing about university pathology departments," Langdon said.

"I thought the real smart doctors were at the university," Dempsey said.

"So do they," Langdon remarked.

"And the guys in the colleges," Willis continued, "think that every new gadget that comes along is perfect for the job. Plug it in, and poof! Out come the answers on a little white tape."

"More likely, displayed on a TV screen," Langdon said, updating the captain gently.

"Then you just read the suspect's name off the tape," Willis scoffed, "listen to the computer tell you why he's guilty, and send a patrol car out to his house to pick him up. If he objects, all you have to do is show him the statistics. He'll agree and come along quietly. Bullshit."

"You've got to admit there are a lot of similarities in these kid cases that would fit very nicely into a memory bank for comparison," Langdon said.

"That's what staff meetings are for," Willis said. "You make some green-assed detective stand up in front of his brothers and tell everything he knows about his case. The things that ring a bell with the other guys will be discussed on the spot. The room becomes a giant living computer and it talks back to itself.

"Greene's computer can't hit the street when the meeting's over. It just stays in its air-conditioned room, humming and jerking off. My detectives are back out in the neighborhoods, a little wiser for the meeting and a little worried about having to get up and strike out again. *That* way each of them wants to go grab their best suspect and beat the truth out of him, if only to get off the hook for the next meeting." Willis ran his hand over his flat gray crew cut and down across his face.

"Now that *never* happens." Langdon smirked.

"Well, it could," Willis said, smiling slightly, "if we could get you and Dr. Davis and Dr. Mazouk to overlook a couple of well-placed bruises on a suspect's ass."

"Fat chance," Dempsey said.

"When are you going to meet with Sullivan?" the pathologist asked.

"I'd like to jump him right away," Willis said, "but I want to know what you find out here first."

"You know what we'll find here, Henry. You've stood at one autopsy table or another for a hundred years," Dr. Langdon said.

"No, not a full hundred," Willis said. "It just seems like it." His tone of voice was that of a man who has come to suspect that this time might be his last. He stuffed his fists into the pockets of his unpressed jacket and stared at the chief medical examiner for a long time before he motioned to Dempsey that it was time for them to go.

12

Bessie Lewis had never met the Reverend Jesse Cadillac before. The God she believed in did not wear velvet jackets or yellow alligator shoes. When Cadillac's men had showed up at her house in a long black limousine, she had assumed they were lost. They asked for Tom Lewis first and then Bessie. With a lot of talk and an advance of twenty-five dollars in cash "to cover expenses," they had convinced Bessie and Tom to attend a meeting at Cadillac's Chapel of Prosperity and to lend them several photographs of Tyrone.

The meeting was scheduled for three P.M. that Sunday. The pictures of Tyrone Lewis and several of the other missing and murdered boys had been copied and enlarged to political-poster size. They hung on the walls of the church like ancient icons or holy tapestries in a Renaissance Italian cathedral. The place was packed. In front of the white-and-gold altar, several chairs had been placed, facing the congregation. In them sat those parents who were willing to go along with the Reverend Cadillac's plan "to bring the issues to the public." "After all," he had told them during their first private meetings with him, "the police and the mayor have not done much." The time had come for the people to do something for themselves, Cadillac had told them. Reporters who had been invited to cover the larger meeting at the chapel concluded cynically that any plan advocated by Jessie Cadillac was probably full of shit but good colorful copy.

Cadillac's men were all over the chapel, looking very much, in their blue suits and dark glasses, like the Tontons

Macoutes. They too were armed, though not as obviously as Papa Doc would have had them. With Jesse's men, nothing showed except their strut and their stance, which silently testified to more than inborn confidence. Each of them carried a thirty-eight-caliber Browning automatic under his jacket. Cadillac knew that with his flock, religious fervor could get out of control and individual disappointments in providence could suddenly flare among the faithful. Divine rewards were not always available for equitable distribution. Excommunications, although not exterminations, had become more and more common as the congregation grew larger and Cadillac became more prosperous. Such excommunications were carried out by the blue-suits whenever Reverend C decided that a vocal troublemaker had "lost his faith" or had exhibited "disharmonious prayer rhythms." One infallible sign of disharmonious prayer rhythms was a persistent inquiry into the church's finances. The dissidents were invited to move on to other corners of the Lord's vineyard without delay or ceremony. An alternative offer was a broken leg or a smashed windshield. As a result of such clear Scholastic reasoning, no disgruntled parishioner had yet risen to nail his demand for ecclesiastical reformation to the door.

There were only hushed conversations among members of the congregation and not even that among the parents as the two groups sat staring at each other and fanning the air with their programs. Most of the parents had never known each other until Cadillac had brought them together, and even now there was an obvious caution among them that inhibited conversation. They were united by only tragedy and shared a common distrust for the police and for the press. Reporters and cops had repeatedly asked them very personal questions, promised more than they had delivered, and still came back to intrude even further. Had it not been for those callous intrusions, Cadillac's offer of sympathy and concern would probably have fallen on deaf ears.

Bessie Lewis was nervous and looked it. She had just whispered to her husband, Tom, that they shouldn't have come at all, when the organist switched from the soft background chords to triumphant entrance music. A spotlight hit the bright red door opening behind the altar as six more men in blue marched in to form a reviewing line. Then, after a calculated pause, the Reverend Jesse Cadillac entered, resplendent in a powder-blue cape that fell to his ankles and fastened at his neck with a gold clasp. Beneath the cape he wore a one-piece pink leisure suit that zipped up the front. His feet were covered by red sequined slippers that glittered in the spotlight as he marched to the center of the altar behind the row of parents. He faced the congregation and slowly raised his arms.

"Jesus said," he began in a sudden loud proclamation, "that *anything* asked of the Father in his name would be granted."

"That's right," one of the blue men said.

"Amen," another added.

"And we are here to *ask*," Cadillac shouted, arms still outstretched.

"Right on," someone in the congregation shouted.

"And we *shall* receive!" Cadillac said.

"Amen," the men in blue chorused.

Cadillac put his arms down slowly and folded them across his chest. An unseen lighting technician lowered the house lights and intensified the spots on Jessie. He appeared to be suspended above the altar. An obedient hush came over the crowd. The parents half-turned in their seats to look at the man who had promised so much. Looking steadily at Cadillac was less uncomfortable for them than staring self-consciously at the crowd, which had no alternative but to stare back.

"My brothers and sisters," Cadillac said softly, his voice increasing as he went on, "you see before you those whose losses have been far greater than your own."

"That's right," a blue man said softly.

"We have *all* lost jobs," Cadillac said.

"Uh-huh," a voice agreed.

"We have *all* lost money," Cadillac said.

"Right on," several blue men said.

"We have *all* lost loved ones," Cadillac said.

"Amen," half of the crowd added.

"But only these brothers and sisters have lost sons to the same killer." Jessie swept his hand along the row of parents before it came to rest on the altar in front of him. There was no reply from the crowd.

"We have a mayor downtown," Cadillac continued, contempt showing in his voice, "who claims to be doing everything in his power to solve these murders. But I tell you he doesn't have the power to solve these murders. Only *God* has that power!"

"Amen to that," a blue man shouted.

"Only *God* can make this killer confess."

"Right on."

"Only *God* can bring him to justice."

"That's right."

"And he will do it," Cadillac continued, "if we ask him to in the name of the Father."

"Amen," the crowd said, almost in unison.

"Now *you* know he can do that," Cadillac said pointing to the left front section of the crowd. Several faces nodded with enthusiasm.

"And *you* know he can do that," he repeated, pointing at those on the right. "And you *all* know what it takes to get him to do that."

He paused for a moment before supplying his own answer with upraised arms, face, and voice. "Sacrifice!"

A chorus of "amens" burst from the crowd, and one obese black woman three rows from the rear seemed to faint against her husband's shoulder. To her, sacrifice meant chicken blood and a village in Haiti. Things her grandmother had told her.

"The more we are willing to give to the Lord, the more he is willing to give to us," Cadillac shouted.

"That's the truth," a blue-suit said.

"And we have testimony," Cadillac said. "Where is Sister McDaniel?" He began to survey the crowd. "Where is Sister McDaniel?" he repeated.

"Here I is," a timid voice said from the left midsection. A heavy middle-aged black woman stood up nervously.

"You had the faith, Sister McDaniel," Cadillac said, pointing at her. Every face in the crowd turned her way. "You came forward right here just last week and showed us that you had the faith, didn't you?"

The woman nodded her head.

"And how did you show us your faith in God?" Cadillac demanded.

The woman mumbled a self-conscious reply.

"Speak up, Sister McDaniel," Cadillac demanded. "It's all right for you to tell us all what you did for the Lord last week."

"I gave five hundred dollars to the church," she said a little louder. There was a small gasp from the crowd.

"And where did you get that money?" Cadillac asked.

"From my aunt in New York," the woman said. "She died and left it to me."

"But you're not a rich woman, are you?" Cadillac boomed.

"No, sir," she said.

"Was that all the money you had in the world, sister?" he asked, sounding sympathetic.

She nodded her head again.

"But you gave it to the Lord!" Cadillac said proudly. "Through *me*!"

The woman began to resume her seat.

"Now, wait a minute, Sister McDaniel," Cadillac said, smiling widely and surveying the rest of the congregation. "Don't sit down yet. There's more for you to tell us, isn't there?"

She stood again and nodded.

"What has happened to you since you gave that money to the Lord?" Cadillac asked.

"My mortgage was paid off," she said loudly. The crowd gasped again.

"The mortgage on your house?" he asked.

"Uh-huh," she said, smiling now.

"Did you pay off that mortgage?" Cadillac asked.

"No sir!" she said. Several faces in the crowd smiled with her. They knew that no one ever actually paid off his mortgage in his own lifetime.

"Then who did?" Cadillac demanded.

"The Chapel of Prosperity!" she sang out triumphantly.

The crowd broke into spontaneous applause and the organist hit a rolling fanfare as Cadillac raised his arms again and smiled. Several ladies joined in the swooning, and Sister McDaniel finally sat down. The applause and the organ rolls continued for a full three minutes before Cadillac adjusted his pose to call for silence.

"When you give to the Lord," Cadillac shouted, "the Lord gives to you."

The "amens" were mixed with occasional "hallelujahs."

"Now, I am going to tell you how *we* are going to get the Lord to help these other people reach the end of their troubles." He gestured toward the parents, although there was no doubt in anyone's mind whom he was referring to.

"I have a plan," Cadillac shouted, sounding very much like Martin Luther King's classic announcement of his dream. "We are going to do what the *mayor* and his so-called police force have been unable to do."

"That's right," a voice chimed.

"We are going to bring the killer to his knees. And make him beg for mercy!" Cadillac continued, his own enthusiasm carrying him away. His brow was beaded in sweat, and white foamy saliva stuck to the corners of his mouth.

"We are going to make him fight the two greatest forces in the world!" Cadillac said. "God and money!"

"Right on."

"Because we *know* God is on our side," he said.

"That's right."

"And because we know that every evil man is attracted to money."

"Uh-huh."

"So we are going to collect enough money to make some-one turn that killer in!" Cadillac shouted.

The "amen" chorus was struck again.

"And it's not just money that we are going to collect to please the Lord." He shook his head ponderously. "We are going to collect sacrifices."

"Right on," said a blue-suit.

"Ain't that right, Brother Lewis?" Cadillac asked, peering over the altar at Tom.

Tom Lewis nodded his head as Bessie looked at him, her eyes widening.

"You stand up right there, Tom Lewis," Cadillac ordered, "and let your brothers and sisters get a good look at you."

Bessie put her hand on her husband's arm, but he stood up anyway. He wore a brown suit coat he had not worn for years, and a pair of green wash pants. Tyrone used to call them his gas-station pants. But Bessie had said that didn't matter if they were clean, and she had seen to it that they were very clean for this church service.

"This here is Brother Tom Lewis," Cadillac announced. "You all know his little boy Tyrone was one of them that was killed."

A collective moan went through the crowd and Tom glanced at his scuffed shoes.

"So you all know how much he has sacrificed already," Cadillac said.

"Amen to that," a voice said.

"But he knows that more sacrifice is needed, don't you, Brother Tom?" Cadillac asked. He paused, took a deep breath, and looked out over the crowd. "I want you to tell us all, Brother Tom Lewis, what you are going to give the Lord so that he will find the killer of your boy Tyrone."

Tom looked at the crowd, tried to swallow, and then said, "My house."

There were gasps and moans of appreciation from the crowd, but Bessie was too shocked to speak. Tom had told her nothing of this incredible donation.

"Your own house?" Cadillac asked, looking at the congregation. "The deed to your house?"

Tom nodded and reached inside his brown suit coat for a folded paper. He held it up in front of him for a moment and then handed it to the Reverend Cadillac. The crowd went wild with applause and shouts of "hallelujah" and "praise the Lord." Bessie tugged at Tom's sleeve, but he shook her off defiantly.

As if on signal, the men in blue began to move closer to the rows of seats as Cadillac began to exhort the people to come forward and empty their pockets, to donate their watches and jewelry and to shout loud proclamations of what they would give tomorrow. Some women shouted they would give their cars, and one said she would give her new color TV set. She immediately fainted into the arms of one of the blue guards.

Orderly pandemonium took over the meeting as Cadillac continued to shout his demands for sacrifice and to intimidate those who hadn't stood and testified. His sign language to the blue guards was operated smoothly, and nothing pledged for even an instant went uncollected. Several of the blue guards with clipboards interviewed hysterical women who promised all sorts of personal belongings and gladly gave their names, addresses, and telephone numbers. Some of them signed promissory notes for hundreds of dollars on forms that the blue men had in abundance. The organist all the while played supportive chords in perfect coordination with Cadillac's staccato demands and praises.

The other parents, most of whom were not members of Cadillac's church, seemed bewildered by it all, and a few of them left, the frenzy of the activities covering their exits. Cadillac had talked to all of them before selecting Tom Lewis as his pigeon. He had not requested direct donations from any of the other parents, although several threw pocket money into the baskets as the blue-suits circulated among the crowd.

Finally, sensing that the immediate harvest had begun to slow down, Cadillac signaled to the organist, and the triumphant march started again.

"You will get it all back from the Lord!" he shouted, his arms again above his head. "All back, and more!"

"Amens" and other praises filled the room over and over as Cadillac made his exit through the red door, pausing over and over to wave to the crowd. Behind him several of the blue guards with most of the money and valuables marched in a solemn line from the main room of the chapel through the red door. Then the blue guard who had been in charge before Cadillac's appearance onstage took the center position behind the altar and shouted praises for the display of generosity and faith and told them it was time for everyone to go home and to pray and to collect whatever they could from their neighbors and friends. Only a united effort would work, he told them.

Bessie, recovering from her shock, finally spoke to Tom, who was still sitting beside her. "What will we do, Tom?" she asked with tears running down her cheeks. "Where will we go? You done gave away our house."

"Hush your mouth, woman," Tom said in a hoarse whisper. "It will be all right." He looked beyond the altar for a signal from the master of ceremonies. It came in the form of a single nod. Bessie grabbed his sleeve again as he got up from his chair.

"Tom," she said, trembling, "don't go back there."

"You stay here, Bessie," Tom said. "I got business to attend to."

"Lord, have mercy," Bessie said. Tears continued to run down her cheeks. "Something's come over you, Tom. That man's got you in some kind of power."

"I'm going to come right back, Bessie," he said confidently. "You'll see." He patted her on the shoulder and walked around the half-empty row of parents to the rear of the altar. The man in blue flashed his eyes impatiently and opened the red door for him before resuming his guard. No one else was allowed to enter.

Inside the room, Cadillac's men were sorting the money, the watches, the jewels, and the papers from the clipboard. Cadillac had taken off his cape and was leaning against a large oak desk, smoking a cigarette. As Tom Lewis came through the door, the minister smiled and held out his hand.

"You done just fine, Tom," Cadillac said, shaking the man's hand athletically. "It went just like I told you it would."

"Not yet it ain't," Tom said warily.

"Didn't I tell you in there you had to have faith?" Cadillac said.

"Don't give me that shit, Weed," Tom said. "I've known you too long for that."

"Oh, well," Cadillac said. "I can't make believers out of everyone."

"Just give me back that deed and the hundred bucks you promised me."

"Gladly, Tom. Gladly." Cadillac reached inside his jacket

and produced the deed. He gave it to Tom, who immediately inspected it to make sure it had not been altered. Then Cadillac took a large roll of bills from his pants pocket and peeled off five crisp twenties. "Are we square?" he asked.

"Yeah," Tom said, smiling for the first time since he entered the room. "But tell me one thing."

"What?"

"How did you work the deal with that McDaniels woman?" Tom folded the twenties and put them in his pocket along with the deed.

"That was no deal," Cadillac said softly. He evidently didn't share everything with his men in blue. "I really did pay off her mortgage. It was eleven hundred bucks."

"That means you're out six," Tom said.

"Almost. Call it bread on the waters," Cadillac said. "Actually, she gave me three hundred back. She was so grateful, you know."

"Praise the fuckin' Lord," Tom said, shaking Weed's hand again.

13

Henry Willis tried to keep Sundays for himself. He lived alone in an older Victorian house near Confederate Park and at one time had kept a ragged garden in the backyard as a place to go to get away from the telephone. Then, to defeat this reasonably selfish plan, he had had an outside bell installed. After a few years of complaining that he could never escape, he moved back inside for good, abandoned the weeds, and took calls in his dimly lighted den. Sundays he sat alone reading and rereading the Sunday paper.

The house had always needed repairs, but Henry was neither handy nor wealthy enough to get such things done. At least, that was the excuse he offered to the occasional detectives who would stop by for a drink. In fact, since his wife had died, he really didn't give a damn. The house had four bedrooms. Three of these were furnished and the fourth served as a junk room for boxes of papers and keepsakes that had accumulated over the years.

He had been without his wife for fifteen years. Other than the arthritic colored woman that came in to tidy up downstairs and change the sheets on his bed once every two weeks, there had scarcely been a woman in the house since Helen's death. On her admission history to the hospital the day she had started to have vaginal bleeding, an intern had listed her as a white $G_1P_0Ab_0$. The intern had been partially correct.

The day following her admission, her doctor and the consultant he had called in from the university had said that it was cancer and that it had spread too far to do anything about it. They stopped the bleeding and let her go home with a promise that she would return right away if she started to spot again. She lied to Henry about the diagnosis and bled to death one afternoon in the bathtub. Her note said she didn't want to ruin the mattress on their bed, but Henry never slept in it again anyway. For a little while he had thought she had committed suicide. He had known several cases where women had done it in the bathtub to be neat. He had felt angry and ashamed of her until the autopsy disclosed the true cause of death. Then he felt angry and ashamed of himself.

This Sunday, as he sat in his den, the majority of the newspaper still unread beside his big overstuffed and badly worn chair, he was again angry. But he was not in the least ashamed. In fact, he felt a little arrogant and a little vindictive. He was also a little drunk. He had brooded awhile about Sullivan and the new task force and then he had tried to write a letter to the chief with copies to Mayor Wilson and Commissioner Greene. The early efforts lay crumpled about his bare feet. Each of them had begun with "I was disappointed to find that you were not in your office yesterday after you and the mayor and Commissioner Greene had announced that a task force would be formed under Captain David Bayberry to investigate the missing- and murdered-children cases." Some of the crumpled letters went on after that for a sentence or two before he felt stuck and generally unhappy with the whole damned thing.

The unfinished letter in his lap began with "I quit. After all my years on the force—years that I'm *very* proud of—I have decided to retire. I wanted to put in thirty years, but you and your stepanfetchit team have decided to put on a black-faced minstrel show called a 'Task Force' and have decided to turn it over to an asshole named Bayberry who couldn't solve a Saturday-night shooting with a hundred witnesses standing around grinning ear to ear through their gold teeth."

Willis knew he would never send that version, but he had to put it down on paper just to get it out of his system. The letter went on to mention several of the more difficult cases he had worked on over the years and ended by telling Sullivan what a great bunch of guys the homicide team was and how men like Bobby Dempsey and Neil McDonald were a couple of the finest, most dedicated cops he had ever had the pleasure of working with. Even his writing was a little slurred.

He carried the letter in his hand as he padded out to the outdated kitchen and poured himself another stiff straight bourbon. He was still wearing the white shirt and blue trousers he had slept in, and both garments looked it. He had not shaved, and a gray stubble had appeared on his face. It was too short to look distinguished and too sparse to encourage him to let it grow out.

He had to put the letter down on the cracked countertop to fight with an ice tray that had stuck to the bottom slot of the freezer compartment, and the letter got wet. He picked it up and shook it after he iced his drink, and noticed that the ball-point ink had not even blurred. He stood in the middle of the kitchen gulping on the top half of the drink, reading the letter out loud. He had gotten to the part about Dempsey and McDonald when his voice cracked. Then, with a swift and vicious motion, he crumpled the letter and threw it on the floor. He looked at the rest of the booze in his glass, swilled it in one long gulp that made him gag and almost throw up on the kitchen floor.

The doorbell rang as he was pouring himself another. He knew it would be Dempsey, and he was glad.

"Bobby, you old son of a bitch," he said loudly as he opened the door.

"Hello, Captain Willis," Joan Burke said simply. She smiled a little and stood her ground as his smile dissolved and his eyes narrowed.

"Women's gift to television," he said.

"I'm glad you're home," she said. "I thought you would be."

"I never talk about the job at home," he said, half-closing the door. He felt a little embarrassed about his appearance.

"Neither do I," she said. "Got any more of that?" She threw her eyes toward the glass in his hand.

Willis tipped the glass toward himself as if to inspect its contents and then looked back at the reporter.

"Are you alone?" he asked.

"Uh-huh."

He hesitated for a moment.

"No hidden cameras or tape recorders, either," she said, holding up her cheap brown shoulder bag.

"Come in," he grunted. He made it sound like a total defeat.

"I think I know how you feel," she said, stepping in quickly while the offer remained open. She was careful not to look around the hallway as she entered. Instinctively she knew this would not be the kind of place where one showered compliments on the furniture or the choice of paintings. She had done her homework about Willis' personal life and knew how her own father had chosen to live after he divorced her mother.

"About what?" Willis said, feeling a little foolish in his bare feet. They were terribly white and had big blue veins, and the toenails needed trimming. Somehow the toenails looked even yellower to him than they usually did.

"About . . ." She suddenly stopped. "You said I could have a drink first."

"It's in the kitchen," he said, leading the way. "All I've got is whiskey."

"Whiskey's fine," she said, hoping it wasn't Scotch.

He got a glass out of one of the cabinets next to the sink, blew in it, and set it down on the countertop. She glanced around the thirty-year-old kitchen when he turned his back to get the ice tray out of the Kelvinator again. There were dried coffee cups in the sink, and the ceiling had been lowered with Sears easy-to-install plastic panels and aluminum frames.

"Say when," he said, slowly pouring the whiskey onto the ice.

"I'll take what I get."

"Water?" He gestured negatively toward the faucet with the glass.

"No, thanks," she said bravely. She never drank straight whiskey, but when in Rome . . .

"Good luck," he said, lifting his own glass to his lips. The toast didn't offer any luck. For Willis, it was just a saying.

"Good luck to *you*, Captain," she said, sounding sincere.

"Did you come over here to see how I was taking it?" He asked.

"I knew how you'd be taking it."

"They're out of their minds, you know." He sipped his drink again.

"With the task force?"

"With the task force, with Bayberry, with the whole damned mess."

"A lot of us think so," she said, sipping her drink. She was careful not to grimace.

"I'll *bet* you do." He sneered.

"Why do you say that?"

"What the hell do any of you care? It'll make a good story. No matter that it will screw up the whole investigation." He took a stronger pull on his drink and refilled it from the bottle.

"I know you don't think much of the press, Captain, and I guess I can't blame you, but—"

" 'Homicide chief retires,' " Willis announced professionally. " 'Film at six.' "

Her half-raised glass stopped in midair. "So you *did* do it," she said, meeting him eye to eye. Hers were not made up, and his were a little red.

"Not yet. But I'm working on it."

"You haven't told Sullivan?"

Willis shook his head but continued to stare at the reporter. He had never liked her before, but it was a categorical dislike. "He was 'out of pocket.' "

"We think he was hiding somewhere with the mayor," she said. "We wanted some aftercomments, but . . ." She shrugged her shoulders, spilling a little of her drink on her hand. Willis noticed that she wasn't wearing a ring. He had never noticed that before.

"Why do you want to do it?" she asked.

"Why? What else can I do? Sit around and go down with the ship?"

"You're convinced that Greene and Bayberry can't pull it off, huh?"

"Oh, they'll collect a lot of fancy equipment and spend a lot of money . . . and they'll burn up a lot of man-hours, too. But the killer is going to stay out there and laugh at them. That's just not the way to catch him."

"You're sold on the fact that there's only a 'him,' right?" She mentally kicked herself in the ass for the question. It sounded too much like Joanie the reporter. She had come to Willis' house to ask the captain about himself, following up on an instinct that said he wouldn't tolerate Sullivan's changes.

Willis sucked on his drink again. Who the hell *is* this girl? he asked himself. What right does she have to come barging into my house in the middle of a Sunday afternoon and ask a lot of stupid questions about the case?

He might have well thought out loud.

"I'm sorry, Captain Willis," she said, offering her hand. "I had no right to pry into your theory about any of the cases. Not here. Not in your own house."

"Oh, that's all right," he said, accepting her hand. It was warmer and softer than he had thought it would be.

"No, it's not all right," she said, managing to keep her hand in his a little longer. "I came over here to see how you were. I didn't come to squeeze a story out of you."

"How I was?" Willis released her hand.

"I'm not an idiot, Captain Willis."

"Nobody said you were," he said automatically.

"I could have gone over to Reverend Cadillac's church. The assignment was open to me. But I wanted to be with you."

Willis grunted. "What's *he* up to today?"

"God only knows. No pun intended," she said. "He gave the media notice that he was going to make 'a major announcement about a major contribution'—his words, not mine—to the solution of the child-murder cases. I figured I'd throw up if I went and heard him again."

"He's a two-bit con artist," Willis said, taking some more of his drink.

"Takes a hell of a lot more than two bits to run that operation of his."

"As far as I'm concerned," Willis said, "it's all bunko, and way off my beat."

She sipped her drink again and noticed it was getting better. "It'll be your beat when he starts fooling around with the kids' cases."

Willis turned around for a moment and ran his hand over his short haircut. Then he said, "Do you know how many soothsayers, clairvoyants, fortune-tellers, and dreamers we've had write in or call us about these cases?" He didn't wait for an answer. "Thousands. Or at least it seems like thousands. And from all over the United States, for Christ's sake. Especially California."

"Of course," she said, although she had never been to California.

"And do you know that some of these cuckoos want a piece of clothing from one of the cases, or a lock of hair? A lock of *hair*, for Christ's sake. From one of the dead kids!"

"I thought all the astrologers needed was a birthdate or something," she said facetiously.

"Don't let the mayor hear you say that. He buys that astrology crap. Only he don't want anybody to know about it."

"Come on," she chided.

"No crap. One of the officers we sent him as a bodyguard caught him working on one of those hocus-pocus charts with a calendar. And right in his office!"

"A little voodoo in the mayor's office," she purred.

"Well, he don't use no chicken bones and incense, but I think he's kind of hooked on the stargazers." He glanced at her drink. "Need more ice?"

She handed him her glass.

Willis forced another cube out of the tray, plunked it into her glass, and added another splash of bourbon. "Do all female reporters drink straight bourbon?" he asked.

"Just the ones with hair on their chests," she said.

Willis waited to see if she winced. She didn't, although the swallow almost killed her.

"Equal rights," he said, raising his glass in another toast.

"Screw that," she said. "I make my own way because I'm good at what I do. It's not because I'm a woman or anything like that. Nobody gives me a break just because I'm a split-tail."

Willis looked at her for a moment before he broke into an honest laugh. "Where the hell did you ever hear that term?"

"My father was a marine," she said.

"Where was he?" Willis asked distantly.

Joan only shrugged. "Hell, I don't know. Nowhere. Every-where. I don't keep up with that stuff. As you said, 'It's not my beat.'"

Willis nodded quietly. She was right enough there, he thought. Once, in a supermarket on December 7, he had asked the girl behind the cash register what the day was famous for and she had said something like "Jefferson High plays the Clayton Panthers tonight."

"What *is* your beat?" he asked.

"People," she said.

Willis nodded again. He was drinking slower now. "Mine too," he said.

Impulsively she leaned forward and kissed him on the cheek. "Why did you do that?" he asked gently. He didn't seem to be offended or shocked. Only curious.

"Because in spite of it all, you're a good man. And you're hurt."

"Hurt by who?" he slurred, a little too loudly.

She ignored his question. "And you don't deserve to be hurt," she continued. "Not by them, not by me. Nobody."

Willis looked into his drink, looking for words. He would have preferred to have heard Dempsey tell him to shit in his hat and pull it down over his ears. He would have known how to reply to that. Instead, there was an ache in his throat that he hadn't felt in years.

"I'll survive," he said hoarsely.

"Men like you always think they can," she said.

"Men like what?" He was curious, not challenging.

"You guys with the barrel chests and the short gray hair and the set jaw and the sad, sad eyes," she said.

142

"And bare feet?" He looked down and smiled.

"Bare feet will do, but I would have expected to see you in your sox." She returned the smile.

"White sox, I suppose."

"Black sox on Sundays," she said, keeping up the mood. "But I'm serious. You guys always end up cops or airline pilots or tanker captains or career military or maybe chiefs of staff at city hospitals. You put it all out day after day and keep nothing for yourselves. I'll bet you've worked every Christmas in twenty years."

He nodded silently.

"And told all those other guys to go home to their wives and kids. While you minded the store."

He nodded again. She was almost right. A couple of those years they had gone over to the Harbor Light Mission and helped carve up the turkeys, and once they had fed the derelicts who were waiting in line at the blood bank to sell another pint. That had been the last time they tried that trick. All the bums got sick when the Christmas food hit their shrunken stomachs, and the head nurse at the hospital had told them to go back to the police department and poison the prisoners with their goodwill and holiday cheer.

"Is that a crime?" he asked.

"Yes, it is," she said firmly. "It's a crime to you and a crime to everyone who cares about you."

"Well," he sighed, "it's all behind me now."

"Sure. Leave it all to Sullivan, Wilson, and Greene."

"And Bayberry," he added. "Don't forget old David. He's waited a long time to draw an assignment that had some teeth in it."

"He should be in charge of school crosswalks, and you know it," she said. She took the rest of her drink defiantly and clunked the glass onto the countertop.

"You got any I.D., lady?" he said, splashing bourbon into her glass.

"What are you? Some kind of cop?" she asked lightly.

"Yeah," he said haltingly, "almost an ex-cop." The bottle in his hand hesitated for a moment over his own glass.

"Oh, God, Henry," she said, putting her arms around his neck and burying her head on his shoulder. "You can't leave them with all this."

"I don't think they'd have it any other way," he said, looking beyond her and out into the backyard through the window over the sink. He listened to her cry softly against him. After a few moments he put his hand on the middle of her back and held her tightly against his chest.

They stood there for longer than either of them expected, and for a moment Henry was transported back in years. The sensation of the young woman in his arms was not Helen. It was someone else now long forgotten but still imprinted on his chest and on his hands. Sometime in the past when he too was young. Then, suddenly conscious of her tears, and ashamed, Joan Burke pulled away from him. She began to fumble in the pockets of her jeans for an absent handkerchief. "Do you have a Kleenex?" she mumbled.

He shook his head and opened the door of the cabinet beneath the sink. "Only a paper towel," he said.

"You must think I'm a real jerk," she said, blowing her nose loudly on the paper towel. "Everybody at the station thinks I never cry," she said, managing a little smile. She made the paper towel into a little ball and tossed it into the plastic wastebasket in the corner. It was filled with a week's worth of trash, mostly TV-dinner cartons.

"They think the same thing about me down at *my* station," he said.

"But with you it's probably true," she said.

He shrugged and nodded and half-smiled.

"I can't picture you as anything but a cop," she said.

"Neither can I," he said.

"And always alone, right?"

"Not always. Sometimes Dempsey comes over."

"And brings a six-pack," she added.

Henry stuck out his lower lip and nodded. "Bobby doesn't like bourbon," he said.

"And you sit around and talk about your cases," she said, relocating her drink.

"Mostly," he admitted.

"That's not enough," she said seriously. "Not for a man like you. You need more than that."

"Maybe." He sighed, trying to sound unconcerned. "But I get along."

"Getting *along* is like describing a meal in an expensive restaurant as 'not bad,' " she said.

"I don't go to any of those, either," Henry said.

She made an obvious glance toward the plastic wastebasket. "So I gathered," she said.

"Brett's diner downtown at noon and Swanson TV dinners here at night," he explained.

"Yuk."

"It's like the guy said," Henry continued, smiling impishly over his drink. " 'All you got to do is take one of them out of the freezer and warm it up.' " He snapped his fingers and then assumed an astonished face. " '*Warm it up?*' the other guy says. 'All this time I've been sucking the goodness out of them and spitting out the ice!' "

Joan squinted for half a second before breaking into a wide grin. She felt better smiling than crying. "But you're not giving up, are you?" she asked confidently.

"On what?"

"On everything. On the kids."

"It's not my job anymore."

"Yes, it's your job," she insisted. "It's your whole life, for Christ's sake."

"I'll follow it in the funny papers," he said, trying to sound disinterested.

"No you won't, Henry. Now's your chance to show them. You can do it all yourself." She reached for the bourbon and refilled her own drink.

"That's a tall order," he said. "Working a homicide series alone."

"You don't have to be alone," she said.

"Who do I get, Dempsey?" He smiled and took another sip from his drink.

"You get *me*."

He stopped in mid-swallow, his lips still stuck to the glass. "You?" he asked, coughing slightly.

"Don't you see? This time we're walking the same side of the street. We both want that guy, and neither of us is going to rest until we get him."

Willis turned away and stared at the ceiling. "Well, if that ain't the craziest . . ."

"It's not crazy," she insisted. She walked around to his other side so that he had to look at her. "I've got the resources. You've got the experience. We'd be a hell of a team."

Willis stared at her for a long moment before he spoke. "Can I see all your film? I mean, over here. Not down at Channel Three."

She nodded enthusiastically. "If I can read your reports."

"I can't let you see raw reports," he said. "It's against the rules."

"Whose rules, Captain? Sullivan's or Bayberry's?" She knew she was hitting below the belt and allowed a smile.

"But I don't even *like* reporters," he said.

"That's just what you tell Dempsey," she said. "Why don't you give me a chance?"

Willis seemed to consider the question for a minute or two. A goddamned female reporter helping him with a case.

"Two weeks into an arrangement like that, and you'd be hating my guts," he warned.

She raised her glass in a toast and clinked it against his. "Who knows?" she said. "It might not take that long. After all, you already don't like reporters."

"Especially female," he said. He smiled at her in spite of his clenched jaw. "Are you hungry?"

"Oh . . ." She shrugged. She made it sound unimportant, even though she had not eaten all day.

"I was going to suggest one of those restaurants you were talking about," he said. He had not asked a woman out to dinner since his wife died.

Joan shook her head, and Henry noticed the way it made her hair bounce against her head. "No place you'd have to put shoes on for," she said.

Henry glanced at his feet and again noticed how white and purple and yellow they were. He moved one over the other, but it didn't help.

"Got any more frozen dinners?" She didn't wait for him to respond. She went to the ancient refrigerator and began to poke around in the freezer. "Salisbury steak, ham dinner, and fried chicken with *fresh* garden peas," she announced, sounding like a French waiter.

"I hate *fresh* garden peas," he said, watching her from behind and enjoying her youthful nonsense.

"So do I," she said, closing the freezer compartment. "What else have you got in here?" She began to scan the shelves of his sparse refrigerator. "Horseradish, mustard, Vidalia-onion relish, and one egg," she announced.

He had forgotten about the onion relish and was glad to hear it was still there. Dempsey liked it.

"Wait!" she called, still half in the refrigerator. "Here's a single wrapped slice of Velveeta." She brought the piece of cheese out of the refrigerator and held it up like a prize specimen. "Want half?" she asked.

He smiled and shook his head. She seemed so happy and so filled with life. All he could do was stand there barefoot in his own ratty kitchen admiring the girl he had always classified as a royal pain in the ass.

She squinted slightly as she picked at the plastic wrapper and teasingly exposed the slice of cheese; it was as if she were taking off so much more. Then, after tossing the crumpled sheet of plastic toward the basket and missing, she carefully tore the cheese into four quadrants and came closer to him. "Two for you," she said, popping the little squares into his open mouth like some ancient and holy communion, "and two for me." She began to chew slowly, her eyes again fixed on his.

"Joan, I—" he began.

She put her finger across his lips. "Don't talk with your mouth full," she said softly. She took the drink from his hand, picked up her own, and turned toward the darkened den. "Come on," she said. "Let's see what secrets you keep in your inner sanctum."

Willis began to follow her, when the phone rang. He watched her disappear into the den as he snatched the receiver off the wall and grunted a gruff hello.

"Captain? It's Dempsey," the voice said. "Is she giving you a hard time?"

"Who?" he said, straining at the end of the short phone cord to see where she had gone inside the den.

"That bitch from Channel Three," Dempsey said. "I saw a car in front of your place and ran a check on it. It belongs to Joan Burke, the one from Channel Three."

"No, it's all right, Bobby," Willis said. "She just came by to ask me a couple of questions."

"You want me to come over, Captain? You want me to come over and run her out?"

"No, no," Willis said. He wondered if he had said that too quickly. "It's okay. I mean, she's almost finished anyway."

Dempsey paused, puzzled by the response. Then, with a tone that said, "Oh well, what the hell?" he said, "Okay, Captain. Let me know if you need me."

"Right, Bobby." Willis tried not to sound impatient.

"And . . . Captain?"

"Yeah?"

"How 'bout later on tonight? You want me to pick up a couple of six-packs of Bud and stop by? The late show or something?"

Willis did not answer immediately, and then wished he had. "Probably not tonight, Bobby. I think I'm going to hit it early."

"Yeah, well, that's always a good idea," Bobby said, unconvinced. "But, y'now, if that crap about downtown starts to get to you, give me a call, you know what I mean?"

"Yeah, Bobby. Okay." Willis glanced at the doorway to the den again and tried to decipher the various shadows inside, but it was too dark with the shades drawn.

" 'Cuz you know how I feel about it. I think it's a rotten stinking mess. And I think somebody ought to tell somebody about it. You know what I mean? Like the governor or something."

"Yeah, Bobby. I know what you mean." His replies weren't going anywhere, and Willis knew he sounded like it. For a moment he worried that he had already sounded too abrupt, because Dempsey hesitated. And when he did speak, his tone had changed. He had that unmistakable sound of someone coming to the end of a telephone conversation. "Well, okay, Captain. I'll be out and about for a while. You can raise me on the radio if I'm not at home."

" 'Bye, Bobby. And thanks."

"Sure thing, Captain. Anytime."

Willis hung up the phone and started talking to Joan Burke even before he got to the den. "That was Bobby Dempsey. He just called to . . ."

His explanation ended in midair as he entered the den. Joan Burke was stretched out on his faded couch, naked.

She wore a smile that got broader as he entered.

14

The following morning Willis felt hung-over, a little foolish, and strangely satisfied. He hadn't experienced any of these feelings in years. He almost demanded of himself that he feel guilty, but somehow the emotion would not come. He was late for the office and hoped that when he went to the kitchen Joan would be fixing coffee. Instead, she was gone. She had left a note:

> *Henry:*
> *Please don't think badly of me. I was not trying to use you. You're too fine a man for that.*
> *I know you don't think I'm worth a damn as an investigator, but I'm going to prove you wrong.*
> *Let me work with you. I know we can help each other if you'll only let me.*
> *I'll check with you later in the day. I'm off to dig up some basic facts.*
> *And don't worry—I won't call you at the office.*
> *Joan*

Willis read the note three times before he made his own cup of instant Maxwell House.

"Everything about you is wrong, Joan Burke," he said aloud. "Well . . . almost everything."

Joan Burke knew that one of the most basic methods of getting a story was to walk in on the subject and ask for it. She also knew that her camera crew had an inhibiting effect on almost everyone. To this rule, politicians were a categorical exception.

Before leaving the station, Joan had had a strategy conference with Arlo Jacobs. She wanted to do a five-part special segment on the state crime lab for the six-o'clock news. Arlo had accepted the theme but cut her to three 150-second pieces and cautioned her about Cyrus Atwood. "The old fart will hem and haw his way from nowhere to nonsense," Arlo had said. "Get a lot of background shots and we'll edit them for voice-overs. Then you can set up a few interviews. Across the desk with Atwood, near some of the scientific machines with a couple of technicians. The usual crap."

Joan had let Arlo run his course before reminding him that he had promised to let her choose her own backgrounds and subjects. Arlo had said, "Lab shots are lab shots. All you'll get are white coats and zoom shots of little dials and machines that nobody gives a rat's ass about. The story is going to be: 'How are they doing with the kid's cases?' Everything else is just horseshit for the file."

As she approached the rear entrance to the crime lab, Joan was determined to make Jacobs eat his words. She was going to make him a horseshit-for-the-file sandwich.

She had parked the Channel Three car halfway down the block rather than tip off everyone that she was there. Her plan was to see how far she could go with a series of unannounced off-camera interviews, hoping she'd get a few "off-the-record" admissions for her voice-overs before Atwood had a chance to announce the ground rules to his lab personnel. She had been to the crime lab once before. Atwood had thrown a "meet-the-press" day and had squired dozens of newspeople through the lab, explaining the equipment, identifying the firearms in the showcases, and dispensing little egg-salad sandwiches cut into triangles with warped edges. Now, as she entered the back door unchallenged, she remembered the sticky red fruit punch Atwood's secretary had ladled out in little paper cups. Lukewarm punch and unexplained chemical smells in the suspicious atmosphere of a crime lab ranked very low on Joan Burke's list of favorite things.

She made it almost all the way down the corridor past the gun racks before she was stopped by a young woman who asked the reporter if she could be of help. "May I help you?" could often be translated as "Who the hell are you and what are you doing here?"

"I have an appointment with Dr. Atwood," Joan said. It wasn't exactly a lie. She did have an appointment with Atwood, but it was for the following day.

"His office is at the end of the hall," the young technician said.

Joan was wearing a plain blue dress with a white rounded collar, a black belt, and low black shoes. She carried her worn, overstuffed leather handbag over one shoulder and looked more like an elementary-school teacher than an investigative reporter. She realized that she looked different from her usual "on-camera" appearance, and it was purely intentional. Nevertheless, she still felt a little offended that the lab technician had not recognized her.

"Thank you," she said. "What's his secretary's name again?"

"Clarke. Viola Clarke."

"Oh, yes," Joan said, feigning recall. "She was so pleasant to talk to last time I was here."

"Never overplay your hand" was not only one of Arlo's worn-out rules, but a subconscious favorite of Joan's. She almost broke it with the Viola Clarke compliment, since almost everyone in the lab thought that Miss Clarke was a disgruntled old bitch.

"Charming," the technician sang. She immediately assumed that Joan was either a distant relative of Viola Clarke's or a misguided missionary from some love-thy-neighbor sect, bordering on insanity. The technician took the opportunity to be busy elsewhere.

Viola was watering an anemic fern hanging near her desk when Joan appeared at her desk. She glanced at the visitor for a split second before returning her full attention to her plant. "Dr. Atwood's not in," she announced. She hoped that would be sufficient to drive the visitor away.

"How about Dr. Putnam?" Joan asked pleasantly. Look unconcerned, sound unconcerned, but burrow in there and remember every word. Otherwise, Arlo had said, you might as well sell shoes.

Viola managed an exaggerated shrug without spilling her water.

After another prolonged moment of silence, Joan got the message. Atwood wasn't in, and beyond that, Viola didn't give a rat's ass. With no explanation demanded or offered, Joan changed her direction and headed for Putnam's office, down and to the right. There she found the scene reversed. Dr. Putnam was obviously in, but his secretary was out. Putnam was standing in the middle of his inner office reading the middle section of a rather thick book.

Joan waited at the doorway for several moments before knocking. "Dr. Putnam?"

He half-turned to look at the reporter, his finger marking the page. "Yes?" She looked vaguely familiar to him, but he couldn't remember where, or if, they had met.

"I'm Joan Burke," the reporter said. She did not enter or extend her hand. So far, there had been no signal to do so from the man. Nonetheless, Joan admired his looks. He was everything she wanted a black man to be: moderately tall, slightly built so as not to constitute a physical threat, conservatively dressed (dark trousers, white shirt with a blue challis tie, and a starched white lab coat), soft-spoken, not too dark, and employed in a health-related profession.

"From downtown?" Putnam asked. He shifted the book to his left hand, his finger still marking the page, and took a step closer.

Joan's mind raced for a moment. She couldn't afford to get him pissed off at her a day or so prior to her filmed interview, but the opportunity afforded her by Putnam's lack of recognition was too exciting to abandon. He *had*, after all, only said "downtown."

"Right," she said positively.

"How are things going with the task force?" he asked, offering her hand.

"Just great, they tell me," Joan said, smiling and shaking the doctor's hand. If he goes much further, she thought, I'll have to 'fess up or be accused of fraud.

"I came to ask you about the latest child case," she said. She took her hand back and marched over to his bookcase. She stood there with her hands on her hips, her back to the doctor, apparently reviewing the titles. If you're going to do it, she told herself, do it right.

"I've heard about it," Putnam said. His voice exhibited the slightest hint of insecurity, but Joan was not skilled enough to recognize it. Her back-to-the-speaker post was working.

"Uh-huh." She reached for a book, but only tipped it forward on the shelf without taking it down.

"I understand the autopsy's been done," Putnam said.

"Langdon did it himself, didn't he?" Joan asked simply.

"Right," Putnam said. He crossed the room and sat behind the desk. He was responding to a subconscious need to repress anxiety by assuming a position of authority.

Joan had heard him sit down and knew that her body language needed to be bolstered. Any more of her back at that point would be interpreted as hostility rather than superiority. She turned and faced him, her arms folded across her chest. "What do you think of it?" she asked.

Putnam made an unpleasant face. "I think it's about what you'd expect from the Birmington M.E.'s office."

"What do you mean by that?" she asked simply.

"It's the usual. No more. No less," Putnam said. "They're not a crime lab. Those guys are too used to looking at diseases and traffic fatalities and sudden death in the operating room."

"You mean, they're physicians," Joan suggested.

"Well, maybe there's some of that," Putnam conceded. "You people on the task force know how it goes. The medical examiner considers himself to be a civilian. I've heard Langdon say as much at seminars. He thinks his office is a repository of public information."

"And you think it shouldn't be," Joan said.

"Not in cases like these," Putnam said, shaking his head. "What we need is a team effort. Police investigators working to inform other police investigators. These cases should all be done by the state crime lab. We know how to do a murder autopsy right and how to pass along the information only to the police. Langdon thinks that's all public information."

"I'm inclined to believe you," Joan said. She wasn't sure where the doctor was headed, but he was definitely warming up. "Why don't you guys take over the autopsy phase of the investigations?" she suggested.

"There is nothing I'd like better," Putnam said. "*I'd* like it, and Mayor Wilson would like it."

"You've spoken to the mayor about it?" She tried to sound reassuring rather than astonished.

Putnam nodded energetically. "Actually, he spoke to me. He wanted to know if there was any way I could be assigned to the task force as the designated pathologist for all the children's cases. But I told him Atwood and Langdon wouldn't stand for it."

"Why not?"

"Dr. Atwood likes to talk about being the chief medical examiner for the state and taking over the cases that are now being done by hospital pathologists and the Birmington M.E., but every time he tries to do something about it in the legislature, Langdon shoots him down."

"How does he manage to do that?" Joan asked innocently. "I mean, where does Langdon get his clout with the legislature?"

"The medical society. All Dr. Langdon has to do is to complain to the state medical society that the crime lab is trying to take over the practice of forensic pathology, and they all line up to lobby against us."

"But why wouldn't they lobby *for* you?" Joan asked.

"Oh, you know," Putnam said, leaning back in his chair and putting his hands behind his head. "We've got Ph.D.'s and they think all pathologists should have M.D.'s. It's the same old argument. They don't realize we've had special training in the investigation of murder. How many M.D. pathologists do you think would be able to read their own fingerprints or do an analysis of the bullet they take out of the body?"

"Beats me," she said. "We thought *all* forensic pathologists did things like that."

Putnam laughed. "Who told you that? Bayberry? It sounds like some of his nonsense. He doesn't know anything about homicide. I don't know why Wilson ever appointed him to lead the task force."

"I thought Chief Sullivan appointed him."

"Sullivan appoints whoever Wilson tells him to. Who appointed you?" he asked.

She was careful not to lie. "I was appointed by Arlo Jacobs," she said. "You probably don't know him. He used to be in Washington." That too was true. Arlo had been employed in Washington for a few years, early in his career in radio. He had never worked Washington as a TV man.

"One of Peter Greene's cronies, huh?" Putnam asked. "There'll be a lot more of those kinds of appointments before Wilson is through."

"But Greene follows Wilson, no?"

"Like a puppet on a string. But I'll tell you something," he said, leaning forward across his desk. "Dr. Greene is going to move on just as soon as these kid cases are solved."

"How do you know that?" Joan asked, matching his confidential tone.

"Peter Greene is a fed. Oh, not right now, you understand, but emotionally. He liked it up there at the LEAA, and just as soon as Wilson and Congressman Scott work out the details, he'll be appointed to some other agency in Washington. You just wait and see."

Joan nodded knowingly. "You're probably right," she said. "I've heard rumors."

Putnam spread his hands wide to demonstrate the simplicity of it all.

"But tell me," Joan said carefully. "Who do *you* think is doing all these murders? That's what they really sent me over here to ask you."

"Who?" Putnam asked, standing up from his desk and moving toward the window. "I've been over that a dozen times with Sullivan and Wilson."

"Well, I've had some training in psychology," Joan said. She had. She had taken a sophomore course in normal psychology in college as part of her degree in journalism. "I think they want me to correlate everyone's opinion on the killer."

"*I* see him as a very intelligent person," Putnam began. "He's able to gain the confidence of his victim and kill him without leaving a mark."

"Is he a homosexual?"

Putnam accepted the question without flinching. Everyone had suggested that a homosexual was responsible.

"Probably not," he said. "I think this man is too smart for that. Everyone thinks he's a homosexual because the victims are all boys. But I disagree. I think that's just a red herring to throw everyone off the track."

"But you're convinced the killer is a man," Joan said.

Putnam nodded confidently. "Very much a man," he said. "A woman would inject too much passion into these cases. She'd get angry. She'd leave scratch marks and injure the boy beyond what is necessary to silence him."

"Why would the man want to silence the victim?"

"Because the boy would know too much about the killer by that time," Putnam said.

"Like what?"

"Like who he was. Like why he was doing the killings."

"And *why* is he killing these black boys, Dr. Putnam?" Joan felt her heart pound with excitement. She knew that Putnam would never discuss his private opinions if he knew she was a reporter. But for the voice-overs, his comments were pure gold.

"Organized racism," Putnam said simply. "Why else would all the victims be black?"

"The KKK?" she suggested.

He shook his head, dismissing her idea as simplistic. "It's bigger than that," he said. "I think it's linked to something on a national scale."

Joan cocked her head to show she didn't immediately follow.

"You remember how Hoover tried to set up Martin Luther King?"

"I remember some of it," she said. In fact, she had covered parts of the story for a network feed right after Hoover's involvement had been disclosed.

"Well, even though he's gone, the men that worked with him aren't. Not all of them."

"The FBI," Joan said slowly.

"The FBI, the ex-FBI, other agencies in the government. They're all scared of black power. They're scared that cities have elected black mayors, and they're scared that police departments are being run by qualified black men."

"So they're trying to discredit them," she said.

"Discredit, embarrass, demoralize. Any way they can. If Mayor Wilson and Chief Sullivan and Bayberry can't solve these cases, they'll look like fools to every white person in the country. Including you."

"Me?" Joan asked incredulously. "I'm on the team."

"I didn't mean *you*," Putnam said. "I meant white women like you. That's why I'm going to do everything I can here at the state crime lab to bring these cases to a close. We'll find the killer, and when we do, he'll be white. I'm sure of that. The evidence will prove it."

"Chief Sullivan has great confidence in you," Joan said.

Putnam nodded modestly. "And I'll be proud to take on the directorship of this agency when Dr. Atwood retires."

"Atwood's going to retire?" she asked, hiding her excitement.

"Sooner or later. He's got his years in. And he's delegated all of the crime-lab investigation on these cases to me."

"That was certainly a wise move on his part," Joan buttered. "I'm sure Chief Sullivan agrees."

"I think I enjoy their confidence," Putnam said. "My training speaks for itself. And beyond that, I'm uniquely qualified to investigate a series of black murders. Don't you agree?"

"Do you have children of your own?" she asked casually.

Dr. Putnam's mood seemed to change abruptly. "No, I don't," he said. "My wife is . . . is not capable of bearing children."

"I'm sorry."

"She suffered a nerve disorder as a child," he said almost absently. "But I'm *interested* in children," he said, recovering.

"Children are beautiful. They're so innocent and so soft." He got a faraway look in his eyes as he spoke.

"Soft?" she asked gently. It seemed like a strange word to use to describe a child.

"And shy." He was going now. He half felt it and wanted to fight it, but he knew the feeling. His hands became moist and the familiar empty feeling appeared somewhere deep in his abdomen. "It's their eyes and their skin," he mused. "The skin is so smooth and so . . . special."

Joan noticed the slight tremble to his hands. She struggled to find a rational explanation for it and rapidly sorted questions to keep him going. Why was he nervous? she asked herself. He had been so confident before.

Suddenly Dr. Putnam's secretary appeared in the doorway. "You're meeting with the technical staff in five minutes, Dr. Putnam," she said.

Putnam was at once returned to reality by the announcement. "Oh, yes," he said. "Thank you."

"I was just leaving," Joan said to the secretary. She desperately wanted to avoid an introduction. "I've got to get back downtown anyway," she said to Putnam. She said "downtown" as if it were a secret destination.

"It was a pleasure to talk with you, Miss . . ."

"Block," Joan slurred.

"I'm sure I'll see you again." He offered his hand.

"I'm sure," she said, quickly shaking the doctor's hand and avoiding the secretary's gaze as she left. "Thank you for your help," she said, almost out the door. "I'll be in touch."

Putnam looked at his secretary and said, "Nice girl. Task force."

Joan was out the back door and down the block in minutes. So far, no confrontations. Now, she thought, if I can only get off this street in that damned Channel Three car without being recognized.

_____

She drove directly to Henry Willis' house and found him still at home.

"He absolutely makes my skin crawl," she told him.

"It's all in your glands," Willis said.

"But he's weird," Joan persisted. "You should have seen his eyes."

"Everybody working in forensic sciences is a little strange," Willis said. "How else would they do a job like that?"

"He thinks there's a national white conspiracy to embarrass the black officials."

"Half the black population thinks so," Willis said. "It's just that most of them are afraid to say it."

"Okay," she said. "I'll grant you that. But there's something else about Putnam and children."

"You told me all that, and I'm not convinced," he said.

"If you don't want to do something about it, I will," she said.

"Like what?" Willis asked, apparently unconcerned.

"Like follow him around. Like checking him out. Hell, I don't know, Henry." She sat down heavily in his battered overstuffed chair.

"And what do you think that's going to accomplish?" he asked. "You'll get Arlo Jacobs bent out of shape because you're spending so much time on Putnam, and get Putnam pissed off just as soon as he realizes you're after him."

"What would *you* do?" she asked. "Tell Bayberry or Sullivan? They think he's God. Or at least that's what he leads you to believe."

"Well, look at it this way," Willis said, turning toward her. "If Putnam is a bad apple, nobody on the task force is going to want to believe it. They've got too much invested. And if they think he's straight—and I'm sure he is—they'll think you're crazier than a bedbug. It's a no-win situation."

"That's just it, Henry. What else can I do but follow it up myself?"

"You could give it to the FBI," he suggested.

"Sure," she said, her voice full of sarcasm. "Now I *know* you think I'm nuts. You wouldn't call in the FBI if the president were killed in Birmington."

"Or," he said, pointing one finger into the air, "you could let an ex-homicide chief give you a hand."

She smiled and quickly stood up.

"Would you do that, Henry? Would you really?" She came closer to him and put her arms around his neck.

"Not because I believe you, you understand. But because I don't want to see you get hurt."

"But there's something there, Henry," she said more softly. "I've been way off the beam a lot of times before, but this one I can feel." She could also feel him. She had pulled him close and he had put his arms around her.

"If I check it out," he said, "it's only to show you that your hunch is wrong."

"Show me I'm wrong and I'll never mention it again."

"Make me an offer I can't refuse," he said.

Joan kissed him firmly, and the offer spoke for itself.

15

Monday afternoons, it was part of Jerry Carson's job to take the various bags of evidence to the state crime lab after Dr. Langdon had finished with them. Much of this consisted of plastic bags of clothing taken off at autopsy. The rest of it, transported in labeled paper bags stapled cross the top and attached to a request slip, was made up of blood to be tested for drugs, samples of head and pubic hair, slides from mouths and vaginas, and fingernail scrapings for microscopic analysis. Much of this material was derived from homicide cases, although traffic deaths and other sudden-death cases required alcohol, carbon-monoxide, and drug-abuse tests as well.

Carson wasn't overjoyed to take these bags to the crime lab. Some of them smelled as bad as the rotten bodies from which they had been removed, and since he went only once a week, he *knew* the odor stuck to his car and to his clothes. He also knew that only friends would inquire or understand about the smell. Strangers would only wince and avoid.

Carson and Langdon knew that a chain of evidence had to be established to carry the case through court if the clothing meant anything at all. Too many links in the chain made it potentially weaker. Carson preferred to shorten it by making himself the only connection between the medical examiner's morgue and the crime lab. This caused him to be called to court more often than the others, but he felt compensated by the knowledge that the job had been done right.

He was careful of the county car as he made his way through predominantly black neighborhoods which had developed around the state crime lab. Dr. Langdon had reminded all of his investigators and associates that it would be more than just embarrassing to read "Medical Examiner's Vehicle Hits Child" in the morning paper. "After all," the pathologist had said, "we will have to do the autopsy and then testify against each other at trial. And no matter what we say, the mother of the child will accuse us of covering up the autopsy evidence to save the skin of our own investigator." Dr. Mazouk had suggested that a rule be established to cover such a situation. He had said that any autopsy done as a result of an accident involving the M.E. should be done by the state crime lab. The suggestion had provoked gales of laughter, since everyone at the meeting knew what Dr. Langdon thought of the state crime lab's competency in forensic pathology. "Let's wait on that until Dr. Atwood hires his first M.D. out there," Langdon had said, ending the discussion.

Carson pulled his car into one of the narrow spaces behind the state lab. The space was marked "For Official Use Only." Its admonition gave Carson a chuckle every time he saw it. For what other purpose would someone try to park behind the state crime lab?

Carson, burdened with an armload of evidence bags, inched the back door to the crime lab open and walked in. As he did, he passed another sign that said "Keep This Door Locked at All Times." It never was, and Carson was able to walk in unseen, unannounced, and totally unchallenged. No one at the lab had ever seriously considered someone sneaking in to alter crucial evidence prior to a big murder trial. In fact, even Carson had to concede that the general chaos presided over by Dr. Atwood and his crew made it virtually impossible for any burglar to find whatever it was he was looking for. No one was ever quite sure how Atwood managed to find anything either.

Carson's routine was to locate a junior clerk or technician who appeared to be free of other duties for a moment, log in the bags of clothing and specimens, chat aimlessly for a few minutes, and get the hell out of the mess. His allegiance was unquestionably to the medical examiner's office downtown, but his unofficial and more subtle role was to serve as a verbal bridge between the two offices.

At the logging-in desk there was, to Carson's mild annoyance, no clerk. In her place there was a hand-lettered card which read: "NOTICE: All specimens from the medical examiner's office are to be brought to the personal attention of the director." It was signed "Dr. Cyrus Atwood." Atwood seldom signed his name "Ph.D.," preferring the more ambiguous title of "Doctor."

Carson studied the card for a moment, resting his armload of paper bags and request slips on the edge of the desk. He had never seen such a directive before, and the formality of the message bothered him.

Suddenly there was a whining voice behind him. "Clear enough for you, Carson?" The voice was clearly that of Cyrus Atwood himself.

"Yes sir," Carson said, shifting his armload and turning around.

"I've moved the logbook to my secretary's desk. I'll handle these things personally after this." The old man squinted above his thick frameless glasses, perched on the end of his long straight nose. He was quite tall and still amazingly erect for his age, so upright that he almost leaned backward. His head was covered by two masses of white hair that defied combing, and he carried his mouth tightly shut with jaw muscles twitching and lips frequently colorless from pressure.

"You want me to check in *all* our specimens with you, Dr. Atwood?" Carson asked. He shifted the bags in his arms to indicate how large the volume of material had grown since the two agencies had started.

"We're going to log everything through *my* secretary's desk," Atwood said, "but I'm only personally interested in the kids' material."

"The child cases?" Carson repeated anxiously. Over the years, he had come to appreciate the individual expertise of several of the lab technicians and criminalists that worked for the state crime lab. The dedication of some of them approached self-sacrifice. Others were just state employees putting in their time. Carson had come to classify Dr. Atwood in the latter group.

"Seems to me you fellows downtown could use all the help you can get," Atwood said.

"You're right enough there," Carson said affably. He still held the bags in his arms.

"How many of those kids are you counting in *your* series?" Atwood whined.

"I'm not sure Dr. Langdon is calling them a series," Carson said.

"The television people certainly are," Atwood said. "Every day the news and the papers run the cases like a box score."

"Oh, *they* do," Carson said. "That's for sure. Seems like if a child is five minutes late for supper, somebody down at the six-o'clock news lists him as 'missing.' But Dr. Langdon says they don't all look connected. At least, not to him."

"No?"

"There's been some with different causes of death and some that don't fit the usual circumstances of how the bodies were found."

"Oh, I know all that, Carson," Atwood snapped. "We get the official copy of the autopsy report for final approval, you know."

"Yes sir," Carson said softly. In fact, the forms that the state provided to each of the medical examiners' offices and coroners' offices around the state had a space in the lower-left corner for "approval by the state crime lab."

"You don't have any *real* crime lab downtown," Atwood added. "Not in the city, and not even in the county."

"Yes sir," Carson said. The director's statement was essentially true. Both the city and county police maintained adequate fingerprint services, and Dr. Langdon had upgraded the medical examiner's toxicology capabilities at the hospital to provide poison studies for the emergency room, but no one could argue that there was another real crime lab outside Atwood's shop. The old man had virtually cornered the market by promising to provide crime-lab services for all the law-enforcement agencies in the state and by pointing out to the legislature that one consolidated, central lab would be cheaper than a couple of dozen smaller units competing with each other.

"So, I see it as a cooperative effort, Carson," Atwood said. "Your Dr. Langdon and his assistants can do the autopsies that have to be done for Birmington, and we will continue to provide the criminalistics."

"Yes sir." Carson eased one buttock onto the corner of the old receiving desk. His armload had become noticeably heavier.

"I've had a meeting with Dr. Peter Greene, the commissioner of public safety, to discuss some of the problems."

"Problems, Dr. Atwood?" Carson asked blandly. As the medical examiner's official fisherman at the crime lab, Carson had learned to choose his own bait. Wide-eyed amazement and feigned cooperation had proved to be his most valuable lure.

"Problems facing the Birmington police and the new task force in solving these cases." Atwood beamed.

"I'm sure the city will be grateful for all the help they can get," Carson said.

"City?" Atwood asked loud enough for the whole lab to hear. "Why just the city? This is going to involve the city of Birmington, the county, the surrounding counties, and anywhere else in the state we think appropriate." He folded his arms across his chest and closed his eyes, enjoying the mental image of this metropolitan crime network.

"Will there be any changes in procedure," Carson asked, "other than checking in the specimens with your secretary?"

"Yes, yes, of course," Atwood said, quickly returning from his fantasy. "I intend to complement Commissioner Greene's task force with one of my own. Come, let me show you." He headed toward his cluttered office. Carson followed with high hopes he would soon get rid of his armload of evidence bags.

At his secretary's desk, Atwood paused and waited for her to look up from her typewriter. She felt uncomfortable on the electric model and had said so daily. Viola Clarke was white, sixty-three, and had been Dr. Atwood's secretary since his arrival. She had not only grown used to the clutter and the chaos but also actually made it worse by her own work habits. Once she had taped a note to his door that said "Dr. Atwood, one of the district attorneys called. It is *urgent* that you contact him." There was, of course, no phone number attached, and since Atwood's lab covered the entire state, there was no way to know which city the call had come from. He had kept the note as a reminder of her incompetence until it too got lost in the clutter. Some said that Atwood kept Viola Clarke around to cover his own bungling. Without her he'd have no one to blame.

"I believe you know Sergeant Carson, Viola?" Atwood asked. He too enjoyed using the old police ranks for the medical examiner's investigators. To him it was slightly demeaning. It made them ex-cops instead of college-trained criminalists.

"Oh, sure," she said, smiling a little too sweetly and extending her limp backhand like the belle of the ball.

"I've told Carson here," Atwood boomed, "that all his specimens are to be brought to your desk for receipt and cataloging."

Viola made an unpleasant face. Bloody clothes, even though they were in stapled bags, did not coincide with her own idea of executive-secretarial work.

"And I told him *why* we are doing it this way, Viola," Atwood continued. "It's to get to the bottom of these child killings."

"Isn't that a terrible thing?" Viola asked incredulously. "Little black boys."

"Terrible," Carson said. He put some of the test-tube bags on the corner of Viola's desk next to a half-edited journal article that Atwood had been "working on" for more than a year.

"Don't put them down there!" Atwood snapped. "That's my paper for the National Safety Council meeting."

Carson began to collect the little bags as Viola said, "No it's not. The paper for the National Safety Council meeting is over there." She indicated another disorganized and unfinished stack of case reports and articles torn from medical journals. "*This* is the article you and Dr. Putnam were working on for the Southern Forensic Society *Journal*." The Southern Forensic Society was a loosely organized collection of crime-lab technicians who met annually. Their so-called *Journal* was typed, photocopied, stapled, and mailed by the secretary of whoever happened to be president that year.

"Well, whatever," Atwood said. "We need someplace for Sergeant Carson to put these specimens down." He looked around Viola's desk and adjacent shelves. It was clearly hopeless.

"I liked the logging system the way it was," Viola said.

Carson acknowledged the woman's remark with a hopeless shrug. He had a disturbing feeling that one of the test-tube bags had begun to leak, but he didn't dare to readjust his burden to find out.

"There's got to be someplace," Atwood said almost to himself. He readjusted his glasses on his nose with a bony index finger, looking like the curator of a disorganized and eclectic museum. "Over here," he said at last. "I'll move these medical journals." He indicated a small round table which could have served as a coffee table in an old New England farmhouse.

Carson felt the urge to help, but he stood there in silence as Dr. Atwood began to push the stacks of medical journals onto the floor.

Apparently Carson did not move fast enough to please the old man. "Over here. Put those things over here," Atwood snapped. Then, turning to Mrs. Clarke, he said, "Now, where is that logbook I asked for? We've got to log these specimens in, you know."

"Nobody brought me any logbook, Dr. Atwood," the woman said defensively. She had become an expert at blaming someone else for everything that went wrong. The talent comes with being a career state employee.

"I told them yesterday to set up a new logbook here at your desk," Atwood insisted. He thumped her desk for emphasis. "Why doesn't *anyone* around here listen to what I say?"

"You were out of town yesterday," she corrected.

"Well, maybe it was the day before," Atwood said, brushing her comment aside with a wave of his hand. "We've got to have a logbook."

"Maybe you could use the same logbook we have always used," Carson said, unloading the specimen bags at last.

"The logbook we always . . ." Atwood mused. He seemed to like the idea at first, but then changed his facial expression abruptly. "No, no, Carson. We will have to set up a *new* logbook. One specially set up for the task force."

"You mean just for the children's cases?" Carson asked. There was no challenge in his voice. He really didn't give a damn how the old man set up the project. He simply wanted to get the hell out of there.

"Well, of course just for the children's cases," Atwood said. "The rest of the specimens will be handled in the usual and customary manner."

"But . . ." Carson said before catching himself.

"You can log your other cases back at the other desk, near the door," Atwood continued.

"I still don't have any logbook," Mrs. Clarke said. She was convinced that with a little resistance and a lot of luck, she could escape this new task altogether.

"Well, you'll get one," Atwood snapped. "Dr. Putnam will see to that."

"Dr. Putnam?" Viola asked cautiously. She disliked working for Dr. Putnam. As far as she was concerned, he was too particular. Putnam wanted everything in its place, with everything properly marked. She preferred her own boss's sloppy ways. They matched her own style and provided her with an excuse for avoiding all responsibility. Besides, she said to herself, Putnam is black. She saw no reason why she had to work for any smart-assed black doctor.

"Is Dr. Putnam going to be in charge of the children's cases over here?" Carson asked. He was glad to hear of it if it was true, but he was careful not to let it show in his voice.

"In charge?" Atwood asked incredulously. "Certainly not. *I'll* be in charge. Dr. Putnam is simply going to look after some of the technical aspects for me."

"I see," Carson said, trying not to sound disappointed. He began to gather up the bags again, looking at the labels to distinguish the child cases from the others.

"Why don't you have him log *all* the specimens in at the door desk until we get something else set up down here, Dr. Atwood?" Viola knew that the slightest diversion from his new plan would detour Atwood further.

Dr. Atwood paused at the suggestion, held his finger across his lips as he thought, and then began to nod his head. "All right. I'll go along with that for the moment, Viola. Dr. Putnam can pick up the specimens down there when he's ready. In the meantime, you can check into what happened to that new logbook."

"Yes sir," she said, smiling gently. She doubted that that problem would ever be back.

"You want me to take them back to the door?" Carson said, gathering the bags in his arms again.

"I believe that's what has just been decided, Sergeant Carson," Atwood said. He sounded as if he were speaking to an idiot.

"Well, I'll get them all down there right away, Dr. Atwood," Carson said.

"And, Carson . . ." Atwood called as the investigator was retracing his steps down the hallway.

"Yes sir?"

"You can tell Dr. Langdon about my new plans for handling things over here."

"Yes sir."

"And tell him we are going to get to the bottom of these cases without delay," Atwood added.

"Yes sir," Carson said. "I'll tell him as soon as I get back downtown." He really wasn't sure what he would tell Dr. Langdon that he didn't already know, except that Atwood had apparently met with Commissioner Greene and together they had hatched some new harebrained scheme which seemed to involve Dr. Putnam. No one at the medical examiner's office was exactly sure what Putnam actually did for the lab. They knew he was slower than hell in getting any results back to them and that too often his conclusions were wishy-washy. More often than not, the Birmington men had little direct contact with Dr. Putnam.

Carson was at the door when Atwood's shrill voice called out, "Tell Langdon this business has gotten bigger than Birmington." Carson kept walking, making believe he didn't hear the aging director.

In some ways, Carson's methods approached genius.

16

While Carson wrangled with Atwood at the state crime lab, Captain Henry Willis was cleaning out his desk. On his way in to the police department, he had stopped to pick up several empty whiskey cases from a local liquor store. His office temporarily resembled an impromptu party, although there were no glasses, bottles, guests, or laughs.

Dempsey stood against the wall, chain-smoking and gnawing on the inside of his lower lip. "Tell me again why you're doing this? he asked.

"Because it's good for me and it's fun," Willis said.

"Like jogging in the cold rain with a stone in your shoe?"

"Something like that." He continued to discover and examine long-forgotten objects from the past and to pass immediate judgment on their salvation. The "keeps" were nestled into one of the Lord Calvert boxes, while the others hit the side of his city-issue steel wastebasket with a clang.

"You're going to look for some of that crap someday," Dempsey said when an unidentified souvenir hit the can after a minimal inspection.

"Fat chance," Willis said. "I've got too much crap at home already. Helen was always after me to throw half of it out."

Dempsey could not remember when Willis had ever mentioned his wife's name before. Everyone in the department knew she had died, but it was not a subject that any of them ever discussed. Not even among themselves. Helen's death had been recognized as the captain's private domain, and no one trespassed.

"What did the chief say when you told him?"

"His feet must have been nailed to the floor," Willis said. "How else can you explain his not leaping into the air and clapping his hands?" A delegate's badge and faded ribbon from a long-forgotten homicide seminar survived ten seconds in his hand before disappearing into the wastebasket.

"But he's going to be absolutely stuck with these kid murders after you're gone, Captain."

"Don't bet on that," Willis said. "Old Gayle and his dancing partners have got a new bag of tricks all lined up for you. And you're going to love it."

"You know that's a lot of horseshit, Captain. Those computers couldn't even find a stolen car if we gave them the license number and the location of the garage where it was parked." Dempsey butted his unfiltered cigarette in a nearby ashtray and started a new one.

"Signs of the times, Bobby. Signs of the times. They don't need any old-fashioned cops around anymore. All they need is a bunch of computer programmers with badges to plug in the data. The arrest warrant comes out the other end, like shit through a Christmas goose."

"If you go, I go," Dempsey announced.

"Don't be an asshole. I've got my time in. You haven't."

"But even so," Dempsey continued, "I don't need to take a lot of shit from the chief and Captain Bayberry. Neither one of them knows their ass from a knothole."

"Careful," Willis said playfully. "The place is probably bugged." A laminated clipping about an arrest in a 7–11 store homicide slipped into the box.

"So what? I could find a job on the police department of some small town somewhere else in the state and—"

"And go crazy by a week from Tuesday," Willis said. "You're about as small-town as the mayor of New York."

"But everything's going to change around here," Dempsey said. "And I don't want to be part of it. Homicide is my life, for Christ's sake."

The remark made Henry Willis pause. It sounded silly to hear "homicide" and "life" side by side, but he knew exactly what Dempsey meant. Homicide was his life too, or at least he thought it *had* been. Once a man was caught up in the detection and solution of homicide, there was no other, more satisfying way to spend his time. "It is a study of one man's *total* disregard for his fellowman," he had lectured the rookies. And he had promised them that if they were fortunate enough to stay in homicide for their entire police careers, they would come out of it with a far better understanding of the murderer's mind than all the psychiatrists, the medical schools, and the courts combined.

"That's why you'd better not leave it, Bobby. *You've* got to hang in there and wait them out. These kid cases will blow by. Some sicko will be picked up and spill his guts on why he did it. 'God made me do it,' " he mimicked. "And when it comes down, it will be due to good old-fashioned police work. It won't have *nothin'* to do with all those humming machines His Honor the ever-loving mayor is going to buy."

Dempsey followed his boss's gaze to the map on the wall. "According to your pins, I'd say the killer is black," Dempsey said.

"The kids are black and the neighborhoods are black," Willis said. "But that don't mean the killer has to live in their neighborhood. He could fly in from New Jersey, if he wanted."

Dempsey gave a casual nod of his head to show he halfway agreed.

"But it don't mean he *can't* live in their neighborhood either," Willis continued. "He's somebody they see all the time but don't see at all. He's common. He's ordinary. It's like I told you about the hen house."

Dempsey began to recall Willis' favorite story for the police academy, but Willis told him again.

"When the man on the street looks into a hen house, what does he see?"

"Chickens," Dempsey said.

"And when a trained police officer looks in there?"

"He sees details," Dempsey said.

"You bet your ass he does," Willis said. "Details and anything else that's out of place. The officer remembers that there were about two dozen chickens in there and how much each one weighed and which one had scuffy shoes and who wore the flashy ring and which ones had dirty fingernails . . ."

". . . and which one wore an overcoat in the middle of July," Dempsey added.

Willis smiled at that one. "You really did listen, Bobby. I'm proud of you." Willis didn't realize he used the same story every year.

"You going to take your map with you, Captain?" Dempsey asked.

Willis shook his head slowly. "I'm going to leave it for you, Bobby. You may need it to tell you what those machines downstairs are cranking out." He paused and allowed a small smile. " 'Course, I might take a couple of boxes of pins with me. Just in case."

"So that's what you're going to do," Dempsey said. "You're going to sit at home and stick pins in the wall to check everything we do."

"If I thought I could check everything you do that way, I would have taken a box of pins home a year ago," Willis said. "Actually, I'm going to spend a little time straightening out that backyard of mine. I've been meaning to do that for quite some time."

"Uh-huh," Dempsey said. He was a good cop. And because he was a good cop, he had noticed Joan Burke's car parked in the same spot all night. He knew that because the pebble he had placed on top of the right-front tire—up under the fender where no one would see it, and small enough that not even Willis would hear it drop if the car moved—was still there in the morning. And he was also a good-enough cop not to ask his captain about the overnight guest. It was none of his business, and yet he knew that it was. A friend does not report the presence of a female television reporter in the home of the chief of homicide, and a friend does not report that she stayed overnight. Bobby Dempsey knew that a friend, particularly an old and loyal friend, would never report such things. But a good cop would. And above all, Bobby Dempsey was a good cop.

"I can just see you puttering around in your garden," Dempsey said sarcastically. " 'Not too many aphids this year,

Reverend?' 'How are your marigolds turning out, Mrs. Jones?'" Dempsey bowed to his imaginary garden guests and made a face.

Willis was about to frame an answer, although he didn't have one totally satisfactory to himself, when Captain Bayberry appeared in the doorway. Unlike Willis and Dempsey, Bayberry wore a deep-blue double-breasted uniform jacket with brass buttons and gold stripes on the sleeves, as well as his captain's bars on his collar. He had mercifully left his cap with the gold-braided visor on his desk. He was pretty, just as he intended, and if it weren't for the fact that he was thirty pounds overweight, sweating heavily, and out of breath, he would have been perfect for the cover of a police fraternal magazine.

"Henry, I don't believe it," Bayberry said.

Willis shrugged slightly and kept packing.

"It's hard for me to think of homicide without thinking of you at the same time," Bayberry said. He took a clean well-pressed handkerchief from his right-rear pocket, and without unfolding it pressed it to his brow. Willis was reminded that his own handkerchief was dirty and crumpled in his pocket. Dempsey was reminded that he didn't have one.

"Good morning, Dempsey," Bayberry said in begrudging recognition.

"Good morning, Captain," Dempsey replied. He stood a little straighter and butted his cigarette while the captain again mopped his brow.

"The chief called me in and told me to get down here and catch you before you leave," Bayberry said.

"Oh?" Willis said without looking up.

"He is going to put me in charge of the homicide aspects of the children's cases," Bayberry said. His face had begun to shine again, although he had recaptured his breath.

"You and the computers," Willis announced flatly.

"I won't have much to do with the computers, Henry," Bayberry said. "I understand the chief and Commissioner Greene are bringing in some outside help on that. Somebody from the statistics-and-finance branch of the city government."

"Good," Willis said unconvincingly.

"The chief asked me to come down here to see what kind of notes or charts you have that might assist me in setting up my team," Bayberry said.

"You mean to make sure I didn't take anything home with me," Willis said. In fact, Sullivan had told Bayberry to get his ass down to Willis' office to make sure that Willis didn't destroy some kind of map or chart he understood Willis had constructed. Sullivan had never seen it personally.

"You have Chief Sullivan's complete trust," Bayberry said. "You know that, Henry." He glanced at Dempsey and felt a little self-conscious. "Do you mind?" he asked Dempsey a little impatiently.

"Huh?" Dempsey said. "Oh, sure. Not at all, Captain. I've got lots of things to do." He looked around the area where he had been standing for anything he might have left, and then, while straightening his belt and his jacket, crossed in front of the desk to approach the door. "I'll see you before you leave," he said to Willis.

"Okay, Bobby," Willis said. He did not offer his hand. Neither of them felt it was a good-bye.

Bayberry watched quietly as Dempsey left the room. He then stepped over and closed the door. The middle of it was glass, but it created a small barrier between Willis' inner office and his secretary's alcove right out front.

Bayberry leaned close to the desk and lowered his voice. "Look, Henry, I know why you're pissed off. You've done a great job with this section over the years. Nobody can take that away from you. But this is now, Henry. We've got to move with the times. The mayor says we are going to be criticized all across the country if we don't show them we're up-to-date. That's where the computers and the task force come in. He's got nothing personal against you."

"And I don't take it as anything personal," Willis said.

"Then what, then?"

"I suppose it's pride more than anything," Willis admitted.

"You? Proud?" Bayberry scoffed. "I don't think I've *ever* heard you blow your own horn about anything."

"No, not pride like that, David. Quiet pride. The kind that makes everything go right and the kind that won't let you be associated with failure."

Bayberry looked at Willis for a moment before replying. He could understand Willis' brand of idealism. He had had some of it himself when he first joined the police force. But whereas Willis had opted for the tight jaw and the closed-fist approach, Bayberry had chosen departmental politics. And politics required compromises.

"And you think this project is going to fail," Bayberry said.

"Guaranteed."

"Because of what?"

"Because of distance, David."

"Distance," Bayberry said, testing the word.

"Homicide investigation is a one-on-one game. The killer goes one-on-one with the victim. The detective goes one-on-one with the killer."

"And Captain Willis goes one-on-one with the detective."

"Simple as that," Willis agreed.

"But why can't a team or a task force collect all the information, put it together, and run it back out on the street for an arrest once identification has been made by the computers?"

"David, you're a dreamer. All that computer is going to give you is numbers and probability. It'll tell you how many blue cars are owned by blue-eyed rednecks and how many rubbers were probably thrown into the river last Saturday night, but it isn't going to be out there to listen to some pissed-off hood spill his guts just to get even with somebody. And your task force isn't going to be in the right place at the right time to make a deal with some punk when he's caught red-handed."

"That's not how it's going to be up here, Henry," Bayberry said.

"Look, if they wanted you to run this place your own way, whatever *that* is, they would have told you so and they would have told *me* so. But that's not the way it is. That's why it's time for me to go, David. Mayor Wilson is stuck between a rock and a hard place. Either way he goes, he's going to feel the pressure. Either he's a black mayor who won't interfere with traditional white Southern police styles or he's an innovator who is willing to bring modern science to the unenlightened South despite the opposition it evokes within the police department."

"You think he's grandstanding?"

"I don't think he has any other choice," Willis said. "Either Sullivan put you in charge of homicide because you're black and beautiful or because you'll stay in line when they have to explain to the media why the task force and the computers didn't work."

Bayberry glanced at the map on the wall. "Is that it?" he asked.

"That's my whole bag of tricks," Willis said. He closed the box he had been packing and Scotch-taped the edges.

"What do the pins mean?" Bayberry said, stepping closer to the map.

"They mean they've got a point on one end and a head on the other and they stick in the wall if you hold them the right way and push."

"Up yours," Bayberry said, still looking at the map.

"It's not black, David," Willis said, "but you can kiss it." He put the box under his arm and headed for the door.

Still looking at the map, Bayberry asked, "Where will you be if I need to contact you?"

"Check with Dempsey," Willis said. "He knows everything."

"You may be right, there," Bayberry said softly. He turned and offered his hand to Willis. Willis had the box under his right arm and awkwardly attempted to offer his inverted left before he mentally said the hell with it, shifted the box to the other arm, and shook Bayberry's hand firmly. Neither of them could fully understand what the other was about to do with his life.

17

The senior staff at the medical examiner's office seldom met
formally. This was because Tom Langdon, M.D., had full
confidence in his colleagues to perform their duties almost
independently. This Monday was entirely different, Langdon
had decided, and in prompt response to his request, they had
gathered in his office.

Burton Davis, technically on third call for the week,
appeared the most relaxed. He had come in from home,
where he had been working on an aged tractor engine which
he hoped to restore sufficiently to use on his forty acre
"farm." The farm did not produce anything except trees, a
few scrub cattle, and an opportunity to get away from the
city. It had taken him an hour and a half to drive into the
city from his isolated retreat, and he was the last to arrive.

Dr. Mazouk had drawn first call in the morgue that week
and appeared in a green scrub suit and old sneakers splattered
with dried blood. Mazouk took the opportunity to light up
an unfiltered Camel. He was the closest thing to a pure
scientist the medical examiner's office had ever seen. Mazouk
still looked up the anatomy before testifying in court about
a run-of-the-mill thirty-eight-caliber shooting. The others
knew the defense attorney wouldn't give a damn about the
course of an injured artery or the origins and insertions of
an obscure muscle in the forearm. All the prosecutor and the
defense would want to know was where the bullet went in,
where it came out, and the official cause of death. What it
went through inside the body was pure scientific bullshit.

"We don't have many staff meetings," Langdon said. "Maybe we should."

Mazouk nodded in agreement, but no one else did.

"The reason we don't," Langdon continued, "is—"

"Chief," Davis interrupted, "if you don't mind, I'd rather hear about why we *are* meeting than why we don't. As for me, I'm happier than a pig in shit if we don't meet at all."

The remark caught Langdon by surprise. "Yeah . . . right, Burt," he said slowly. "We may have a problem, and I don't want any of you to be caught off guard."

"Libby's pregnant," Davis offered, grinning from ear to ear.

"It involves the mayor," Langdon said flatly.

"Florence Potter's pregnant," Davis said, persisting in his uninvited humor.

"The mayor has a hair across his ass about the kid cases, and he's gotten to Sullivan and Peter Greene," Langdon said.

Mazouk raised his eyebrows expectantly, and Carson nodded in silence. At a meeting of the pathologists, Carson knew he was expected to shut up until called on.

"All *my* cases are signed out," Davis said. His record for tardiness in completing his autopsy reports was almost legendary. But in the childrens' cases he had managed to keep up-to-date. Such was the pressure exerted by the police, the D.A.'s office, and the press. Mazouk's cases, on the other hand, were always up-to-date, even when no one was interested in his findings.

"He's organized some kind of a computer-assisted task force and turned all the kid cases over to it," Langdon continued.

"How many are in *his* series?" Davis asked. "Twelve or fifteen?"

"They're going to check every child death for the past three years," Langdon said. "What's that come to, Jerry?"

"Fifty-eight," Carson said, looking at his notes.

"I'll bet Henry Willis is fit to be tied," Davis said.

"Worse," Langdon said. "He quit."

There was a collective gasp.

"*Henry* Willis?" Davis asked.

"And Bayberry's taking over homicide," Langdon said. He pronounced the black captain's name with such contempt that no one was invited to think it was a good idea.

"I cannot believe that," Dr. Mazouk said.

"It's true, Kal," Langdon said. "And that's not all. Jerry's been over to the crime lab, and Dr. Atwood has already joined the new team." He called on the chief investigator with a glance.

"Dr. Atwood had me checking in all new evidence directly to him," Carson began to explain, "but he couldn't figure out how to do it. At least not for now. I got the feeling he is going to put Putnam on the children's cases and leave himself free to play with the press."

"Now, that figures," Davis said. "Old Cy would never pass up a chance to get on-camera."

"The main thing is for us not to get stuck in the middle of all this," Langdon said. "I've got some ideas, but I want to hear yours first."

Burton Davis shrugged. "Business as usual, I guess. I'll do my cases, dictate a report, and bump the top copy to the crime lab. Atwood can send it to any asshole he chooses."

"Kaleb?" Langdon asked.

"It's rather mysterious," the Lebanese pathologist said. "Why should there be a shake-up when we are just in the middle of such important cases?"

"That's exactly why," Langdon said. "As I see it, the mayor wanted to orchestrate a takeover, and the kid cases are providing him with suitable cover."

"A takeover?" Mazouk asked, mulling the word. His mind flashed to the political coups his own country had experienced when he was a young man at the American University of Beirut. Until this very moment he had never associated that type of political upheaval with the United States.

"In real estate, Kal, the three most important things are location, location, and location," Davis said, counting on his fingers. "With Mayor Wilson, the three most important qualities for anybody he appoints are black, black, and blacker."

"I wish I didn't have to agree with you, Burt," Langdon said. "But Bayberry's appointment makes it a little too obvious."

"The guy couldn't find his ass with both hands," Davis said.

"And you think that's why Dr. Atwood is turning all the cases over to Dr. Putnam?" Mazouk said.

"He's light, but he'll do," Carson said.

"I don't believe it," Mazouk said, folding his arms across his chest.

"Got a better analysis?" Davis asked. Teasing Mazouk was one of his more enjoyable pastimes, and usually the Lebanese didn't know it was happening.

"The mayor is getting pressure from the press," Mazouk said, giving it a try, "and Sullivan is feeling a little frustrated by the lack of an arrest, and . . ." He stalled, unable to continue the logic. "What do you want us to do?" he finally asked. "You're more familiar with downtown politics than we are."

"I'm not so sure about that," Langdon said, glancing at Davis. "Burt's had his finger in a few pies down there. He knows how the game gets played."

"The city provides the cases and the county foots the bill," Davis mused.

"And that may be our out," Langdon said, leading gently.

"Lay it on me," Davis said.

"Rather than get caught up in the city infighting," Langdon said, "it may be time for us to remember that we are a *county* office."

"You mean, not do any city homicides?" Mazouk asked.

"We can't go *that* far," Langdon said, "but it's similar to how we have stiff-armed the feds from time to time. When we didn't want to be bothered with the FBI, we simply told them we were a county agency and not authorized to deal directly with the federal government. Remember?"

"Yeah, but the mayor and the chief of police aren't going to put up with that kind of bullshit, Tom," Davis argued.

"Who knows? It worked with the Fee-Bees didn't it?" Langdon said.

"When they want something from us," Carson agreed, "they are part of the community. But when we want to look inside one of *their* facilities to check the bloodstains or the cell where a death happened, they suddenly become federal and immune."

Davis shook his head. "But Sullivan isn't going to go away just because you shut the door in his face and say 'Sorry, we're county, not city.' Shit, he'll have Bayberry himself over here attending autopsies and throwing up all over Bubba's nice clean morgue floor."

"I may have to check it out with the county attorney," Langdon said, thinking out loud.

"He's black too," Carson warned.

Dr. Langdon looked at his chief investigator and emitted a long low sigh.

"I'm not sure I completely agree with the suggestion of a racial conspiracy," Mazouk said slowly.

Langdon turned his gaze from his investigator to the face of his Lebanese colleague. In some ways Mazouk was so thorough and so perceptive, he thought. And in other ways he was simply Lebanese. "I don't think I used the word 'conspiracy,' " he said.

"The implication was there," Mazouk said, his tone reminiscent of his British training.

"I'm simply trying to bring everyone up-to-date and look for ways to cover our asses," Langdon said.

"I suggest, for one, that my *ass*, as you put it, Dr. Langdon, does not need covering," Mazouk said. "All of *my* cases are in order, and I don't care who is nominally in charge of the investigation."

Dr. Langdon was partially stunned and fought hard not to show it. Mazouk had never called him "Dr. Langdon" except when they had all gotten drunk and argued over Watergate, Nixon, and the constitutionality of the tapes.

"I hope you're right, Kal," Langdon said gently. "Maybe I'm reading too much into all this."

"I don't think so," Carson said. He received a sharp glance from Langdon that shut him off.

"Dr. Mazouk has made a good point, Jerry," Langdon said. "Just because the mayor felt it necessary to try another investigative technique, we shouldn't feel too defensive. After all, we haven't given it a fair chance. Isn't that right, *Doctor Davis?*"

Davis had been equally stunned by Mazouk's remark and hadn't heard all of Langdon's last statement. The sound of his own name and title brought him back to reality. "Huh? Oh, yeah. Right, chief," he said quickly. "I've always liked Captain Bayberry."

Carson still didn't get it, and the confused expression on his face showed it.

"Well," Langdon said, standing up from his desk, "that's about all I have to say. Sorry to spoil your day off, Burt."

"No problem," Davis said expansively. He stood up and began to stuff his plaid workshirt into his beltless jeans. "I had some things to get in town anyway."

"What about you, Kal?" Langdon asked pleasantly. "What are you up to today?"

"Oh, I have a few topics to look into at the university library," Mazouk said. His tone had softened considerably.

"Another paper?" Langdon asked casually.

"Actually, I'm checking the references to that paper the New York group wrote on narcotic emboli in lung sections. I was rather skeptical about some of their conclusions, and I intend to see if they cited their sources accurately."

"Well, if anyone can do it, you can, Kal," Langdon said. He offered his hand, and the Lebanese pathologist shook it warmly, smiling ear to ear and showing a lot of very white teeth.

"You want Carson to drive you over there?" Langdon asked. "Parking can be a bitch."

"Oh, that won't be necessary," Mazouk said, gathering the few papers he had brought into the office with him. "I have a current decal."

"I envy your energy," Langdon said. "There are a few things I need to check out at the library too. Maybe next week."

"If I can be of any assistance . . ." Mazouk said.

Langdon waved off the offer with a flip of his hand. "No, thanks, Kal. I'll get to it. It's something I've got to do for myself." He looked down at the papers on his desk and seemed instantly preoccupied.

"Be careful with all of that farm machinery," Mazouk told Davis as he turned to leave. "Injuries to the eyes and the extremities are very common in the agricultural environment."

"I'll cover my ass," Davis said softly. His remark drew a quick glance from Langdon and a narrowing of the Lebanese eyes. As usual, Mazouk was unable to completely comprehend Davis' comment.

"Right," Mazouk said curiously. "I'll be on my way, then."

"Take care, Doctor," Carson said.

Mazouk nodded as he left, closing the door with a small precise click of the mechanism.

Langdon immediately pointed at Carson and threw his head toward the door. The gesture was quickly understood. The investigator crossed the room. Langdon didn't really believe that Mazouk would be listening at the door, but these were troubled times. He made eye contact with Davis but said nothing as Carson casually opened the door and took a step or two into the main clerical section. There was no sign of the Lebanese pathologist.

"What the hell is he up to?" Davis said a little too loudly.

Langdon put his finger across his mouth as he waited for Carson to come back and close the door.

"He's on his way to his car," Carson said.

"You think he's serious?" Davis said.

"Who knows?" Langdon said. "It's probably just in his genes. He expects everyone who has a Ph.D. to be a gentleman, I guess."

"He gave me the creeps," Davis said.

"Don't sweat it, Burt," Langdon said. "But let's not drop our guard, either."

"You think he's been talking with Sullivan?" Davis asked.

"I doubt it," Langdon said lightly. "Why should he? What's he got to gain?"

Davis gave a shrug. "How 'bout your job?"

"God. There are days when I'd be happy to let him have it," Langdon said. "I could find myself a little hundred-bed hospital in the hills and retire looking at gallbladders. But I don't think we have to worry about that. Kaleb's not black."

"He ain't no redneck, either," Carson said, sounding very Southern.

The three of them stood silently for a moment until Davis finally said, "Let me know what you want to do, chief. I'll go along with whatever you say."

"You'll be up at the farm?" Langdon asked.

"Maybe," Davis said. "Now that I'm here, I just might see if there are any bored nurses at the hospital."

"Uh-oh," Carson said. "Should I call over there and warn them?"

"Give me a break, Carson. It's my day off." He turned to leave and gave Langdon a thumbs-up gesture. "Hang in there, chief."

"Check in with me, will you, Burt?" Langdon asked. "Things might break faster than we expect."

"Yeah," Davis said without looking back.

Carson watched him cross the outer-office area before he said, "He's a good man."

"You got that right, Jerry."

"How 'bout the other one? You want me to watch him?"

Langdon winced at the suggestion. "Jesus, Jerry, I couldn't ask you to do a thing like that."

"Who said you had to ask?" Carson replied softly.

Langdon's expression was dead serious as he shook his investigator's hand.

18

The main campus of the university had been laid out on the northwestern edge of the city, far from the noise and bustle of the commerce downtown. But that had been a hundred or so years earlier. Now it occupied an oasis still inside the city and yet somehow removed from it. All of the main faculties were there—law, medicine, engineering, the arts—and each building faced its own portion of a patchwork of grassy quadrangles. The buildings were brick, the ivy traditional, the walkways crooked, the oak trees bent and gnarled, and the student body unkempt, but in an expensive and practical style. The school was typically Southern, private, and ninety-four percent white. The other six percent kept the civil-rights hawks in Washington off the backs of the board of trustees.

Dr. Mazouk had kept his word to Dr. Langdon—in a way. He had gone to a library, but it was located deep within the lower levels of the *law* school. Hardly the place where a careful researcher would expect to find the technical references to refute or support the New York group on the embolization of narcotic debris.

Mazouk carried a thin black attaché case that shut with expensive clasps and a four-digit combination lock just beneath the handle. He entered the law library by pushing aside a mechanical arm in front of the checkout desk. The machine gave a few electronic clucks indicating he was not carrying magnetically coded material in or out. The student at the checkout desk was engrossed in an 1874 U.S. Supreme Court decision on a dispute between two Midwestern states each claiming rights to regulate the flow of commerce along the only river between them. He was engrossed only because Fuzzy Dawson was likely to call on him the following day. The student had no extra interest to waste on Mazouk. He wouldn't have known him from a Middle Eastern rug salesman anyway. Dr. Langdon handled all of the forensic lectures at the law school.

The pathologist took the small elevator to the subbasement floor and emerged among the stacks of forgotten reports of an obscure federal regulatory agency having to do with rural electrification. Some of the male law students liked this level of the library because it was cool, quiet, and virtually unused. The female students found it musty, spooky, and too isolated to be seen by good-looking men.

Mazouk made his way along the dimly lighted stacks (energy conservation had prompted the president of the college to extinguish every other light down there) and found a cubicle reserved for "Research and Typing." He needlessly glanced over his shoulder and then turned the doorknob slowly, as if to minimize the clack he anticipated from the aging brass mechanism. There was no light on inside the tiny cell as Mazouk closed the door behind himself. He was neither surprised nor frightened to realize he was not alone.

"May I open the light?" Mazouk asked, his phrase suggesting his foreign origins.

"Please," the male voice said from the corner.

Mazouk threw the switch, and the study lamp suspended above the table in the center of the room made a yellow cone. The other man's hands were folded in the middle of the lighted circle on the table and his tie, white shirt, and blue suit were easily seen. But not his face. He sat a little taller than the edge of the bright light, and it was difficult to make out his features until Mazouk was also seated. Mazouk laid the briefcase on the table beside him.

"Did you bring the latest?" the man asked.

"Copies of the report and the slides," Mazouk said.

"Excellent."

"It's not always easy to get a duplicate set of the slides made. The histology tech sometimes seems suspicious."

The man gave a low grunting laugh. "Of you? Everybody knows you make an extra slide of everything that comes along and seems interesting. No one will think anything of it."

Mazouk nodded sullenly. He placed his hands palms down at the edge of the lighted circle and squinted through the brightness at the man across the table. It was the same man he had met several times before. The man was in his mid-thirties, smooth-shaven, and moderately tall. His hair was dark, closely cut, and combed back in a severe part that distinguished him from the average unkempt law student. His hands were soft and the nails were neatly cut, although there was no evidence of any manicurist's buffing.

"Dr. Langdon would be very upset if he knew I was here," Mazouk said.

"Understandable," the man said.

Mazouk waited for him to say something more, but as usual, nothing came.

"There should be another way for you to obtain this material," Mazouk said. "It has not yet been finalized or sent to the crime lab."

"I agree with you, Doctor," the man said without sympathy.

Mazouk waited again, but still there was nothing. After a moment, the man gave a slight ripple of his fingers on the table. It was minimal impatience. Mazouk responded by sliding his briefcase closer and adjusting the combination. He flipped the clasps with a precision usually reserved for a fine watch and opened the lid. Inside, there were a few sheets of typed paper and a plastic box of glass slides. Mazouk glanced at the man again and then handed him Langdon's preliminary autopsy report and the slides. Each slide contained a thin slice of Martin Luther Peale.

The man took the report, glanced quickly at each page, and nodded silently. He seemed pleased with the findings. "Excellent, Doctor. We'll depart in our usual manner." He folded the report along its long axis and slipped it into his inside coat pocket with the plastic box. He did not offer to shake the pathologist's hand as he stood up, adjusted his jacket, and stepped toward the door. "I anticipate you'll remain here for at least thirty minutes."

"Right," Mazouk said.

As the man departed, he paused in the doorway and allowed the smallest and coldest of smiles. "I'm sure you'll be able to find something interesting to read. If you're interested in rural electrification."

Outside the cubicle, the man departed, apparently unseen, by avoiding the little elevator and walking the two flights of stairs to the main reading room. There, arriving just ahead of him and quickly assuming a studious attitude behind a volume of decisions on the Unifom Commercial Code, sat Jerry Carson. The man looked quickly around the room but took no interest in the law students studying there. He could see parts of Carson's face behind the UCC reports, but since he did not expect Carson to be there, he did not recognize him. The man had evidently not been trained by Henry Willis to look beyond the obvious. He was unable to distinguish the hens in the hen house.

Carson, on the other hand, needed no arcane clues to identify the man Mazouk had met. The man heading for the main exit of the law library was Dr. Barry Putnam.

Suddenly Carson was faced with a devil's choice. Without backup, he was forced to choose following either Putnam or Mazouk. His years of police training did not fail him. He knew that whatever the purpose of the secret meeting, it had probably been achieved. Mazouk had arrived carrying a briefcase, and Putnam was leaving without one. If Putnam had brought something to give to Mazouk, there was a chance that it would still be in the briefcase when Mazouk returned to the office. On the other hand, if Mazouk had brought something to Putnam, there would be only one opportunity to identify it. Carson would have to follow the crime lab's deputy chief and abandon Mazouk. He bolstered his logic with an even more fundamental truism. His subject's contact was leaving in front of him. The subject's location was now technically unknown. Carson could only hope that Mazouk would remain in the cubicle long enough for him to reestablish the tail. If he had already left the cubicle, Carson would lose both of them.

Carson allowed a decent interval and left the law library, turning left just as Putnam had. Putnam had already made it halfway to the parking lot. He was walking normally, apparently unaware he was being followed. In the parking lot, his plain state car was parked dangerously close to Carson's. As he inserted the key in the door, he paused and looked around. Again he saw people but not persons. Instinctively Carson turned away from the man from the crime lab and bent sharply over the hood of an adjacent car, apparently inspecting a scratch. As Putnam drove off, Carson was confident the ploy had worked. He got into his own car and resumed the surveillance. Putnam's casual manner of driving convinced Carson even more that he had not been seen.

Putnam's route took him in the general direction of the state crime lab, and Carson's heart leaped for joy. He knew he could invent a legitimate excuse for arriving at the lab shortly after Putnam and capitalize on the chance that Putnam would attempt to put away whatever he was carrying without delay. If he was carrying, Carson reminded himself as he stopped at a red light and carefully studied Putnam in the traffic ahead of him. A sudden intrusion into the doctor's office could easily be explained as a mistake, he reasoned, and Putnam would be caught with the goods. Then he reminded himself that nothing ever went *that* well. Putnam's car followed the expected route with almost boring precision. Carson's driving skills and knowledge of the city were so good that he could have followed a motorcycle driven by a fleeing bank robber. Putnam's route was so direct and so obvious that Carson began to worry he had chosen the wrong man to follow. He picked up his radio transmitter and gave his identification number to the dispatcher at the county police department. "Patch me to a phone at my office, will you?" he asked.

"Negative, M.E. five," the dispatcher said. "Equipment is down."

"Shit," Carson said on the air.

"I can *relay* by phone if you like, sir."

Carson wrestled with a message for Langdon that could stand the light of day. He knew there were hundreds of

Nosy Nellies and police buffs out there monitoring the channels. He also knew the TV and radio people recorded everything the cops put on the air.

"Tell M.E. one that M.E. three is coming home with an interesting case." Carson flipped his microphone switch to Off and reconsidered his message; he hoped Putnam was not on the same channel or able to recognize Mazouk as M.E. three.

"I copy that, M.E. five," the dispatcher said. "Is that all?"

Carson was still lost in worried thought as he studied the state car several vehicles ahead of him.

"M.E. five?" the dispatcher repeated. "Is that all?"

"Yeah. Thanks," Carson said. Radio formality was one of the habits he had quickly abandoned after coming over to the M.E.'s office. He had always thought that signing off was a lot of crap.

Unexpectedly, Putnam made a sharp turn. Carson was suddenly concerned that the doctor had picked up the message, recognized that it was too strong not to be right next door, and realized he was being tailed. Recognized or not, Carson knew he had no one to pass the ball to. He bit his lip as he approached the right turn and entered the side street slowly. A block ahead of him was Putnam's car. His route was no longer direct to the crime lab, but his manner of driving was the same. He had neither slowed to get a better look at his tail nor sped away.

"Son of a bitch," Carson said, half-astonished, half-confused.

There were fewer cars on the side street, and Carson had trouble staying behind the old woman in front of him while keeping Putnam in view. Then, as if to prove that everything *can* go wrong, the old woman signaled for a right turn into a convenience store. The street between him and Putnam seemed dangerously empty. Putnam was only a block away. Impulsively Carson pulled halfway into the 7–11 behind the woman, his left wheels straddling the sidewalk. He waited until Putnam had increased his lead to three blocks and then resumed the tail.

The side street became more residential and then almost vacant. Carson passed a sign that said, "County Park—No Camping." "Where in God's name are you going, Dr. Putnam?" he asked out loud.

In another six-tenths of a mile Putnam's left turn answered the question. Confederate Park. The land had been donated to the county by an industrialist who had moved his business to another state when the racial riots had erupted in the sixties. In fact, his plant had not been anywhere near the riot area, and several investigators suspected that the fire that destroyed it had been economic arson. But no charges were filed. The investigation was finally closed when he donated the land as a park. The county had erected a playground, two softball fields, and a picnic area, but hardly anyone used them. It was too far from downtown and contained no interesting sights. Sundays it attracted a few dozen people who wanted to get out of town, but weekdays it was dead.

Carson knew he could not follow Putnam into the park. Theirs would be the only two cars in the place. Instead, he drove by the entrance, found a remote area, turned around, and parked halfway back. He could see Putnam's car at the far end of the picnic area, but he could not make out what the doctor was doing.

"In the movies I would have a pair of binoculars," Carson said, slamming the steering wheel with his palm. "Damm it." He looked at his watch, anticipating the report he would have to write, and began to time Putnam's visit. Then, almost as quickly as he had arrived, Putnam drove out of the park and headed back to the city.

"This time, you can go by yourself," Carson said. "You didn't come all the way out here to collect beer cans." He waited for Putnam to disappear down the road and then turned into the park. The picnic area was not only abandoned but also looked unused. There were no ashes in the fireplaces, and none of the grills were warm. Evidently, Carson thought, Putnam didn't come here to burn something. He scanned the dozen or so picnic tables. There was nothing on or under them. Then he noticed the lid to the nearest trashcan was ajar.

"Bingo," he muttered. He removed the lid with a stick, even though he knew it was worthless for fingerprints. Some crime-scene habits were hard to break. Inside the trashcan there was a medium-sized paper bag, the kind that every grocery store used. Carson studied the bag for a moment, wondering if he should leave it intact and call Dr. Langdon or open it up.

"There's probably nothing in it except the leftovers from somebody's lunch," he said. "If I get Langdon out here and it turns out to be six beer cans and a McDonald's wrapper, I'll never hear the end of it."

Suddenly he was seized by a stronger idea. Almost running, he toured the other trashcans, throwing each lid on the ground and looking in before rushing on to the next. All of the other trashcans were empty.

Half-disappointed, he returned to the original trashcan and pulled out the paper bag. The top had been rolled down and there was no name on the outside to identify the grocery store. It was a plain paper bag similar to those he used to carry evidence to the crime lab. He carried the bag to the nearest picnic table, and feeling a little foolish, opened it.

"Son of a bitch," he said loudly. "A dress! The guy is a goddamn transvestite!" He reached into the bag with his thumb and index finger as if the contents were contagious. Then, with a slow extracting motion, he lifted the first red satin sheet out of the bag and emitted a long low whistle.

19

Florence Potter stuck her head into her boss's office and said, "Check Channel Three, Mr. Mayor." Wilson glanced at Chief Sullivan for a moment and then rushed across the room to turn on the TV set in the bookcase.

". . . was a veteran of many years," Joan Burke was saying. "Reached at home today, Captain Willis had no comment. That was his style: work hard, say nothing until the case was over. But Channel Three has learned that Henry Willis did not resign to take a well-deserved rest. He left the police department in disgust, forced out by the advent of a team of nonexperts and a roomful of computers. Mayor Wilson believes these machines and his newly assembled task force are the answer to the murdered and missing children, but Captain Willis did not agree. Willis believed in hard work by trained investigators in the field. And over the years, he has been right more often than he was wrong."

The camera moved in to frame Joan Burke's face. Her eyes were glistening and her voice was a little thicker than usual as she continued. "We will all miss Captain Henry Willis. He leaves us at a time when more than ever we need his talents. If changes in the police organization are such that he felt he could no longer stay, perhaps the time has come to question those who make changes. From Channel Three, this is Joan Burke."

An anonymous male voice added that the program had been a Channel Three special announcement, as Joan Burke continued to stare into the camera.

"That bitch!" Wilson said as he angrily snapped the set off. "She's making Willis some kind of a martyr."

"I'm surprised Channel Three let her get away with that kind of stuff," Sullivan said.

"That's Arlo Jacobs," Wilson said. "You remember how he was during my campaign, Florence. He never gave me a fair shake."

Florence did not recall the TV coverage of Wilson's mayoral campaign with the same paranoia, but she knew when to agree and when to differ from her boss. "I think he would have preferred Roger Freeman," she conceded.

"Preferred?" Wilson shouted. "Jacobs should have announced himself as Freeman's campaign manager and been done with it. But we showed them. No white man is going to win in this town unless he has the black vote. I don't care how many inner circles of business he belongs to."

"A lot of people thought pretty highly of Captain Willis," Florence said, staring at the blank television screen.

"So did I, Florence," Sullivan said. "So did I. But that's not the point. Willis could have stayed if he wanted to. Nobody walked into his office and asked him to resign. We all thought he was one of the best homicide men we had ever known."

"And Chief Sullivan has a doctorate in criminology!" Wilson told her.

"I know," Florence said softly. The mayor pointed out Sullivan's academic status to everyone who visited City Hall, but she didn't see why he had to repeat it so often to her.

"Willis just couldn't grow with the times, Florence," Wilson continued, pacing as he spoke. "That's all it was. Chief Sullivan and Dr. Greene and I have given this whole matter a great deal of thought. We're convinced that these cases call for a new system. An approach with science to back it up. And if Henry Willis doesn't think that's a good idea, then he *should* retire. Only I don't see why this little honky bitch from Channel Three wants to hang it on me."

"Maybe she thinks you wanted to get rid of him to put Captain Bayberry in charge," Florence said.

"Bayberry's a good man," the mayor said a little too

defensively. "He'll need some experience and some time on the job to show the men he knows what he's doing, of course, but that'll come in time."

"Uh-huh," Florence said neutrally.

"And once they get behind him and see that he knows how this task force is going to work, they'll be happy with him. Just as happy as they were with Henry Willis." Wilson wasn't talking to Florence Potter anymore. He was filling the room with the sound of his own voice. Arguing with unseen foes. Convincing the world that he was right.

"We've got a lot of smart young black officers moving up over there. They'll fill in behind Bayberry. They'll see he's the right man for the job. And once the task force gets fully organized and swings into action, the mayors in all the other cities will sit up and take notice of how we get things done down here. They'll say, 'Cleland Wilson's got himself a *team* down there.' They'll see we know how to use men in the right places and how we're not afraid of new ideas and new systems."

He paced to the window and back again before continuing. "Dr. Greene knows *all* about these new things, Florence. He was with the Federal Law Enforcement Assistance Agency! They thought their job was to send new riot-control equipment to the cities to keep down racial turmoil. But Peter Greene showed them a thing or two. He's got his Ph.D. He showed them that we can use some of that stuff too! He showed them it isn't just the white police departments that know how to use radios and printout computers to cross-check on information in the cities. He's a good man, that Peter Greene.

"This city is going to be a model," he continued. "The whole world is going to see how far we've come. And they're going to copy us for years to come. *Years* to come." He had begun to perspire now, and his eyes flashed with excitement.

"The best fire department anybody has ever seen, and sixty-two percent black," Wilson said loudly, as Chief Sullivan and Florence exchanged worried glances. "And the parks! Just look at what we've done with the parks. *I* appointed the new parks director, and he's doing a fine job. A *fine* job. We have got more people employed in the parks system than any administration before me. And it shows!"

"It shows to you and me, Cle, but not everybody in Birmington sees it our way," Sullivan said. "A lot of them think you're just filling out the top positions with black faces."

"You got no call to talk to me like that, Gayle Sullivan," Wilson said. He sat behind his desk heavily.

"You want me to leave?" Florence said.

"No," Wilson said quickly. "I want you to hear some of this, because you're in the same boat as the rest of us. I'm sure a lot of people think you got your job because you're black."

"We all may be moving on," Florence said.

The mayor loosened his tie and tugged at the button that held his collar uncomfortably tight around his neck. "Peter Greene is getting us some federal help, isn't he?"

"Peter Greene is up in Washington," Sullivan said, "but talking to a couple of black congressmen isn't going to solve all our problems."

Wilson looked at his watch. "He should be in Jack Scott's office right now. See if you can get him on the phone, Florence."

She placed the call on the mayor's desk phone as both men waited in silent anticipation.

"This is Mayor Cleland Wilson calling Mr. Scott from Birmington," she said, sounding official. She nodded excitedly as she passed the phone to the mayor.

"Cle! How the hell are you?" a booming, raspy baritone said. The voice said cigarettes, campaign speeches and yelling at ball games, and whiskey.

"Just fine, Jack," Wilson said exuberantly. "How are you holding up?"

"Passably, thank you kindly, Mr. Mayor," Scott said in his best darky-off-the-plantation tone. Jimmie Jackson Scott was the congressman from the all-black, all-Democratic Southwestern district of the city. He was thirty-four and a lawyer, although he had flunked the state bar exam three times in a row before he gave up and devoted himself full-time to urban politics. He was known, as he would tell it, as "Jimmie" to the street niggers, "J. Jackson" to the property owners, and "Jack" to the inner circle. No one except an occasional newscaster looking for cheap support among white listeners ever referred to him as "Scotty."

"When you coming down here?" Wilson asked.

"Anytime you say, Mr. Mayor," Scott said, continuing his plantation tone. "I'll do almost anything to get out of Washington and return to my native South." Scott was more than a little hung-over.

"What I need you to do might be easier for you up there, Jack," Wilson said.

"Greene gave me part of it," Scott said. "Sounds like a tall order."

"You know which doors to knock on," Wilson said.

"But when I do, some of these honkies up here think I've shown up to cater their lunch."

"Pick and choose, Jack," Wilson said. "Pick and choose."

"The president's nigger liked your task-force idea," Scott said.

"Can he deliver?" Wilson asked.

"I suspect he gets glad-handed and promised like the rest of us, but even he has to wait to see what's in the morning mail," Scott said.

"He's window dressing," Wilson said.

"No, not really, Cle," Scott said. "I think the president listens to him. Not in public, of course, but he relies on his own man a lot more than the pros from the NAACP."

"We've *got* to have this, Jack," Wilson said. "We're going to look like shit if we don't crack these cases."

"You know how they are up here, Cle," Scott said. "They are either going to take over the whole scene, federalize the living shit out of you, or totally ignore you and let you dry in the wind."

"Aim for something in between," Wilson said. "This is Gayle's show, and I want it to stay that way."

Chief Sullivan nodded at that one. "I want the FBI to stay in their cages," he said.

"Gayle says to stay clear of the FBI," Wilson repeated.

"You guys want some kind of a fucking miracle," Scott said. "You want federal money, but no muscle."

"See what your friends in the black caucus can do for us," Wilson said. "Their cities are in the same shape as ours. If we can grab onto a federal tit, so can they."

"They haven't got a string of little-boy murders to feed the flames," Scott said.

"Bullshit," Wilson said. "Their murders may not be little boys, but they're just as black and they're all in the inner cities. You just look at the statistics."

"All those cats know the statistics," Scott said. "They know who gets killed and who does the killing in their cities."

"Just get us some money," Wilson said.

"Too bad you're not a member of a prominent minority group," Scott said.

"I am," Wilson said. "I'm black and I can read."

Chief Sullivan, sensing the conversation was ending, waved his hands to extend it.

"Wait a minute, Jack," Wilson said. "Gayle wants to put in his two cents' worth." He handed the phone to the police chief and sat back in his high-backed leather chair.

"Jack? This is Gayle. How's it going, babe?"

"Everything's cool up here, brother," Scott said. "How are things in the land of parking tickets and petty thievery?"

"If that's all we had to worry about, we'd be in heaven," Sullivan said. "Right now we've got our hands full."

"I thought your homicide section was one of the best," Scott said seriously.

"Oh, it is, Jack," Sullivan said. "No doubt about that. 'Course, you heard that Henry Willis quit on me."

"Quit?" Scott said. "When did all this happen?"

"Right after he heard about the special task force and the computers," Sullivan said. "It was bound to happen."

"Losing Henry Willis is a tough blow," Scott said.

"Tell me about it," Sullivan said.

"And I suppose you reached into your grab bag of experts and came up with an instant replacement," Scott said.

"Bayberry," Sullivan said. "We've got him in homicide and Barry Putnam at the crime lab. That's the team."

Mayor Wilson nodded appreciatively.

"It will probably be easier to shunt some money to the state crime lab than it will be to fund the city police department," Scott said.

"Do what you can, Jack," Sullivan said. "With a little help from the feds, it will all fall into place."

"You're going to get all the help I can find," Scott said. "You can count on it."

"And stay in touch, Jack," Sullivan said. "Don't let me find out about things on the six-o'clock news, for Christ's sake. Pick up the phone."

"When I know, you'll know," Congressman Scott said.

"Peace, brother," Sullivan said. He offered the phone to Wilson, but the mayor shook his head.

"He'll come through," Sullivan said, hanging up the phone.

"Those computers are costly," Wilson said heavily.

"So was losing Henry Willis," Sullivan added. He turned to look out the window.

"Now, don't you start on me too, Gayle," the mayor said. "You knew the whole plan. It was a calculated risk."

Chief Sullivan nodded. "Maybe we're moving too fast," he said.

"Maybe so," Wilson said. "But we're not going to get another chance."

20

The following day, Willis drove to the medical examiner's office and found Tom Langdon. At the same time, Joan went to the station and convinced Arlo Jacobs that the time was not ripe for a special series on the state crime lab. Jacobs quickly agreed and said, "I told you so." He didn't have to hear her reasons for the cancellation. He had all the lab shots he wanted on file.

Dr. Langdon met Willis in his office and told Libby to hold his calls. It was always a pleasure to see the old homicide chief, even under these circumstances.

"What are you doing to stay busy, Henry?" Langdon asked, handing him a steaming mug of coffee.

"Stamp collection," Willis said, adjusting the cup to find the handle.

"My ass." Langdon sat in one of the chairs in front of his desk as Willis took the other. Langdon always preferred the equal setting when talking to Henry Willis. This was particularly true now that he had retired.

"I'm enjoying a luxury," Willis said. "I've found time to sit and think. The phone doesn't ring and I can read over some of the cases six or seven times without interruption. I wonder how it would have been if I could have done that when I worked for the department."

"You would have been bored to tears," the doctor said. He took a loud sip from the surface of his hot coffee.

"Yeah," Willis said. "That's probably right." He rotated

the cup between his palms, enjoying the sensation of the hot cup.

"We're still plugging along over here," Langdon said. "The cases are the same, but the names keep changing."

"That's how it gets after a while," Willis said. "That's when you know it's time to quit."

"I think I'm getting there, Henry, but I just have to wait and see how it affects you."

"If I don't go completely bananas, you'll consider joining me out on the pasture, huh?" Willis returned the pathologist's smile. Each knew the other would never quit completely, regardless of how the political wind blew.

"Maybe someday," Dr. Langdon said.

Willis assumed a more serious attitude, glanced at the closed door, and leaned closer to the pathologist. "Is there *anything* new?" he asked.

Langdon shook his head slowly. "Nothing really worth a damn," he said. "How 'bout with you?"

"I'm pretty well shut down," Willis said. "I don't think Bayberry would give me the time of day if I asked for it."

"What makes you think he knows the time of day?" Langdon said. He shared the growing concern that under Captain Bayberry's direction the homicide section was producing less and less, even on routine cases.

"You're the only one that keeps me even halfway up-to-date," Willis said.

"You know you can have anything we have," Langdon said.

"I appreciate that, Tom. But I hope you won't get your ass in a crack by talking to me."

"*I* run this shop, Henry. Wilson know that, and so does Sullivan. The only way they can raid my positions is to get rid of me first."

Willis nodded and took a swallow of his coffee. "What do you hear from the crime lab?"

Langdon shrugged. "Same old shit. Atwood's been talking to a couple of out-of-town civic groups about statewide consolidation, but he's been doing that for years. I think he's getting senile."

"And Putnam?" Willis asked casually.

"Now, *there's* a strange duck," Langdon said.

The characterization caught Willis' attention, but he was careful not to show it. "Oh?" he asked. "How so?"

"There's a little something going on between him and Mazouk."

"Your Dr. Mazouk?" Willis asked.

"Uh-huh. I don't think it's serious, Henry, but Carson developed it and I'm not sure I understand it all." Langdon proceeded to tell the ex-homicide chief about their recent staff meeting at the MEO and how uncomfortable he had felt at Dr. Mazouk's attitude. "He wasn't . . . how should I put it? He wasn't one hundred percent, Henry. You know what I mean?"

Willis nodded and adjusted his seat, obviously interested.

"I put Carson on him, and he tailed him out to the law-school library," Langdon continued. "Carson said he went to some little study room way down in the basement and met with Putnam."

"Putnam?" Willis said. His attitude was no longer casual.

"We don't know why he met with Putnam, and I haven't asked him. But frankly, Henry, I'm concerned."

"A little maneuvering for a state job?" Willis suggested.

"Maybe. But why such a cloak-and-dagger meeting? Kaleb can move over to the state lab anytime he wants to. He knows that."

"You mean anytime Atwood agrees to hire an M.D."

"Yeah. Well, Carson figured something was going on and decided to follow Putnam after the meeting."

"And?"

"Let me show you something." Langdon got up from his chair and crossed the room to lock the door. Then he went to a file cabinet and slid the bottom drawer open. He took out a bulging plastic bag and brought it to the desk. "Carson has been with me a long time, Henry."

"And with the county P.D. even before that," Willis said. "He's straight as an arrow."

"Well, at least he's not full of shit, you know what I mean? I mean, he's not the kind of guy that would find something and then make a mountain out of a molehill." The medical examiner opened the thin plastic bag widely and exposed the crumpled paper bag inside.

Willis leaned over the desk and inspected the paper bag closely without touching it. "What have you got?" he asked.

"I'm not sure, Henry." Langdon began to unroll the top of the paper bag. The bag had a dusky, slightly iridescent cast to it. Willis recognized it immediately.

"You had the bag printed?" he asked.

"As best we could," Langdon said. "We didn't want to involve the technicians from the P.D.—city or county—until we were a little more positive of what we had. Carson and I did the best we could, but God knows we're not experts in fingerprints."

"Lift anything?"

"Smudges," Langdon said. "Nothing we felt anybody could work with."

"Uh-huh," Willis said, looking at the pathologist.

"Carson trailed Putnam from the law school to Confederate Park," Langdon explained. "He was too far away to see anything definite, but—"

"Putnam was alone?"

"Yeah. Nobody else with him. So Carson parked just outside the park and waited for Putnam to leave. He only stayed five minutes or so and then headed back to town."

"You know where he went?" Willis asked.

Langdon shook his head. "Carson figured he'd better check out the picnic area instead." He opened the paper bag slowly and held it for Willis to see the contents.

"What the hell is it, Tom?"

"Sheets, Henry. Red satin sheets."

Willis wrinkled up his face and stared into the bag as the doctor reached in and lifted one of the sheets into the air above his head. The bottom of the sheet stayed in the bag.

"Putnam's?" Willis asked.

"As far as we can tell," Langdon said. "Anybody could have used those trashcans, but all the others were empty." He lowered the sheet into the bag and dusted his hands together.

"Pretty fancy," Willis said, meeting the medical examiner

eye to eye. "But other than suggesting that Dr. Putnam has expensive tastes and an odd way of disposing of unwanted sheets, what have you got? Stains? Hairs?" He paused for the answer.

"We did find a dried stain in the middle of one sheet. It tested positive for semen. Again, we were a bit handicapped, considering the source of the material. After all, we couldn't send it to the crime lab, could we?"

"So you and Carson checked it out by midnight chemistry?" Willis asked with a grin.

"Carson and I and Davis."

"You got old Burton Davis to come in to do extracurricular lab work?" Willis asked. "I thought he was up to his ass in sheep, horses, and farm equipment."

"He became *very* interested when I told him who it was that Mazouk met," Langdon said. "I think he's always been a bit uneasy with Mazouk. Foreign training and all."

"Davis would suspect anyone who graduated outside the ACC. But tell me about the hairs," Willis said.

"Carson and I went over the sheets with hand lenses and found a dozen or so black pubic-type hairs."

"So?" Willis asked. "I believe Putnam is of the Negro persuasion. The hairs are probably his own."

"Oh, yeah, Henry. We all agree. But it's still interesting that he went so far out of his way to dump the sheets."

"If he did," Willis added.

"If he did," Langdon agreed.

Willis got up and paced the room once. "So what are you going to do with all of this now, Tom?"

"Well, we're going to keep an eye on Mazouk. Not so close, mind you, that he'll get pissed off and quit if we're wrong about him, but close enough to find out why he would go to all that trouble to meet with the deputy director of the state crime lab, who, after all, could walk in here any bright afternoon and ask us for everything we've got."

"You don't suppose *they've* got something kinky going on between them, do you?" Willis asked.

"Davis suggested that, but we didn't find any Lebanese

hairs. They were all pure Afro under the microscope. Frankly, I don't see either Putnam or Mazouk in such a posture."

"If the sheets were Mazouk's," Willis mused out loud, "he could have dumped them by himself. It doesn't make sense. There's something more."

"He would have had to bring them to Putnam in the briefcase, Henry," Langdon said. "And why to the law library?"

"Maybe he's checking on his own wife," Willis suggested, "and he doesn't want to make a stink until he's got the goods on her."

Dr. Langdon shook his head. "She's in Beirut and has been for almost a year. Something to do with her mother's family."

"I don't suppose you've got a label or a laundry mark on those sheets," Willis said.

"Nope. They're clean except for the hairs, the semen, and the fibers."

"Fibers?" Willis asked, turning to face the pathologist.

"A couple of red synthetic fibers that look like carpet or some such, under the scope."

"Let's see," Willis said.

Dr. Langdon opened his middle desk drawer and brought out a sealed plastic envelope. He held it over his head briefly, framing it against the light.

"There in the lower-left corner. You want a hand lens?"

Willis repeated the inspection routine and said, "No. That's okay. They look like little red fibers to me. I'll take your word for it that they're synthetic carpet."

"Now, that's just me and Carson and Davis, you understand. We're no experts on fibers. But we thought we'd keep it close to the chest until we figured out who's who."

Willis nodded and stuck out his lower lip as he returned the plastic envelope to the pathologist. "Did the semen type?" he asked.

"Davis thought he got a B-neg on it, Henry, but hell, he hasn't actually done a stain test for years. It's tough to work without a lab tech."

"If it's not a B-negative, what else could it be?" Willis asked.

"Well, it *could* be an AB with the A too weak to react, and it *could* be A-pos that has degenerated. I'm not all that sure, Henry. I just wouldn't want you to rely on it."

"*Me* rely on it," Willis said. "What's all this to me? I just stopped in to shoot the shit with you."

"Well, Henry," Langdon began gently, "we've all come a long way. You and I have known each other for years, and . . ."

"And you want me to check out Dr. Putnam," Willis said.

"While we watch Mazouk."

"I haven't got any of my men, no radios, nothing," Willis said, holding his arms wide, helplessly.

"A mere trifle of a handicap for a man of your talents, Captain," Langdon said, smiling.

Willis stuffed his thumbs into his rear pockets and traced the pattern of the carpet with the edge of his shoe. "Nothing for nothing," he said.

"Fair enough, Henry. What do you want?"

"Well, I haven't exactly lost interest in all those kid cases," Willis said. "And you know I can't go downtown for information."

"Uh-huh."

"So if I check out this Putnam-Mazouk thing for you, will you give me whatever I need on the children?"

"Henry, you can have a key to my files, for all I care," Dr. Langdon said. He came closer to the detective and slapped a hand on the man's shoulder. "How are you really getting along?" he asked. He sounded like a doctor.

"Oh . . ." Willis sighed. "It's tough not to be busy. Y'know what I mean?"

"Yeah, Henry, I know how that must be for you. You haven't the faintest idea how to retire."

"And you know what else?" Willis said, looking into the face of his longtime friend. "I don't think I really want to learn."

Willis felt discontented as he drove away from the medical

examiner's office. He didn't have time for Putnam *or* Mazouk. If they wanted to play games with each other, that was up to them. What he wanted were the children's cases. Pure and simple. He had heard about Putnam from Joan Burke, and now he was hearing it from Tom Langdon. Okay, he admitted to himself, Putnam is some kind of a squirrel. He gives Joan the willies and he plays games with a Lebanese pathologist. But that doesn't make him crazy enough to be involved with those kids. Or does it? he asked himself. There still are no coincidences. The connection bothered him, but he knew it was absurd.

At the first stoplight his hands gripped the wheel in a twisting action.

"All right, you guys," he said aloud to Langdon and Burke. "If you want me to check Putnam out, I'll check him out. Only he's not worth it."

He had ignored the green light and the horns behind him. The tap on the window brought him back to reality.

"C'mon, move it," the cop began.

Willis looked at the officer blankly.

"Oh. Excuse me, Captain."

"What?" Willis said, rolling the window down. "Keenan, isn't it?"

"Kiernan, sir," the cop said gently. "Is anything wrong, Captain?"

"If something isn't wrong, Kiernan, we're *all* out of a job," Willis said. "Keep your eyes open." He drove away on yellow, leaving the traffic officer confused and the other drivers still angry.

21

The lead editorial in the morning paper, ghost-written by Homer Lavine, had come down hard on the lack of progress in the kid cases. The implication was that politics had interfered with good police work and Willis had been driven out. The subheadline had asked: "When will the child killer strike again?" The paper had not even wrapped its first fish before the question was answered. In midafternoon another boy was found.

The boy was about thirteen, and like the others, he was black. He was wearing brown corduroy pants, sneakers without socks, and a faded green sweatshirt that advertised a rock band. Captain Bayberry had never heard of the band and didn't know their lead drummer had fatally OD'd on cocaine and heroin several months before. Henry Willis wouldn't have known it either.

Jerry Carson was having trouble repressing the anxiety he felt at the scene. Bayberry and Chief Sullivan were there with dozens of uniformed and plainclothes officers, but it didn't look like anyone was in charge. The TV and radio people were there too, but for this scene, no one had bothered to stake out the perimeter with yellow rope. Cameramen walked wherever they wished and filmed whatever they wanted.

Joan Burke was at first astonished and then saddened by the total lack of discipline.

Sullivan and Bayberry were in full uniform and their brass buttons glinted in the sun whenever they moved to give directions to the officers searching the area.

"What are they looking for, Chief Sullivan?" Joan Burke asked, thrusting her microphone into his sweaty face.

"Clues. Just clues," he said. "You never know what you might find." He glanced at the disorganized search activity and swept his hand across the scene for Joan Burke. "Get a picture of all that," he said. "Those men are working hard to solve this case." Joan nodded her head. She had often bitched at Henry Willis from the other side of his yellow rope, but she could instantly see the difference in his scenes and this one.

"This may be something, Chief," Captain Bayberry shouted from the smaller knot of men hunched over the boy's body.

"Excuse me," Sullivan said to Joan Burke. She had never seen a body this close before, and Sullivan gave no signal to exclude her. She motioned to her camera crew to film it all.

"Carson just noticed that the boy's fingernails are painted," Bayberry said. Each of the nails was lacquered an off-red with a deep luster.

"You think the kid's a chicken?" Sullivan asked Carson.

"Where there's a chicken, there's a chicken hawk," Carson said. "It just doesn't fit with the rest of him."

Sullivan nodded, but his face did not register comprehension. "What do you mean, Carson?"

"It doesn't fit with the clothes. The sneakers and the old sweatshirt. A real pro would be dressed better. At least that's the way I see a chicken working the streets."

The boy's face was turned toward his outstretched right arm. The tongue protruded slightly from his mouth and a persistent fly kept landing on the boy's face to feast on the unseen pieces of salt.

"You find any injuries?" Sullivan asked.

"Nothing yet," Carson said. "But we'll get a better look at him downtown."

"Maybe we should take this one straight to the state crime lab," Bayberry said.

"He's inside the Birmington city limits," Carson said flatly.

"You think you ought to call Dr. Langdon out here?" Chief Sullivan asked.

Carson stood up and arched his back to relieve a cramp. "I

don't see why," he said. "There's nothing more to see out here. I'm sure Dr. Langdon would prefer to work on him at the morgue. But if you insist . . ."

"No, no," Sullivan said, holding up his hand and sounding conciliatory. "If you think he wouldn't be interested in coming out, we'll do it your way."

"It's not a matter of interest, Chief," Carson said. "It's just the way we've divided things up. The pathologist is called when the investigator from the medical examiner's office thinks it's necessary."

"And *you* don't think it's necessary," Sullivan said, making certain Joan Burke caught it all.

"Frankly, I don't," Carson said.

"Dr. Putnam goes to all of his scenes," Bayberry said.

"Dr. Putnam has to work with rural cops and hasn't got a crew of investigators trained in forensic observation," Carson said more forcefully. "Maybe he doesn't feel as confident with the crime-scene crew as Dr. Langdon does."

"That may be a matter of opinion, *Sergeant* Carson," Sullivan said.

Carson felt his eyes narrowing despite his effort to maintain self-control. "Yes sir," he said, "I suppose it is." The lines of authority and crime-scene protocol had already been hammered out by Dr. Langdon and Sullivan's predecessor.

"We may all have to sit down someday soon and discuss how we handle murder scenes from here on," Sullivan said.

"But in the meantime, Chief," Carson said, "if you have no reason to delay the removal of the body to the morgue, I'll see to it that he is wrapped and transported."

Sullivan stared at Carson for more than a moment and accepted the fact that this was not the appropriate time for a confrontation.

"How about it, Captain Bayberry?" Sullivan asked without looking at the man. "Is that all right with you? Do you have any objections to letting *Sergeant* Carson remove the body from the scene?"

"We have our pictures and just about everything we need, Chief," Bayberry said hesitantly. Sullivan and Carson were still staring at each other, neither backing off an inch.

"All right, Sergeant," Sullivan said. "*This* body is yours." He turned abruptly and marched off toward a group of his men who had found an old beer can and several other items of trash.

"Would you tell Dr. Langdon that I'll get by to talk to him after he's completed his examination?" Bayberry said softly.

"You're not coming to the autopsy?" Carson said loudly.

Bayberry shook his head and made a slightly unpleasant face. "I don't think so," he said. "I have an awful lot of paperwork to attend to downtown."

Henry Willis could have told Carson that the last time Bayberry attended an autopsy was during his training at the academy, and even then he almost fainted.

"I'll relay your message to the doctor," Carson said. He was careful not to smile. He motioned to his ambulance crew. A clean sheet and a transportation bag were brought, and in a few minutes they had the boy loaded into the vehicle. Carson felt unusually happy to leave the new homicide squad behind him at the scene. Arriving at the medical examiner's office ahead of the body, he found Dr. Langdon putting the finishing touches on an industrial-accident autopsy. An elevator repairman had evidently connected the wrong wires and had called the elevator car down to crush him against the floor.

"The latest child case is right behind me," Carson said to Langdon.

The pathologist shook his head wearily. "Let's get a good set of pictures," he said. He snapped his right glove off before writing on the body diagram for the elevator case, to avoid smearing it with blood. Langdon had a thing about sending bloody diagrams upstairs for filing.

"Bayberry's scene was a mess," Carson said.

"You're not surprised, are you?" Langdon asked.

"I guess I'm not," Carson conceded. "It's just that it's hard to accept less than what Henry Willis would have tolerated."

"Was Sullivan out there?" Langdon asked.

"In full uniform, playing to the cameras."

"Who covered the scene for Channel Three?" Langdon asked.

"What's-her-name. Joan . . ."

"Burke."

"Yeah. Joan Burke," Carson agreed. "She was having a field day. No perimeter line. No restrictions. We had newspeople and cops running all over each other."

"And no I.D. on the boy?"

"Not as yet," Carson said. "I almost had it with Sullivan."

"Oh?" Langdon said, halting his writing for a moment to look at his investigator. "What was *he* up to?"

"He made some asshole remarks about you not being out at the scene and said that Dr. Putnam always came."

"Maybe he'd prefer Putnam and the crime lab to cover the next one," Dr. Langdon said.

"Don't say that," Carson warned. "He's right on the edge."

"It is only a matter of time," Langdon said flatly. "You know they won't be happy until they take over just about everything."

"What's the latest on Dr. Mazouk?" Carson said, glancing around the morgue room to make sure they were alone. Bubba Hutcheson was off delivering a specimen to the tox lab.

"He's still at the resident committee meeting at the medical school, as far as I know," Langdon said. "You can catch up with him later. We can't watch him twenty-four hours a day. As a matter of fact, I'm not sure we want to."

"If we don't know where he is, we won't know what he's doing," Carson said. Deep down inside, he was still a cop.

"That's true enough, but tailing a professional colleague makes me feel uneasy."

"Well, it doesn't bother me a bit," Carson said. "I'll keep him in my sights for as long as it takes."

"You're still convinced he's passing information to Putnam, huh?"

"I feel it in my bones," Carson said.

"God, I hope you're right. A thing like this could tear us all apart if we are accusing him falsely."

"What I can't figure is *why* he's fooling around with Putnam," Carson said.

"Probably security," Langdon said. "He can feel the pressure on us from downtown and is probably worried whether we'll survive. Maybe he sees the state crime lab as our logical successor."

"With Putnam as chief," Carson added.

"That may not be so farfetched," Langdon said.

Just then the big doors to the walk-in cooler opened and Billy Cashman entered, pushing the still-wrapped body of the latest child on a cart.

"Be sure to check the nails," Carson told his chief. "We never had one with fingernail polish before."

"Fingernail polish?" the pathologist said.

"Sure as I'm standing here," Carson said. "Let me show you." He carefully unwrapped the sheet as Cashman steadied the cart. "And it's no sloppy job, either."

"That's a new twist," Langdon said, bending closer to inspect the boy's hands.

"Sullivan brought up the chicken-hawk angle when he saw it."

Dr. Langdon nodded over the plausibility of the suggestion. "Who knows?" he said. "It certainly is different."

"But the rest of him isn't," Carson said. "Look at the neck. I think there are some very light abrasions there, but I can't be sure."

"There's *something* there," the pathologist said. He adjusted the overhead light to create a cross-illumination. "You'd better get back on the outer door, Billy," he said to the attendant. "Homicide will probably be showing up any minute."

"Fat chance," Carson said as the attendant left the dissection room. "Captain Bayberry was scared shitless that Sullivan was going to make him come over here and watch."

The idea made Langdon chuckle. "Bayberry will find out about the autopsy when he reads the report," he said.

"But that won't be until the report is sent to the crime lab," Carson said. "It might take weeks. It seems to me that if he wanted to know anything about the preliminary findings, he'd attend the autopsy itself."

Dr. Langdon looked at Carson as if he had just made an outstanding observation. "That's it!" he said. "That's what's going on with Mazouk."

"What is?" Carson said.

"Mazouk is their pipeline for the preliminary findings," Langdon said, excited by his conclusion. "They could never get anything out of Henry Willis until he was ready to tell them, and Putnam can't help them until he gets our final report. The preliminary findings don't go to the crime lab."

"I still don't get it," Carson said.

"Sure. It's simple," Dr. Langdon said. "And it's not as sinister as we all may have thought. Wilson and Sullivan want to get autopsy information about the children's cases without having to ask *me* for it."

"And without having to wait for the final report," Carson said, catching on.

"Right. So they made a deal with Dr. Mazouk, and God knows what they promised him to pass along the information as soon as it was available."

"With Dr. Putnam interpreting the results for them," Carson added.

"That way, they look smarter than we are and weeks ahead of our final report," Langdon continued.

"But why would they care?" Carson asked. "Why wouldn't they just sit back and let the process take its course?"

"Come on, Carson," Langdon said. "You know what their game is. Everything that is good coming out of these cases is going to be credited to Sullivan and Greene."

"Or Putnam," Carson said.

"And ultimately to Wilson," Langdon added. "Meanwhile, everything that looks stupid or is botched up in any way will be blamed on the rest of us." He used his fingers to count off the possibilities. "You, me, and Henry Willis!"

"Son of a bitch," Carson said, delighted with his chief's analysis. "They take their politics seriously, don't they?"

"Wilson wants his team to win," Langdon said, "and he doesn't care how they get there."

"So Wilson is going to use the children's cases to embarrass you, make Putnam look good, and replace you with somebody of his own choosing," Carson concluded.

"Right. And that's either Putnam himself or Mazouk."

The concept intrigued Jerry Carson. Langdon could almost

see his mental wheels spinning. Then he seemed to reach an impasse. "Why Mazouk?" he asked. "He's not black."

"That's why it's Putnam all the way," Langdon said.

"You mean they'll give Birmington to the state crime lab?" Carson asked incredulously.

"Why not? That way Wilson will have one of his own men in control at all levels," Langdon said. "His sights are set a hell of a lot higher than just the city."

"Who can we go to, then?" Carson asked. "The governor?"

"Oh, we could take that route, Jerry, but why should he believe us? He'd probably think we are suffering from urban racial paranoia. Wilson and Putnam would deny everything anyway."

"So they're just going to lay out there and gobble us up one by one?" Carson asked.

"They could," Langdon said, "but that approach doesn't seem to be fast enough for them. They don't want to conquer by attrition. They want to sweep us clean." Langdon was acutely aware that his was the only county office without a black employee above the level of clerk. He had not planned it that way, but black M.D. pathologists in the country could be counted on one hand.

"What can we do about it, then?" Carson asked. "If Wilson manages to replace you with one of his own, he can have my job too. I'm not going to be the chief investigator under Putnam."

"Well, don't quit yet, Jerry," Langdon said. "I think we can play their game a little better than they can and make it blow up in their faces."

"I'm listening," Carson said.

"If Mazouk is their pipeline to the early findings in the kid cases," Langdon said softly, "we might be able to pass along something that will lead them down the primrose path. If they grab it and run, and it later proves to be bullshit, the media will never let them forget it."

"A ringer," Carson said, obviously pleased.

"Something like that. And to make it work, you'll have to give Mazouk his head."

"Unless he's already spotted me on his tail," Carson said. "If he has, he'll wonder why I dropped him."

"I'll leave that up to you, Jerry. But in the meantime, we want him to have every opportunity to run through the files, confidential memos and all. Let him get to Putnam however he wants."

"As far as I can tell," Carson said, "he doesn't know I have the slightest interest in him."

"Keep it that way," Dr. Langdon said.

"What are you going to do for them?" Carson asked.

"I think Putnam has given us just the thing we need," Langdon said. "The sheets."

Carson looked astonished. "You're going to tie him to the kid cases with his own sheets?"

"No. That wouldn't be honest or fair," Langdon said. "He doesn't have any more to do with these cases than you do."

"You lost me," Carson admitted.

"Putnam got rid of those sheets because he used them to entertain a lady who was not his wife," Langdon explained. "It was just a coincidence that he dumped them the same day he met Mazouk."

"Okay," Carson said, going along with the theory.

"But we found hairs and carpet fibers on the sheets," Langdon said. "Why don't we make them work for us? Look. I'll do this autopsy in the usual way. I'm convinced we'll find pretty much the same thing—a gentle strangulation, with no other clues."

"Yeah." Carson was still not with him.

"And in my preliminary report, I'll mention that we found racially identifiable hairs and unusual carpet fibers on the body and that we have them under investigation."

"But Putnam will wonder why we didn't send them through his lab for analysis," Carson said.

"We'll say in the report that we're going to send them to the FBI lab in Washington," Langdon explained. "Everybody knows Atwood has no use for us, so why should we have to explain that we went straight to the FBI with our evidence? We've done it before."

"But Wilson's going to want Putnam to come up with an identification of the hairs and fibers before the feds do," Carson argued.

"And we're going to let him," Langdon said. "All we have to do is let Mazouk know where they're kept and let him sneak them over to Putnam."

"The hairs and fibers from Putnam's own sheets," Carson said, beaming with the irony.

"Exactly. Putnam will run a quick analysis, photograph the shit out of those hairs and fibers, and give them back to Mazouk to return to my desk."

"And in about a week," Carson predicted, "*Doctor* Putnam and Chief Sullivan will announce that they have discovered suspicious hairs and fibers from a crime scene and promise the public the cases will soon be solved."

"Right on," Langdon said, adopting an accent.

"But since there aren't any hairs and fibers on these bodies, Wilson and his boys will be running down a blind alley."

"From which they cannot return, if they have given it enough publicity," Langdon said. "The *final* autopsy report will, of course, contain no reference to any hairs and fibers, and no one, not even Mazouk, will be able to ask us about it."

"Delicious," Carson said.

"It's even better than that, Jerry," Langdon said, smiling. "Even after he knows he's been set up, Putnam won't realize that he's been studying his own hairs and his own carpet fibers."

"Or maybe his girlfriend's," Carson added.

"Either way, there's a poetry there that is precious," Langdon said. "But first, let's finish this autopsy."

22

Dr. Mazouk was right on schedule when he passed Langdon's preliminary report on the still-unidentified child to Putnam. This time, they were truly alone at the law library. Carson had remained at the M.E.'s office. Later that day Putnam called Mazouk, ostensibly to ask about a carbon-monoxide level in a routine truck fire. He told Dr. Mazouk to call him back on a safe pay phone and left a number. Mazouk did so in less than ten minutes and was astonished by Putnam's demand.

"I cannot do that," Mazouk said. He was in a foul-smelling phone booth two blocks from the morgue.

"You have to do it," Putnam said.

"But Dr. Langdon said that material was going to be sent to the FBI lab in Washington."

"That's why *we* have to have an opportunity to examine it first," Putnam said. "How will it look for the task force and the crime lab if the break in the case comes from the feds?"

"That's why I don't understand why Langdon is handling it this way. He always goes through the state crime lab first."

"I don't think the task-force idea makes him any happier than it did Captain Willis," Putnam said. "They were old friends."

"Still . . ."

"Look," Putnam said, taking charge of the Lebanese pathologist. "Things are going to be a lot different around here when these cases are closed. And I thought we agreed you want to be on the winning team."

"I do," Mazouk said simply.

"Then get me those hairs and fibers. I'll only hold them for a couple of hours. Long enough for microphotographs and a couple of tests."

"Nondestructive analysis," Mazouk bargained.

"You'll get it all back, and no one will ever be able to tell I've been into the envelope. Trust me."

"If they find out, I'll be ruined," Dr. Mazouk worried aloud.

"If they break the case before we do, we'll never get the reorganization approved. You still want to be chief pathologist for the state, don't you?" Putnam waited for Mazouk's reply.

"I'm not bringing them to your lab," Mazouk. "It's too risky."

"Use the law-school parking lot," Putnam said. "After it closes."

Mazouk worried for a full minute and then agreed. "Midnight exactly," he said.

"I'll need a couple of hours with the material," Putnam said. "Till three, maybe four A.M. at the outside."

"I've got to put them back in Langdon's desk by morning. The maids start cleaning at six-thirty."

"You'll have plenty of time," Putnam said, growing a little impatient. "After you give it to me, you can go home and worry. I'll call you when I'm finished."

"By four o'clock in the morning, I'll be a nervous wreck," Mazouk said. "I don't know what I'll say if someone catches me coming out of Dr. Langdon's office."

"No one's going to be around there at that time of night," Putnam said. "Besides, aren't you on first call?"

"Yeah," Mazouk said, brightening a little.

"Well, then . . ."

"Midnight," Mazouk said firmly as he hung up.

Dr. Putnam had made his call from a fast-food restaurant several blocks from the crime lab. He seldom ate there. He said he couldn't stand the smell of the frying, but what he really hated was the soul music that filled the place day and night. As he left, he passed by a darkened booth where a white man sat alone reading the menu and sipping his mug of coffee. The menu hid his face and there was nothing distinctive about his clothes. For a moment Willis thought his gray crew cut would give him away among so many Afros, but Putnam seemed very preoccupied.

The doctor returned to his car and left the parking lot in the direction of the state crime lab. Willis gave him an extra thirty seconds before resuming his surveillance.

As he left the greasy-soul-food restaurant, Willis' practiced eye scanned the parking lot. The unmarked car at the end of the row nearest the curb stood out to him like a sore thumb. Impulsively he changed his direction and walked over to the car. A white male sat alone behind the wheel. The man seemed busy with paperwork as Willis approached.

"Going in for soul food, Dempsey?" Willis said after tapping on the window with his keys.

"Well, hello, Captain," Dempsey said. "Just catching up on some routine reports. What are you doing over here in this part of town?"

"I just love pig-ear sandwiches," Willis said.

Dempsey assumed a pleasant expression and said nothing more. He knew it was impossible to bullshit a man like Captain Willis.

Willis reached into the car and patted the detective on the shoulder. "Give Bayberry my best," he said as he turned to walk away.

"Will do, Captain," Dempsey said. He attempted to resume his writing on the clipboard on his lap, but could not. The clipboard was blank and he knew Willis had seen it. "Shit," he said softly. He watched the captain get into his own car and drive off before he cautiously resumed his tail. Spotted or not, Dempsey had an assignment to carry out.

In a few minutes, Willis was able to put Putnam at the state lab by turning down an access road and looking across the motor-pool parking lot. Putnam's car was in its assigned space. Willis knew the move would tip Dempsey that he was interested in the state crime lab, but he could live with that. Unless Dempsey had spotted Putnam leaving the soul-food restaurant (a hen leaving the hen house), there would be no way for him to know what or whom at the crime lab Willis was interested in.

Willis found a shady spot under an isolated tree and parked his car. From there he could see the rear entrance to the crime lab and everyone coming or going to the employees' parking lot. The move put Dempsey at a decided disadvantage. He was forced to take a parking space even farther away and was only able to observe the captain's car. As they waited, each of them wondered whether he didn't have something better to do. The ability to handle boredom, Willis used to lecture, was a sign of a good detective.

Neither Willis nor Dempsey had ever learned to read for enjoyment or to study unassigned police materials. Waiting, for Dempsey, meant a ritual of fingernail-filing and rhythmic drumming on the dashboard of his car. Willis idled his time by slumping down behind the wheel and pretending to be half-asleep.

Putnam sat at his desk brooding over Dr. Mazouk's announcement. If Langdon was excited enough by some hairs and fibers from the last child case to send them to Washington, it could only mean one thing, Putnam reasoned. The hairs were foreign to the victim and the fibers were indicative of the environment in which he was killed. The forensic conclusion was a basic one.

Langdon's selection of the FBI lab in Washington instead of the state crime lab as a place to study the hairs and fibers worried Putnam more than he cared to admit to himself.

"Langdon has no idea who he is after," he said softly. He felt his pulse race as he reassured himself over and over. "He just wants to cut us out. That's all it means. He's keeping it all to himself and the M.E. office. *That's* why he's going to the FBI."

Putnam knew that without known hairs and fibers for comparison, the evidence would be worthless. Even the FBI lab could not work magic. He felt his pulse race and his palms crawl with sweat as he mentally argued with his own conclusions. Black hairs were black hairs. No distinction. He had seen that often enough in other cases sent to the state lab for comparison. But carpet fibers were another matter. As long as his own carpet existed at the apartment, he was at risk. But no one knew about the apartment. He was sure of that. Or did they?

Putnam paced his office and fought the panic rising within him. Then, resigned to what he had to do, he left the crime lab. There was no one in the parking lot to be seen, and he scolded himself for looking. As his car entered the street, a short unnoticed parade began: Willis on Putnam, Dempsey on Willis.

The drive to the apartment was without incident. Putnam found a space on a side street. It was one that he had used before, but he knew he would not be long. Arriving alone, he would be free from suspicion. Even the black man cutting his lawn across the street paid no attention to Putnam as he locked the car and disappeared around the corner.

There was no one at the front door of the apartment building. Putnam was sure he had entered without being seen. His luck held out on the stairway and along the hallway to the back. There still was no one.

Inside the apartment, he quickly went to work. With forceps and separate plastic envelopes, he took fiber samples of the red carpet, the angora pillows, the bedspread, and the towels in the bathroom. He was confident he had a sample of every fiber in the apartment. As he turned to leave, his heart froze. The sheets! The bed had been recovered with new sheets, but the old ones were gone. His mind raced to the trashcan at the park, and he found it difficult to swallow. He rushed to the bed and ran his hand over the silky smoothness of the new sheets as beads of perspiration popped out on his brow. The cool, smooth touch of the expensive fabric gave him comfort. He saw Tyrone and Martin Luther and some of the others.

"Mazouk said *carpet* fibers," he said aloud. "We don't have to worry about the old sheets." His eyes were a vacant stare and his mouth twisted into a strange smile. The bed was filled with naked boys.

Downstairs, Willis had decided to risk a meeting with the doctor if that's what it took to find out where he had gone. He was reading the names on the mail slots just inside the front door when he heard hurried footsteps above him on the stairs. Instinctively Willis jammed his hands into his pants pockets, hunched his shoulders, and staggered casually down the hallway away from the door. He half-sang, half-hummed an old ballad as he shuffled along, apparently fumbling for keys and searching for someone's name on every door.

At the bottom of the stairs, Putnam gave him hardly a glance. He hated drunks. Especially daytime drunks that sang to themselves. Outside, nothing had changed. Cars were parked along both curbs, but no one seemed to have any interest in the man from the crime lab. Not even the man still cutting his lawn around the corner. And not even the man in the car parked near the fire hydrant at the end of the block. Dempsey had assumed Willis' favorite surveillance pose and was scarcely visible behind the wheel.

For a moment or two Dempsey was divided over whom he should follow. He recognized Dr. Putnam but really had no interest in where he had been or where he was going. Dempsey was interested only in Willis. But if Willis was interested in Putnam, Dempsey felt that *maybe* he should switch subjects. But that didn't make sense, Dempsey convinced himself. Putnam was working with the task force, for Christ's sake. What would they care if Dempsey came back with a report that he had seen Putnam leave a second-rate apartment house and return to the crime lab? Bayberry would probably kick his ass and assign him to some burglary investigation.

Then, as if to solve Dempsey's problem, Willis appeared at the corner. He glanced toward Putnam's parking space and quickly bent over to tie his shoe as Dr. Putnam sped by, totally preoccupied. Willis then rushed to his own car and resumed the pursuit, ignoring Dempsey's obvious departure. Willis made a mental note to tell Dempsey that as a covert observer he was about as invisible as a polka-dot moose.

Willis was disappointed when Putnam returned to the crime lab, parked his car in his assigned space, and went inside. The

brief excursion to the apartment house had made no sense at
all. Putnam hadn't been there long enough to visit a girlfriend. He could have been making a delivery, but he hadn't
carried anything obvious. He must have gone there to pick
up something. But what? And from whom? Wearily Willis
wrestled with these options and then decided to hell with it.
Putnam was back at work and would probably spend the
rest of the day there. If Dempsey wants to watch the back
door of the state crime lab, Willis thought, let him. I'm going
home.

As he left the crime-lab area, he glanced in his mirror.
Dempsey was still on his tail, lagging back about a block and
a half. Suddenly he gave a little smile. "Okay, Bobby," he said,
"let's see if you're any good." He inched his speedometer up
fifteen miles an hour and began to take unexpected turns,
complimenting Dempsey after each one when he reappeared
in the mirror. He became harder to follow, but Dempsey did
not disappoint him.

"You're not bad, Bobby," Willis said as he wheeled onto
the entrance ramp to the parking floors of a high-rise bank-
and-office complex. "Let's see if you can handle this one." He
paused to take the parking stub from the machine and then
squealed his way up several floors before pulling into a space.
Then he rushed to the nearby elevators and pushed the
button. The down car arrived before Dempsey. The elevator
opened into the busy bank lobby and in a minute Willis was
on the street. Then he hailed a cab and baffled the Cuban
driver by telling him to drive around the block and enter the
parking complex. The five-dollar tip eased the driver's concern as Willis got out next to his car and drove off humming
to himself. In his mind, he could see Dempsey checking
random floors and finally discovering that Willis' space was
now empty or occupied by another car.

At home, he parked boldly in front. A joke was a joke, and
he didn't really care if Dempsey knew he was there. He also
didn't give a damn that Dempsey would spot Joan Burke's
car parked across the street. Even Dempsey had to be getting
used to that by now.

She was at work in the den when he walked in. She had a

pencil across her mouth and a serious expression as she studied the map, but he kissed her anyway.

"What have you figured out?" he asked, slipping his hands around her waist.

"That I missed you," she said. "What have you been doing?"

"Watching Putnam." He took a colored pin from a box at the end of the small writing desk and squinted at the map. The desk was no longer a cluttered heap of old bills, paycheck stubs, and clippings. It had been organized, and each child's case commanded its own color-coded folder.

"Putnam?" she said, half-astonished. "You said you weren't interested in him."

"Uh-huh," he grunted as he located the apartment on the map and pushed in the pin. "I wasn't."

"What's that? Another murder?"

"Nope." He spanned the distance from the apartment pin to several of the murder scenes with his thumb and little finger. "It's an apartment Putnam visited today."

"Apartment? Whose?"

Willis shrugged and continued to study the map. "Beats the shit out of me," he said. "All I know is, he went from the crime lab to this apartment house, stayed about fifteen minutes, and went back to work."

"So what's that got to do with the murders?" It was her turn to play devil's advocate.

"Probably nothing," Willis said heavily. "But *you* were the one that thought he was acting strangely. I just figured we'd give him a pin of his own. We've got plenty of them."

Joan looked at the map for a moment and then turned to face Willis again. "But who lives there? In the apartment, I mean."

"I only got a quick glance at the names on the mail slots," Willis said. "He started to come out, and and I had to get the hell out of there. But one thing's for sure. His name isn't on any of the slots."

"Girlfriend," Joan said simply.

Willis nodded easily. "You're probably right. But if it is a girlfriend, I don't think she was home. He didn't stay long enough to even say hello."

"Maybe he forgot his watch," she offered.

"Could be," Willis said, unconvinced. "I can check the names out tomorrow."

"I've been running a distance check from kid scene to kid scene," she said, staring at the pin that marked the apartment. "I'm trying to see if a pattern falls out."

"Get anything?"

She shook her head. "They're all different. I thought maybe I could come up with the same number of blocks from somewhere to somewhere. If it's there, I haven't found it yet."

"One kid was last seen at a movie," Willis said. "Can you overlay all the movie houses and see if it makes anything?"

"Sure," she said. "That will only take me a week. Who do you think I am—Dempsey?"

"If you were, you'd be trying to get out of the bank and whipping your ass to get over here, still mad as hell." He laughed and told her how he had temporarily shaken Dempsey off his tail.

"Why's he so interested in you all of a sudden?"

"Beats me," Willis said. "It's probably Bayberry. He can't stand the thought of me free-lancing these cases."

"But you told him you weren't."

"And of course he believed me."

"Did Dempsey see Putnam at the apartment?" Her tone implied that Dempsey was an intruder into her private suspicions about the doctor.

"Maybe. Maybe not. But who cares? He can check Putnam out anytime he wants to. He just doesn't have any reason to. And I'm not really sure that *we* do."

"Aw, Henry, don't start that again," she pleaded. "The guy makes my skin crawl. Don't make me argue the case again."

"Case? What case? The guy is a little weird, and that bugs you," Willis said. "But that's a long way from his being involved in these kid cases."

"I never said he was *involved*," she snapped.

"Hey, hey. Don't get upset," he said, putting his arms

231

around her. "If you want him checked out, he'll be checked out."

"It's just that . . ." She put her forehead on his shoulder.

"We'll check out all the angles," he said softly. "I'll even shadow the mayor's limousine if it makes you happy."

"You're patronizing me, Henry Willis," she said in a sing-song.

"No I'm not," he half-whispered. "I'm holding you close to me and I'm smelling the perfume on your neck . . ."

"It's my shampoo," she said softly.

". . . And I'm thinking what an asshole I was not to get to know you sooner."

Had Willis known how fascinated Joan Burke would be about the location of Putnam's apartment, he would have put the pin in the wrong place on the map. Instead, he had provided her with a lead she couldn't resist.

She had left him a note:

> *Henry:*
> *You looked too comfortable on the couch to disturb. I've gone to the station to cut some material coming in from network for the eleven-o'clock. Arlo says do it or else.*
> *I'm glad you liked the chicken. It was my grandmother's recipe.*
> *I'll see you tomorrow.*
>
> *Joan*
> *P.S. I'm glad you liked me too. But I was better than the chicken.*

She found the neighborhood without a hitch and parked a block away because she had the damned Channel Three car. The few stores that had survived in that section of town were already closed, and even with the streetlights, the area was dark. The gaudy sign in the window of one store confirmed it by offering neck bones, snout, and pig ears on sale. Joan Burke was definitely not at home.

There was no one on the street as she turned the corner and headed for Putnam's apartment house. An occasional yard was trimmed, but most had gone to seed and trash. Dim lights burned inside the small wooden houses, and somewhere the immature bark of a puppy begged to be let in. She walked with a quick, determined step that suggested she belonged in the neighborhood and was unafraid. Neither was correct.

As she approached the front door to the small apartment house, she had a sinking feeling that Henry's pin was in the wrong spot. Everything about the building felt wrong. Too small. Too dark. Too quiet.

Then, with a mental conversation that ridiculed her lack of courage, she opened the front door and went in. The hallway was dimly lit and the mailboxes were just to the right, exactly as Henry had described them. She was at the same time excited and terrified that she had found the right place. With her nose on the mail slots, she was able to read each name, and with a quivering hand she wrote them all in her tiny spiral notebook. Only one mail slot was blank. None of them said "Barry Putnam."

She made her way along the first-floor hallway, pausing briefly at each door, evaluating the noises from within. Almost all of it was midevening television; the rest, muffled domestic conversation. The names on the doors matched the mail slots. On the second floor in the back, there was a door without a name. She walked quickly away from that door on her first pass. It was as if it would suddenly open and Putnam would be there. But after she had nervously inspected all the other doors on the second floor, she returned and hesitantly pressed her ear to it. Inside she heard only the false echoes of her own heartbeat and anxious breathing.

Suddenly, from behind her, a curiously high-pitched voice broke the silence: "He don't come here too much."

Joan whirled around to look at the woman across the hall. She held her fat little dog tightly on his leash. The dog gave an ineffective grunt, the closest he could manage to a growl. "Hush, Murphy," the woman said.

"I'm looking for Dr. Putnam," Joan said. She had obviously

been startled and felt a little foolish about it when she saw the harmless-looking old woman in the doorway behind her.

"Don't know his name," Mrs. McCroughough said, stepping out of her apartment and snapping the door shut. She tugged at the reluctant Murphy. "He only comes and goes. The door used to say 'Bernard Parsons.'" Her years had taught her to appear unconcerned and to bury her curiosity.

"The man I'm looking for is a . . ." Joan hesitated, gauging the effect of the word that stuck momentarily in her throat. ". . . Negro."

Mrs. McCroughough nodded confidently and started off along the shabby corridor. "That's him," she said.

"I'm a friend of his," Joan said, hoping the woman would stay.

"Yep," the woman said. It was no concern of hers. She understood that "these days" some black men knew white women.

Joan wanted to ask the woman if the man brought a child, a son perhaps, to the apartment, but the question seemed too abrupt, and the woman did not stop. Even her dog seemed more concerned with leaving than with the young woman in front of the quiet door.

Joan listened again after the woman disappeared down the front stairwell. She was calmer then, and the silence inside seemed louder. She raised her hand to knock, but she couldn't make it strike. She wanted him to be there but was frightened he might open the door.

Her fear embarrassed her as she retraced her steps down the back stairway. She told herself she had learned enough and that she should get Henry Willis before proceeding further. But another voice inside her said she was only being chicken and that Henry would laugh when he heard of her retreat. She paused on the first landing of the back stairs. A *reporter* would investigate. A *reporter* would . . .

Her internal lecture on bravery was suddenly cut short by a gentle hand on her shoulder. She turned with a shudder and looked into the man's face, her mouth suddenly dry and a chill racing across her cheek.

"You're Miss . . . Block?" Putnam said.

Joan nodded rapidly.

"What brings you here?" he asked. His hand continued to rest on her shoulder. The grip tightened ever so slightly.

"I'm . . . I'm . . ." she stammered. "I'm looking . . . for *you.*"

"For me?" Putnam said curiously. His eyes stared into hers, and he offered a small crooked smile. "Why would you look for me here?" he asked.

Joan glanced at his other hand. It was empty.

"They told me at the lab I might find you here," she said. She knew that wouldn't fly as soon as she said it, but it was all she had.

"Oh, they did?" Putnam said calmly. He was confident that no one at the lab knew of the apartment. Not even TD knew. "Well, then," he said, "let me invite you in." He slid his hand from her shoulder to the back of her arm and walked her up the stairs.

Putnam glanced appreciatively at the reporter as he slid the key into the lock with his left hand. His grip on her arm was firm but not enough to cause alarm.

"I really don't have that much time," she said, subduing her nervousness.

"But you came all this way to find me," Putnam said, swinging the door wide. Inside, the apartment was dark. The dim light from the hallway made an ineffectual triangle on the floor.

Joan shook her head and tried to smile politely. Her mouth became a crooked line.

"This is my own place," he said, ushering her through the doorway. "I *want* you to see it." He closed the door as soon as they were inside, and the room became pitch black. Putnam let go of her arm and moved away. She still felt his presence nearby and heard a heavy click. She wanted to turn and run, but felt frozen to her spot in the darkness.

"I'll find the light," he said from somewhere else in the room. She had not heard him move across the thick red carpet. The blackened silence roared in her ears. She felt he *must* be able to hear the pounding of her heart.

Then, with a half-twist of a dimmer switch, the room became an amber glow. Putnam was next to the wall in the living room, smiling widely. Joan glanced around the apartment quickly, half-expecting to see someone else.

"How do you like it?" he asked.

"It's . . . charming," she said. She turned and glanced at the door. Somehow he had removed the doorknob.

"No one else knows about this place," he said. He held his hand out invitingly.

Joan did not move, but asked, "Do you come here often?"

"Every now and then," he said strangely. "Come. Let me show you the rest."

She took a hesitant step toward the doctor. The lack of furniture in the living room made the distance between them seem longer.

Putnam came to her with catlike smoothness, his hands outstretched to grasp her wrists. He continued to smile, and his eyes were opened widely.

Disbelieving her willingness, she let him take her wrists in his hands. His grasp was strong, but he was not hurting her.

"Who are you?" he asked gently. His teeth gleamed in the softened light. "In my office, I thought you were from the task force," he said, looking into her eyes. "But I don't believe that anymore. I can feel you tremble."

Joan found herself fascinated by his eyes. Her mouth refused to form words. "I'm . . . a . . . reporter," she said at last.

"A reporter!" he said, apparently praising her choice of work. "How nice. And you came to report on me."

"Not just you," she said. "It's your work. The crime lab. Everything you do." Her tone was almost apologetic.

"And would you like to *see* what I do?" He nodded his head encouragingly.

"You're holding my wrists very tightly," she said.

"I'm so sorry," he said, loosening his grip a little. "I didn't mean to hurt you."

"Our file says you live with your wife. Over by the university."

"I do. I do," he insisted. "This is just a place I come to."

"To get away? To be alone?" she asked quickly. "Everybody needs a place like that sometimes."

"Of course they do, Miss Block. That's not really your name, is it?"

She shook her head. "It's Burke. I'm from Channel Three."

"Television," he praised. "Would you like to see *my* television?" He seemed quite pleased with the offer and led her by both arms toward the bedroom.

"Please . . ." she said softly.

"You'll like my television. I make my own cassettes."

"I'd like to see them sometime," she said, struggling a little as he brought her near the bed. She began to wonder if this was inescapable rape. But surely, she argued with herself, he couldn't afford such a complaint. An attempt at seduction, maybe, but not forcible rape.

Putnam spun her around skillfully and sat her on the edge of the bed. Her hands felt the unusual coolness of the smooth sheets as Putnam let go of her and reached for a hidden panel at the head of the bed. A television began to flicker, sending rolls of gray and then pink light across the room and onto the wall. The actor on the screen was a small black boy in a baseball uniform. He seemed unafraid and smiled as he took his cap off and waved it to an unseen crowd. Joan did not recognize the boy's face.

"One of my earliest films," Putnam said from behind her.

"A relative?" she asked hopefully.

"Call him a friend," Putnam explained almost absently.

"He's a good-looking boy," she said, making small talk.

"He's beautiful," Putnam said, breathing heavily right behind her. Joan spun around to look at the doctor. His penis, half-erect, was in his hand.

"Oh, God, no," she pleaded softly.

"Don't you think he's beautiful?" Putnam asked. His attention was fixed on the screen. It was almost as if he had forgotten she was there. His slow stroke continued.

She turned back toward the screen with a muffled gasp. The boy had taken off his baseball uniform, and Putnam, naked and erect, was kissing him on the shoulder. She felt her heart die in her chest as she watched the action on the tape. Her skin began to crawl and her throat began to ache with dryness. Although she didn't recognize *this* boy, she knew what she had found. Her brain began to scramble for survival.

"*Some* people," she began, pacing her words and fighting to appear calm, "would be offended by such a film." She paused in her attempt to swallow. "But I'm not."

Putnam, close behind her, said nothing. She could feel his careful, rhythmic motions.

"As a matter of fact," she continued, "I have seen films like these in New York." Her mind flashed to the absent doorknob and she tried to recall if she had seen any windows. The dim light in the living room had prevented her from recognizing the foil-covered sliding doors to the balcony.

"I told Malcolm not to be afraid," Putnam mused.

"He doesn't look afraid," she said. She watched the action on the screen progress and felt her stomach tighten. Fear was welling up inside her. She began to doubt how long she could last before she would have to cry.

"He made us do it, Mama," Putnam said, his voice sounding years younger.

"None of this is your fault, Dr. Putnam," Joan said. She still could not turn and look at him. He was also in front of her on the screen, and she hated what she saw.

"Doobie, doobie, doobie," Putnam chanted with the voice of a little boy. His movements seemed more rapid.

"In some parts of the world," she said flatly, "such things are quite acceptable. I've done some research on it. I could show you some of it down at the station." The overt sexual activity with the boy seemed to be ending as Putnam raised his head and kissed the child on the cheek. The boy still seemed unafraid. He had done nothing in the film to reciprocate Putnam's advances. Then, to Joan's horror, she saw the doctor's hand move up the boy's abdomen, along his chest, and onto his neck. The boy's expression changed from enjoyment to fear and then to panic as the hand closed around his throat. She wanted to rise, to scream, to run but she couldn't. Putnam had slipped a fabric cord around her neck. His strong hands pulled it tight as pulses pounded in her head and the last flutter of the boy's ineffectual struggle flashed into her eyes. She tried to call out for Willis, and in her hypoxic brain, the boy's face became green before fading to black.

Outside, in the hallway, Murphy sniffed at the door before reluctantly retiring to his own apartment for the night.

23

Mazouk left his house at exactly ten-thirty. He was uneasy and his hands trembled slightly. When he got to the medical examiner's office, only one car was in the parking lot. It belonged to the night doorman, and Mazouk knew he'd be watching television downstairs in his room next to the morgue. There were no windows on the street floor. The morgue man had no way of knowing a car had pulled up. Mazouk let himself in through the staff entrance on the opposite side of the building. He held the heavy door with both hands until it closed with an almost silent click. The stairway was dimly lit by a night light, and Mazouk paused for a moment to listen for any sounds. There were none.

He took a deep breath and quietly climbed the stairs to the office floor above. Upstairs, he switched on all the lights. He knew they could not be seen from the morgue man's room and reasoned that if an investigator were to come in from a late call, he would have no excuse for being there in the dark.

Mazouk made a rapid tour of the office floor, walking lightly and even looking into the ladies' room. There was no one anywhere. Then he went to his own desk, picked up a couple of routine files as decoys in case he was caught, and took them to Langdon's office. There, instead of putting on all the lights, he switched on the one in Langdon's private bathroom and swung the door open wide. It was enough to light up Langdon's desk area and still make it difficult for anyone to see what he was doing from the street.

Mazouk put the file folders on Langdon's desk and took a

clean, still-folded handkerchief from his pocket to open the middle drawer of the desk. He was slightly surprised to find it unlocked, but he knew how trusting the chief pathologist was. There, lying in front of him in the drawer, were two plastic envelopes. One was marked "fibers" and the other was marked "hairs." Each bore the number of the latest child murder.

He used his handkerchief to put the envelopes into his jacket pocket and to close the drawer. Then, returning to his office, he replaced his files and turned out the lights. In a minute he was out the side door and into his car. The night was cool and black. It had threatened to rain, and there was no one on the street.

He drove around anxiously, killing time and looking at his watch every five minutes. He wanted to arrive at the law-school parking lot exactly on time. He had already made up his mind that if Putnam was not there, he'd abort the whole plan, put the plastic envelopes back in Langdon's desk, and go home to throw up.

At a quarter of twelve Mazouk approached the university area, driving slowly and stopping at every yellow light. Students bustled here and there across the campus with books under their arms, arguing whether they'd go straight back to their dorms or grab a beer at the local hangout. Behind one dorm an insomniac group of students had organized a game of Frisbee under the streetlights.

Ahead of him lay the law school, already closed and darkened. He drove by the law building to case the empty parking lot and decided to round the block once more. The last thing he wanted was to be challenged in the parking lot by the campus police.

On his second pass, the lot was still empty. It was one minute after twelve. Mazouk did not realize how slowly he was driving until an overloaded convertible rushed by, its occupants shouting something about winning the game and waving beer cans in celebration. Then, with a heavy feeling in his chest, Mazouk turned into the driveway, passed under the student walkway, and entered the parking lot. He drove slowly to a darker corner partly protected from the sentinel lights by a large tree, turned around to face the main exit, and shut off his lights. His engine idled while his heart raced. He was determined to wait five minutes and only five minutes before abandoning the whole ridiculous plan. He began to worry about Langdon, about his career with the medical examiner's office, and about the blind faith he seemed to be placing in Wilson, Sullivan, Bayberry, and Putnam. Touted as the new and permanent order of things to come, it began to sound like a harebrained scheme orchestrated by disenchanted blacks to whom he owed no allegiance and from whom he had heard only unproved promises. He remembered his childhood in Beirut and the constant fighting which tore the city apart; his good fortune in obtaining a postgraduate appointment in London; the thrill of landing in the United States; his instant acceptance by his American colleagues. Now he saw himself exposed, accused, and implicated in a racist conspiracy that failed; the public humiliation; the ignominious return to Lebanon or a retreat to some obscure African nation building a new medical facility on American aid.

Suddenly his agony was broken by the upward flash of headlights, a car moving quickly, entering the parking lot from the other direction. The blinding lights bore down on him, sending spasms of panic through his body. The campus police he thought. The city police! The FBI!

The car pulled into the space next to his own and faced the opposite direction, each driver adjacent.

"Did you bring it?" Putnam asked.

"God." Mazouk sighed. He tried to swallow but was unable.

"Well, come on, come on," Putnam said, his arm outstretched between the cars.

Mazouk reached into his jacket pocket, found the envelopes still wrapped in the handkerchief, and handed them to Putnam. "I have tried to keep my fingerprints off the plastic," he said.

"Yeah. Good," Putnam said. He took the packets, handkerchief and all, and put them into his own pocket.

"When . . . when will I get them back?" Mazouk stammered.

"You go home and wait there," Putnam said firmly.

"They have *got* to be returned tonight," Mazouk warned.

"You have my word," Putnam said. "Now, get the hell out of here." He threw his own car into drive and wheeled away from the sweating Lebanese pathologist with an air of finality that left Mazouk suddenly feeling alone, insecure, and half-double-crossed.

When Putnam's car reentered the street, Mazouk switched on his lights and drove out the side driveway. His only expectation was an empty house and a silent telephone.

Putnam drove straight to the state crime lab, oblivious of the late-night traffic around him. At the lab he parked in his assigned space. He went directly to his office and private lab alcove and turned on the lights. Putnam unlocked a deep drawer in his desk and took out the plastic envelopes he had brought back from the apartment that afternoon. Then, after adjusting himself in front of a large comparative microscope he seldom used for anything but bullet examinations, he extracted Mazouk's handkerchief and its contents from his coat pocket. From his other coat pocket he removed a plastic envelope containing fibers from the oriental rug. He looked at *that* envelope and gritted his teeth. If he had not forgotten about the oriental rug in the closet on his first trip to the apartment, he would not have run into Joan Burke. Dr. Putnam was intolerant of mistakes, particularly his own.

He studied the medical examiner's envelopes carefully, using forceps to avoid fingerprints. Dr. Langdon had folded the edges and secured them with common staples. Putnam felt a surge of superiority and contempt for the chief medical examiner. Langdon could have sealed the envelopes with a red plastic tape so thin it would tear when anyone attempted to open it. The FBI used it, and so did Putnam whenever he wanted to transmit evidence to Washington. But then, he thought, what would Langdon know about the niceties of evidence preservation? He was, after all, only a medical pathologist.

With the skill of a watchmaker, Putnam removed the staples and emptied the contents of the envelopes into sterile petri dishes. Under the microscope, the hairs and fibers would seem as big as electrical cables. Then, putting them aside for a moment, he made similar preparations of the fibers from the apartment, and with quick, determined movements plucked several hairs from his head. He placed these on individual glass slides and winced as he secured a few more from his own pubic region. He was now ready for the actual comparison.

Putnam's hand trembled as he adjusted the focus of the microscope on the known and the test fibers simultaneously. The small beads of sweat that formed on his brow were annoying, but he denied himself any movement to brush them away and restore his comfort. The hair from Langdon's envelope came slowly into focus. The edge of the cortex glinted in the bright light, while the central pigmentation and shape of the hair screamed "Negroid" to Putnam's expert eye. Then with the opposite lens he focused on one of his own pubic hairs lying in the center of the slide. The match was perfect.

Putnam knew that hair comparison was a less exact science than fiber analysis or ballistics. Racial characteristics and pigmentation of hairs could be easily distinguished for exclusion but seldom matched for positive identification.

Dr. Putnam put the glass lids on his hair-sample slides and moved them off the microscope stage. He then began the comparison of the fibers from the Langdon envelope and those from his apartment. Langdon's carpet fibers came into view with startling clarity. They were obviously synthetic. A monofilament with inherent dye, crimped and braided at manufacture to inhibit unraveling. The highlights of the bright beam of his microscope dazzled at the edges of the strands as he adjusted his fine focus.

Putnam chose the slide with fibers from the oriental rug for his first comparison. As they came into view, he recognized the internal structure as animal hair; probably wool. He began to smile and his anxiety lessened a bit as he returned the slide to the desktop. He repeated the process with the slide from the angora pillows. The structures were also hair, quite distinguishable from the Langdon sample. Still no match.

He felt his contempt for the medical examiner's incompetence rising within him as he prepared a slide from his carpet. An inner voice was beginning to say that Langdon had nothing! A few Negro hairs. Meaningless.

Then, with unmistakable clarity the carpet fibers in the two microscope lenses came into simultaneous focus. Putnam was stunned. Every detail of every fiber was the same.

Putnam covered his slides and slowly got up from his microscope desk. The property room was only two doors down the hallway. He walked deliberately but quietly to the property room, opened it with his master key, switched on the light, and went in. There was a logbook on a chain just inside the door, looking like a metropolitan phone book. He balanced it on his knee as he flipped through the pages. Then, using a file number he found there, he located a bag containing the clothes of Tyrone Lewis.

Back in his own office, he opened the bag and partly extracted the clothes onto several sheets of typing paper to protect the articles from further contamination.

Putnam went over the garments with a hand lens and a pair of forceps. Within minutes he had retrieved several hairs and a few fibers. His hands trembled as he brought them to his microscope. This time he matched not only the red carpet but also one pillow *and* the oriental rug.

———

Langdon's bedside phone rang distantly but impatiently. His dream told him it was somewhere else and that sooner or later his secretary would get it, but midway through the fifth ring he fumbled it to his ear. "Dr. Langdon," he said numbly.

"Dr. Langdon?" the voice said quickly. "This is Dickinson at the morgue."

"Yes, Bailey, what's up?" Langdon recognized the voice of the old man who covered the morgue door from midnight to morning.

"Sorry to bother you, sir, but Mr. Willis called and said he had to see you right away. At the crime lab."

"At the crime lab?" Langdon asked. He paused for a moment and forced the rest of his brain to wake up. He thought he had given Henry Willis his unlisted home number, but . . . "What else did he say, Bailey?"

"That's about it, Doctor. Only he said it was real important, and not to call him there. He said he'd be in Dr. Putnam's office."

"Okay, Bailey," Langdon said. "I'll get right on it." He dressed quickly and put on a dark nylon windbreaker. In the kitchen, his ancient black Labrador struggled dutifully to his feet and flapped his tail against the refrigerator.

"Not this time, boy," Langdon said as he paused to scratch the dog behind his ears. "You get to go back to bed. Only humans have to go out at this time of night."

As he drove along the empty streets, Langdon worked on Willis' discovery. It had to do with the Mazouk connection, he reasoned. And it had to be big. Otherwise Willis would never risk the exposure. Surer than hell he's got the goods on Putnam's political scheme, he said to himself. And there is going to be one hell of a stink when the conspiracy between Sullivan and the mayor and the state crime lab hits the fan. Internally, Langdon was delighted. He liked to win.

The drive to the crime lab took thirty-seven minutes with every traffic signal obeyed. Langdon did not want to explain where he was going to some patrol officer. And he particularly didn't want to say whom he was meeting. Willis' retirement and police politics had seen to that.

As he entered the staff parking lot behind the lab, Langdon was surprised to see Putnam's car but not Henry's. That didn't make sense, but then, Willis never made mistakes. He found the back door unlocked and the hall lights on. Somehow he had expected Henry Willis with a flashlight and a contented smile on his face. He shouted a hello and received an answer from down the hall.

"We're down here, Tom," Putnam said loudly. "Lock the door."

Langdon snapped the dead bolt on the rear entrance and made his way toward Dr. Putnam's office. His expectations were baffled. What the hell *is* Putnam doing here? he wondered. Did he have it all wrong? Was Mazouk on the trail of something all along? Was Putnam in on it? He began to feel a little foolish about his earlier doubts and looked forward to Willis' explanation.

Putnam was seated behind his desk looking calm and confident as the medical examiner walked in.

"*Doctor* Langdon," Putnam said strangely without getting up. "It's always a pleasure to see you."

" 'Morning, Barry." Langdon glanced around the room. "I thought Henry Willis would be here."

"Shut the door," Putnam said.

Langdon hesitated but complied. "You got something to say to me?" he asked.

"I've got a shitload to say to you," Putnam muttered. His voice was not friendly.

"*You* made the call. Not Willis," Langdon said. He came closer to the desk but remained standing.

"Another brilliant deduction," Putnam said. "You're full of those lately, aren't you?"

"What's this all about, Putnam?" Langdon's tone said there would be no nonsense.

"It's about you."

"Me," Langdon confirmed. His thumb was toward his chest.

"You and your goddamned medical examiner's office." Putnam sat close to his desk, his hands out of sight.

"At four in the morning?" Langdon said. "You called me out to talk interdepartmental politics at this hour?"

"Not exactly."

"Maybe you *are* a little crazy," Langdon said. "Carson thinks so."

Putnam stiffened at the remark, and the left side of his face twitched. "Sit down," he snapped.

"Up yours. You can see me in *my* office. And you can bring Sullivan and Atwood." He turned to leave.

"Sit down!" Putnam shrieked. He sounded like a small boy who was angry and suddenly in control of both the ball and the bat.

"What?" Langdon said impatiently. He didn't need any crap from this asshole. Maybe this was a good time to settle it. He turned toward the desk again, and his challenge froze in his throat. Putnam had a large-caliber revolver in his hand.

"You went too far," Putnam said. "You and your fibers."

"So Mazouk *did* bring them to you," Langdon said. He sat slowly in the chair opposite Putnam's desk.

"Among other things."

"I knew it was true," Langdon said. "I could feel it. You want it all, don't you? You and Mazouk."

"I did, but it's all over."

"And you think threatening me with a gun will solve everything, huh?" Langdon was concerned but not alarmed. Putnam was still his inferior, and Langdon could not escape the attitude.

"You're not going to break this case, Dr. Langdon."

"When Sullivan hears about this, you'll be finished, Putnam. Nobody will give you the Birmington office."

"I almost had it," Putnam said.

Langdon looked at the black scientist's strained face. "You need a rest. I'll explain it to Atwood for you."

Putnam did not seem to be listening. "Nobody really cared about them, you know. They were just kids from the street. Sooner or later they'd all end up in jail anyway." He was looking at Langdon, but his eyes were focused beyond.

"Who?" Langdon asked softly.

"And none of them showed any marks. No *real* injuries. Tyrone was bad. He had to be punished. He knew that." Putnam's voice became gentle now. "My mama said so."

"Your mama?" Langdon coaxed.

"Reverend Roony made us all undress," Putnam said. The gun in his hand suddenly wavered, and Langdon swallowed hard. He remembered the man who ran amok on the psychiatric ward during internship and stabbed a nurse before crashing through the eighth-floor window.

"Did you *see* those boys, Barry?" Langdon asked gently.

"And all my life I worked hard to be somebody," Putnam mused. "I got my doctorate."

"Sure you did," Langdon soothed.

"I could have run the crime lab better than Atwood."

"A lot better." Langdon started to get up slowly from his chair, but changed his mind as the gun moved clumsily in Putnam's hand.

"I would have found those fibers quicker than you," Putnam said, returning a little from his fugue. "I know criminalistics."

"You're good at it too, Barry." Langdon looked out the window behind Putnam. The parking lot was dark and quiet.

"*I* made the match," Putnam said. "You didn't." He was proud of his accomplishment. "The reporter from Channel Three didn't get any fibers for comparison. I found her first."

"You were too smart for her, Barry."

"All those boys had dirty feet," Putnam said absently. "I had to wash them first."

Langdon's mind raced through the cases. All of them *were* washed clean. Willis had noticed that. The hairs on the backs of his arms felt suddenly alive. "Did they have painted fingernails, Barry? Pretty red ones?"

Putnam's stare was even blanker.

I don't want to play this game no more, minister. I want to go home.

The boy was Martin Luther Peale, and he was frightened.

"You can get treatment," Langdon said. "I'll see to that for you."

"They'll put me away," Putnam moaned.

"Only to help you."

"They'll send me to prison!" he declared.

Dr. Langdon shook his head slowly. "No, they won't, Dr. Putnam. They'll see that you're sick. And they'll all want to help you."

"They'll send me to prison because I'm black." He seemed to drift back in touch with reality. "But I'm not going to let them." Putnam shook his gun menacingly at Dr. Langdon, holding it like a man unfamiliar with firearms. Langdon winced inside and braced himself for the bullets. After all these years of being the courtroom expert on gunshot wounds, he said to himself: I'll finally find out what it feels like.

"Your wife," Langdon began, maintaining his outward calm,

"won't understand why you did this, and it will hurt her."
Crisis-negotiation formula. A psychiatric straw floating along
in the stream of the pathologist's memory and eagerly grasped
at.

Putnam stared at his colleague as he considered the remark.
Langdon had met TD once at a faculty social. He had exchanged meaningless pleasantries as one does at such functions
and had even asked her about the origin of her paraplegia.
As a pathologist he felt he had the right to ask about obvious
diseases without embarrassment. Putnam had been taken aback
by the question, but TD had simply said, "Polio." Langdon
had replied, "I'm sorry. It's an interesting virus, isn't it?" And
she had agreed, even to the extent of describing some of her
latest research in fetal pig brains. Doctor-to-doctor talk.

"TD is not involved in this," Putnam said heavily. "She
never even knew about the apartment." He squinted his eyes
as if to check his memory more accurately. "Not even the
address," he said confidently.

"I'll bet it is a beautiful apartment," Dr. Langdon said.
Confrontation-crisis rule three or four or whatever. Langdon
was dimly recalling from a seminar he and Willis had attended
several years before: change the subject. Follow any lead. Be
complimentary. "Tell the terrorist how well oiled he keeps his
automatic weapon and keep telling him until he blows your
head off with it," the instructor had said.

"You know it has a lovely red carpet," Putnam said,
enjoying the irony.

"Red's my favorite," Langdon said as lightly as he could.
"I've always wanted an apartment to get away to that no one
would know about." He paused to see if Putnam was buying
any of his horseshit. "Did it have red satin sheets too?"

Putnam's mind flashed to the red sheets and the park where
he had stuffed the bag into the trashcan.

"Why would they bring you the sheets?" he asked obviously baffled by some complexity in the medical examiner's
organization that he didn't understand.

"They bring us everything like that, Barry," Langdon said
with exaggerated confidence. "They always think there's an

abandoned stillborn baby wrapped up in them. The parks department never wants to look."

Putnam frowned and nodded slowly. He appreciated that kind of thoroughness and knew he couldn't even approach it with his rural deputies. "Did you do an acid phosphatase on the stain?" he asked. He was a diamond cutter admiring another cutter's stroke.

"What do you think?" Langdon asked.

Putnam nodded and put on a sly face. "Not much gets by *you*, Dr. Langdon."

"Nor you, Barry." Langdon put his hand out slowly, palm upward. "Now, why don't you give me the gun and we'll let somebody straighten this all out."

Putnam looked at the pathologist as if to test the offer. He seemed distant and tired again. The muzzle of the revolver sloped toward the desk but the butt remained firmly in Putnam's hand. Langdon considered a quick grab for the weapon but dismissed the idea as only worthy of TV movies.

"I suppose it was only a matter of time until you found the apartment," Putnam mused absently.

"Nothing stays secret forever," Langdon said.

"None of *them* could have told."

Dr. Langdon nodded. "You above other people would know there are other ways to find out things like that." The pathologist's pulse quickened in anticipation. Putnam is going to spill his guts, Langdon thought. And what for? His only witness would be dead with a bullet in the chest. God, he thought, make it a clean shot through the chest. Not one of those through the pancreas with weeks of surgery and post-operative rotting and tubes coming out of every hole. . . .

"The old lady and her dog," Putnam said after a moment of silence.

"There *was* a dog," Langdon lied.

"Tyrone liked the dog," Putnam said, his eyes half-closed. The light from the desk lamp cast long shadows across his face, accentuating his nose.

"Boys always like dogs," Langdon said soothingly. "You liked him a little too, didn't you, Barry?"

Putnam nodded slowly. Only part of him was in the office now. The rest had returned to the apartment. "The old woman was nosy," he said. "She was always taking him out."

"And she saw you, didn't she?"

"She saw me, but she didn't know anything."

"But you can't be sure of that, Barry. She might have been the one—"

"She let him shit on the sidewalk."

"In front of the apartment?"

Putnam shook his head. "Down the block. Near Hill Street."

Langdon's mind raced through the city map. There *was* a Hill Street. He could remember it from a questionable suicide a year or so earlier. "Near the fire station?" he probed.

Putnam glanced wearily at the pathologist. "There's no fire station on Hill," he said.

"Uh-huh," Langdon said gently. "There's a substation at Hill and Fortieth."

"That's the other side of the throughway. I'm on the blind side. Where they cut Hill off."

Langdon conceded Putnam's accuracy with wider eyes and a motion of his head. "Your apartment building is not very big, then."

"Two floors," Putnam said. "You *do* know the city."

"After all these years?" Langdon said. "Every parking lot, every abandoned store . . ."

"*I* had to worry about stupid little towns around the state."

"But you served the state well, Dr. Putnam. The deputies admired you."

"We could have worked well together, Dr. Langdon."

"We may yet," Langdon said. "It's not too late. All of this was only an unfortunate mistake. We can straighten it all out and then—"

"No!" Putnam shouted. He stood up from his desk, gun in hand. "There's no time for that now. Someone else will have to carry on for us. You and I are finished."

"But why, Dr. Putnam?" Langdon bargained. He tried to look at Putnam's face and not at the muzzle of the revolver.

"Why waste our experience? Together we know more about forensic science than anyone else in the country."

"Because *they* won't ever let it work," Putnam said sadly. "*They* won't ever understand. It's all gone now. The crime lab. The medical examiner's office. Everything."

Dr. Langdon could feel the despair in the man's voice. The psychologist from the crisis seminar had told them to listen for the despair. "When it comes," he had said, "the end is near. Shoot him. Storm the place. There will be nothing to lose."

Langdon stood up slowly, his arms half-extended, palms up. His was a helpless gesture or a furtive posture of prayer. He was a monk facing his last sunrise. The hopeless man on the roof of a burning building. A sailor on a sinking ship. Resigned.

He closed his eyes. He thought of his ex-wife. Willis. His job and all of the cases he'd leave undone. He thought of the smell of strawberry ice cream just before the cold spoon entered his mouth.

Suddenly there was the unmistakable roar of a cannon, curiously muffled. Langdon's mouth flew open in a muted cry and his hands grasped his chest, but there was no pain. He strained for a breath that wouldn't come, and another crash filled the room.

Langdon opened his eyes to find Putnam sprawled across the desk. The bullet had exited from the top of his head and blood gushed out to join the oozing brain. The gun had fallen on the floor with Putnam's last saliva still glistening on the barrel.

24

Dempsey's car arrived at the apartment house near Hill Street a few seconds before the others. The flashing blue lights swept the houses on either side of the street and mingled with the gray dawn. Dr. Langdon sat in the right-front seat of Dempsey's car. He was still shaking, but not as badly as he had when he had tried to use the blood-spattered phone in Putnam's office.

"This is the only two-story south of the throughway off Hill," Dempsey said.

Langdon nodded numbly. His mouth still tasted sour, and he felt distantly ashamed for having vomited in Putnam's wastebasket. He knew it had been due to the stress of coming so close to his own death, not the sight of Putnam with his brains splattered across the wall. Still, Langdon thought, pathologists, especially forensic pathologists, are supposed to be able to take it.

"You don't have to go in, Doc," Dempsey said.

Langdon flapped his hand silently. "I'm going in," he grunted.

The detectives assembled in front of the apartment house and exchanged mumbled instructions. Three of them went around to the back. At the front door, Dempsey paused and bent over to free his extra gun from his ankle holster. He handed it to Langdon. "Here," he whispered hoarsely. "You might need it. But for Christ's sake, be careful."

The pathologist accepted the snub-nose with vague familiarity as Dempsey stepped in front of him and opened the door. They stopped to read the mail slots, and Dempsey intuitively tapped one with no name. "Let's start with this one," he said. He glanced down the hallway and saw the other men entering through the back door. Each held his revolver in the air. Dempsey made an obvious gesture toward the second floor. Two detectives started up the back stairs, while the third remained at the rear door. Despite their quick motions, there was not a sound.

Dempsey and Langdon and two more detectives made their way up the front stairs and down the hallway to the un-marked apartment. They flattened themselves against the wall and crept quietly toward the door. Dempsey made eye move-ments and small gestures to assign everyone to a station before he slid up to the doorway. He strained to inspect the door in the dim light, and was puzzled to find it splintered around the latch. It had been broken in and was still slightly ajar.

Dempsey pushed the door with his toe and allowed it to swing open. He waited for a moment as every detective stopped breathing. Inside, the silence was broken only by a moan.

Dempsey made eye contact with the detective on the opposite side of the door before he assumed a fast noiseless crouch in the doorway. He held his .357 in front of him with both hands.

The moan was repeated.

The apartment was lit only by a yellow triangle across the carpet. It came from the open bathroom. Nothing moved.

Dempsey straightened up halfway and stepped cautiously inside. His position in the door was immediately filled by another crouching detective. Still another held Dr. Langdon against the wall, protecting the pathologist with his own body.

Dempsey crept forward, his eyes flashing from side to side, searching the semidarkness. When the moan came again, Dempsey swung to his left and froze. In the corner of the empty living room he made out the huddled figure of a man sitting with his back to the wall, his head cradled on his arms and drawn-up knees.

"One move and you're dead, sucker," Dempsey said, sighting his revolver at the form.

"Oh, God, Bobby," the man moaned.

"Captain Willis?" Dempsey said, not quite believing what he saw. He scrambled forward and took a safe position next to Willis, his eyes still searching the room. The other detective moved out of the doorway and to his right, covering the rest of the room with his gun.

"I *knew* she came here," Willis sobbed.

"Are you all right?" Dempsey whispered. He stole another glance at the captain's face. Willis appeared to be in agony.

"When she didn't come home, I *knew* she came here," Willis said loudly. His tone told Dempsey there was no further reason to fear an ambush.

"Where is she?" Dempsey said, standing up and looking around the room.

Willis did not answer. He put his head back onto his knees and moaned again. Dempsey motioned to the detective to hold his position as he walked quickly to the bathroom and glanced in. The bathroom was empty and undisturbed. Dempsey then moved to the bedroom and switched on the lights. There was no one there, but the door to the closet was open partway. Dempsey approached it with extreme caution and swung it open with his foot. He brought his gun down sharply at the crumpled form on the floor.

Her hands and feet were tied behind her with towel strips and a twisted coat hanger. Her panty hose had been tied behind her head, with one leg binding the gag in her mouth. The panty hose flattened her cheeks in a tight horizontal line, and her eyes were opened widely. Around her neck, cutting deeply into the skin, was the cord from a bathrobe. Dempsey felt for the absent pulse in her neck and realized instantly that she was cold and stiff.

Dempsey came out of the bedroom, suddenly exhausted, his gun held loosely at his side. He looked across the room at Willis. The sounds of the captain's sobs filled the room.

"Send Dr. Langdon in here," Dempsey said heavily.

"No!" Willis shouted. He struggled to his feet, leaning against the wall for support.

Dempsey met him halfway across the living room and held him in his arms. The side of Dempsey's gun pressed absurdly against the captain's back. Willis' gun still lay on the carpet where he had been sitting.

"It's my fault, Bobby," Willis said. "She had a gut feeling, and I gave her the address."

"Let it go, Captain," Dempsey said. "It's over. The whole damned thing is over." He felt the captain sob once more in his tight embrace.

25

For the first time in his career, Henry Willis did not go to the morgue to witness the autopsy on a body he had found. Dempsey had persuaded him to come home. They sat in the semidarkness of the captain's study. Dempsey kept Willis' glass filled with whiskey and said almost nothing. Neither did Willis. Dempsey had only a couple of drinks. For him there was still a lot of police work to do that day, and he knew that somehow he would do it.

"You think Langdon's through with her?" Willis mumbled.

"Don't think about it," Dempsey said.

Willis took a long pull on his drink and gagged after he swallowed it. His face showed how hard the tears had come. Dempsey had taken his gun away and had stayed with him for hours.

"I should have gone with her," Willis said again.

"You didn't know."

"As soon as she saw that pin . . ." Willis moaned, staggering to his feet. He lurched toward the wall and pulled the pin for Putnam's apartment out of the map. He weighed it in the palm of his hand for a moment and then threw it against the opposite wall, spilling half of his drink.

Dempsey said nothing. His captain needed room to react, and Dempsey was there to see that he got it undisturbed.

Then, as if possessed by an uncontrollable idea, Willis began to pull the other pins from the map. One by one he fired them around the room, oblivious of his friend sitting on the couch. Dempsey did not flinch. His jaw was set as tightly as Willis'.

Finally, with the last pin still clenched in his hand, Willis turned on the map and ripped its center section from the wall. He beat the wall with his fist and let his glass crash to the floor. A trickle of blood ran down his arm from the injury the map pin had caused in his palm.

"He cheated me," Willis sobbed, resting his forehead on the wall.

"He cheated us all," Dempsey said.

"*I* wanted to blow his brains out," Willis shouted.

"I would have helped you, Captain. But he beat us to it."

Dempsey quietly went to the kitchen and made Willis another drink. He was still at the wall when Dempsey returned.

"I'm hanging it up," Willis said after a while.

"You need some time alone," Dempsey said. "Go somewhere. Do something else for a while. Florida, maybe."

"No, I mean it, Bobby." He took another swallow of his drink. "I don't want any more. No kids, no 7–11 shootings, no domestic ax murders. No more."

Then, as if someone had deflated his legs, he slid down the wall and sat on the floor, his new drink still in his hand. Dempsey watched his head flop forward and waited for the sound of heavy breathing. It came in about a minute. He walked over and slipped the glass from the captain's hand and stretched him out on the floor. He used a sofa cushion for his head.

When he used the phone in the kitchen to call in, Dempsey muffled his voice. "He'll make it, I think," he told the lieutenant. "But I'd better stay with him."

"Take whatever time you need, Dempsey," the lieutenant said. "Nothing is going anywhere down here."

"And probably never will," Dempsey said softly. He hung up the phone and looked absently out of the kitchen window. Several blocks away, through a clearing in the trees and houses, Dempsey saw a patrol car speed along the highway with its blue lights flashing and its siren wailing in the distance.

"Christ," he said, and finished the captain's drink.

Epilogue

Willis went away for a while but came back when he felt healed. The mayor offered him the chief-of-police slot after Sullivan quit in disgust, but he refused. Then the mayor ran for state senator and lost. He accepted a salaried position on a national committee for the United Negro Fund and moved to New York.

Dr. Atwood retired as predicted, and Mazouk accepted the job, but only after Dr. Langdon asked him personally to do so. He had threatened to return to Lebanon, mouthing something about dishonoring the medical examiner's office. But Langdon and Davis had convinced him that he was naive and a little stupid but not dishonest.

Dr. Greene went off to teach at some university in California, and no one really tried to remember which one.

Channel Three named their six-o'clock news program in honor of Joan Burke, and within a year less than ten percent of the viewers knew anything at all about her, the murdered children, or the crazy doctor from the crime lab.

Henry Willis cleaned up his backyard and began to grow azaleas with a fervor that frightened even Bobby Dempsey, who despite his being made homicide chief still drops in from time to time with a six-pack or a bottle of bourbon.